BLOOMS ON THE BONES

BLOOMS ON THE BONES

Flynn's Crossing Romantic Suspense Series Book 5

Yvonne Kohano

K
E

Nanokas Press

A Division of Kochanowski Enterprises

BLOOMS ON THE BONES
FLYNN'S CROSSING ROMANTIC SUSPENSE SERIES BOOK 5

Nanokas Press/KE Press books may be ordered through booksellers or by contacting:

Kochanowski Enterprises/Nanokas Press
PO Box 1274
Clackamas, OR 97015-9594
www.yvonnekohano.com
yvonne@yvonnekohano.com

Blooms on the Bones is a work of fiction. People, places, events, and situations are the product of the author's imagination. Any resemblance to actual persons, living or dead, or historical events, is purely coincidental.

This book contains an excerpt from the forthcoming book *Wine Into Water* by Yvonne Kohano. This excerpt may not reflect the final content of the forthcoming edition.

Any people depicted in stock imagery provided by Thinkstock are models, and such images are being used for illustrative purposes only.

Certain stock imagery ©Thinkstock
Cover design: John Kochanowski

ISBN: 978-1-940738-35-2 (sc)
ISBN: 978-0-989330-50-3 (e)

Original Publication: 4/29/2013
Nanokas Press re-release date: 6/19/2015

Also by Yvonne Kohano

FLYNN'S CROSSING ROMANTIC SUSPENSE SERIES
Pictures of Redemption, Book 1
(Serena & Dane)

Flashes of Fire, Book 2
(DK & Vince)

Naked Intolerances, Book 3
(Gabby & Rick)

Tastes and Consequences, Book 4
(Mac & Roxy)

Blooms on the Bones, Book 5
(Tess & Powers)

Wine Into Water, Book 6
(Marguerite & Deke)

Love and the Christmas Tree Nymph, A Flynn's Crossing Seasonal Novella

Love's Touch of Justice, Book 7
(Jake & Marlee)

This Proposal Between Us, A Flynn's Crossing Seasonal Novella

Measure Twice, Love Once, Book 8
(Geno and Agnes)

And more to come!
Learn about upcoming releases at
www.YvonneKohano.com.

Subscribe to Yvonne Kohano's enewsletter to be among the first to learn about new releases and special offers. Visit www.yvonnekohano.com for more information.

Follow Yvonne at www.yvonnekohano.com, on Facebook as Yvonne Kohano, and on Twitter @yvonnekohano to learn what tickles her about being a writer, and at www.GooseYourMuse.com for creativity tips.

BLOOMS ON THE BONES

Prologue – Seven Months Ago

The graceful flute notes triggered by the swing of the front door informed her that another customer had arrived. The holiday season was always hectic, one of the few times of the year when she hired on extra help, both for delivery and to work in her flower shop. Escaping for a brief break, she hoped that a wave of the peace of the season would wash away her pain and sense of foreboding.

"Hello? Is anyone here?" Heavy footsteps tread on creaky old oak as the voice's male owner moved around the downstairs rooms.

Damn, where was Jan? The girl was supposed to be taking care of customers today for the last of the holiday arrangements.

"Hello, I have flowers to pick up…" The man's voice escalated in frustration, and it trailed away as he moved further from the front stairs. His rant grew fainter, this time from her kitchen, off limits to customers. Then, blessed silence.

Her head pounded, and the migraine that had begun as a mild annoyance earlier in the day was now a resounding hammer, complete with flashing lights behind her eyelids. Every noise was magnified a thousand times, and even the scents of her favorite flowers were vile and bitter. She needed a few more minutes for her energy to rebuild to a point where she could function.

The chimes hadn't sounded again, but she might have missed them. She concentrated on fighting off the brutal pain scraping across every nerve ending. Over the years, she'd learned to live with the odd voices that accompanied the pain. Sometimes, like today, she felt compelled to talk back to them, the urgency in her voice intended to send them away, along with the visions they sparked. Her Native American mentors assured her it was normal with her powers, though at times like this, she was more likely to believe Western medicine's diagnosis.

It was only a symptom of her chronic migraines.

At the raw edge of her agony, she sensed him more than heard him, a spirit to take notice of, as compelling as any she'd ever felt. Strong and commanding, an angry current swirled around him. A woodsy aroma came to her next, strangely comforting despite her pounding head. Usually the pain triggered her senses into overdrive, and yet his presence eased her.

The force moved closer. He was here, in her space, invading her privacy. What was the man doing in her bedroom? She needed to correct the situation immediately. These were her personal quarters, and yet he ignored the signs and came up the stairs anyway.

She opened a cautious eye in the darkened room. His big frame filled the doorway, backlit by natural light coming from below. Dark hair was close-cropped and his arms hung at his sides. His build looked fit in a bomber jacket and tailored slacks.

Both eyes wide opened now, she felt a surge that had nothing to do with her pain as a deep spark of recognition lit up her heart. In moments, the cacophony in her head was nowhere nearly as insistent as the magnetic pull she felt from the stranger grew stronger. The emotions surrounding him sucked her in.

"I'm, ah, sorry. I thought maybe someone up here could help me. I'm here to pick up an arrangement?" His husky voice boomed in the small space, and she felt it in her bones. "I heard someone talking up here," he added, by way of explanation. He stared at her, and she wondered what he could see in the dimmed room.

"I'll be with you in a moment, if you could just wait in the display area downstairs..." Her voice was as husky as his, though her tone was low and breathless. Where was this coming from? She hadn't had this kind of reaction in years. And the tumultuous feelings rolling off him were too much to contemplate right now.

The man hesitated, his hands flexing at his sides. She felt the intensity of his stare despite the induced gloom of the space. "I can come back later..." His voice trailed off as he waited for her to comment.

When she didn't immediately respond, he took a slow step into the room. "Are you all right?" His energy changed to worry – she could feel its shift – and he was advancing even further towards her bed until she swore they were breathing the same air. She felt their connection, his eyes seeking out hers in the dark.

She had to get him out of her refuge. He was too much of everything and the odd sensations he was raising had nothing to do with migraines or invasion and everything to do with his spirit.

Who the hell was he?

They both heard it at the same time and eyes jointly turned towards the bedroom door. "I'm sorry, I was out back on the phone. Hello? Is someone here?" The girl's voice sounded uncertain and faint as her light steps squeaked around the downstairs rooms.

His face in faint profile was chiseled and rugged, his expression holding both concern and frustration. Then his eyes flashed back to hers, and while she knew he couldn't see anything in the darkness, she sank deeper into the covers and hoped that her own confusion was hidden from his view.

"I am sorry to have disturbed you." His voice pitched deeper now. He hesitated once more, torn it seemed, between waiting for her reply and making his presence known to the voice below. He glanced between the door and the bed again, and his hand came out towards her. She sat up slightly, pulled by the strange energy that seemed to pour off him.

It felt like destiny.

They froze that way for who knows how long. Then he shook his head and backed out the door as quietly as he had arrived. The release of his potency came as a whoosh sucking everything out of her. It left her breathless and itchy.

And oddly, her migraine was gone.

Chapter 1

"I feel like we've waited forever to see these pictures." Tess Willowspring turned the ceiling fan above her covered patio to a faster setting and turned off the misters. Despite the heat, the sheltered alcove overlooking her garden was still the best place to hang out with her friends.

And every one of the girl tribe would be in attendance to review photo selections of Serena Williamson Ashland's wedding. Being the maid of honor meant obligations extending past the big event itself, but Tess didn't mind. It was enough to see the joy and peacefulness on her best friend's face. For some people, love conquered all.

"This would be easier on a big screen TV, you know," DK McGiven observed. The diamond on her finger shown as brightly as her smile in anticipation of her own wedding, date as yet unannounced.

Serena shot her a censuring glance. "No, it will be perfect like this. After all, we're not going to be blowing these shots up to poster size. They'll be in an album, both the paper kind and online, and viewing them on the laptop screen is ideal. And it's only been less than two months since the wedding."

Tess wrapped an arm around her shoulders. "Besides, this is where it all began, right? You told us about Dane on an evening like this last summer." She squeezed a little harder, reflecting on everything that had happened over the past year to her friends in Flynn's Crossing.

Serena and Dane fell in love and had an exotic Hawaiian beach wedding. DK met Vince and turned a friends-with-benefits relationship into her own engagement with the brusque writer. Gabby Cooley-Burke found her new love Rick, and finally set aside her past to honor a future that was as romantic as the novels she wrote. Roxy LaFollette reconnected with her old flame Mac, cooking up new ways to aggravate her actor/director boyfriend.

On cue, Roxy appeared at the back door with a large tray in her hands. The Hawaiian-themed snacks reminiscent of the Big Island were piled high, and yet she moved with ease between their chairs, handing out napkins as they grabbed for their selections. For a change, today she'd traded chef's whites for shorts and a t-shirt, and it was always a shock to see her dressed as a civilian.

"It is hard to imagine how much has changed, isn't it?" Roxy shook her head. "I can't wrap my brain around it sometimes. What's next for the girl tribe, do you think?"

All eyes shifted to Tess as the only unattached member currently in attendance. She fidgeted under the combined intensity of their gazes.

Without warning, her mind's eye focused on the memory of a tall powerful man standing across the sand from her on a sunset-lit beach. His gaze was intense, the vivid sheen of the water lapping a few feet away reflecting in the deep brown color of his eyes, giving them a surreal golden tint. The tenderness in his expression didn't have anything to do with her, but the emotion moved her just the same.

Shaking her head to clear it, she spun quickly and fussed at the sideboard, straightening things already lined up with precision. "Hey, don't look at me. There isn't a man on the horizon for me. Maybe it's Marguerite's turn."

"My turn for what, *cherie*?" Marguerite Devereaux picked that moment to come around the corner of the old Victorian, hip-checking the gate with a case in her arms. As

Tess rushed forward to lend a hand, she added, "It was my turn to bring the wine, *non*?"

With good-natured laughter, they assured her she'd done a fine job of it too. There would be more than enough to go around at the next couple of girl tribe get-togethers. She flipped her exotic mane of hair as she commented on it. "I am a woman of large appetites, *oui*?"

"Now if Gabby would get here, we could get started." Serena checked her phone and frowned. "Late again."

"Maybe she was having a hard time getting the boys settled," DK suggested.

"I can only imagine, though you know she has the organization skills of a general. But two eleven year old boys? I'm surprised she and Rick find any time alone together."

"Yeah, I'm almost feeling guilty about taking her away from them, even for the evening." Serena's face brightened again. "But the wolf pack is meeting tonight too. Dane is having them over to look at the groom's album. We get to pick and choose from the bride's – and the groom's too if we want to be nosy."

A sudden whirlwind of activity burst out of the back door. "Sorry! I'm sorry, I tried not to be late tonight. Rick took the boys with him to the wolf pack meeting, and they wanted to make sure they had every electronic game they own with them." Gabby shook her head vigorously. "The boys said that looking at wedding pictures is mushy, and they can't understand why the men want to do it. I'm not sure the guys realize what they're in for."

"See, told you," DK chimed in as they all chuckled and Gabby reached for a glass of wine.

Tess looked around at her best friends, the women who had brought so much richness and pleasure to her life over the last few years. Their bond was only growing stronger, even as it expanded to include the men in their lives. Still, the opportunities to get together like this, all six of them, were growing fewer and the times in between sometimes stretched for weeks.

Change was good, she assured herself. How many of those possibilities had they discussed for hours at gatherings like this? Even the slight warm breeze and the lowering sun were reminders of times past. But she shivered in the heat, sensing that more change was coming, and she might not appreciate the challenge.

"Oh, look how well-matched the two of you are! Tess, come see this." Serena held out a hand to her, and Tess hesitated, afraid of what the pictures captured. When the laptop was turned towards her, it verified worst suspicion.

It was Powers, standing rugged and tall, his arm wrapped around her shoulders and a hand resting tightly on her upper arm. She could still feel the imprint of it, weeks later. Even in his stillness, she felt his restless protection.

But it was his face that caught her attention. Behind his forced smile, pain and longing warred an unsuccessful battle against neutrality. Tess grabbed back her hand just as it started to lift, unable to stop herself from wanting to reach out to him even now.

The echo of pain marking the start of another migraine misted the edges of the picture in front of her. With it, faint voices chanted angrily in her mind and an unsteadiness shook her body. Focusing once more on the face of the man before her, she traced an unsteady finger down the picture where their bodies touched. And the pain and noise subsided.

Chapter 2

If Powers Ashland was a color, he'd be black. As in black and white, with no in between. As in distinct and direct and to the point. As in his mood when his brother called him to insist he host this event.

"It's what the best man is supposed to do, you know," Dane told him.

"I thought I did everything I was supposed to do before the wedding, and in Hawaii. Now this?"

It wasn't that he was actually angry about it. In fact, he was ecstatic that Dane had found his way back to society with a woman who loved him despite the demons he carried. For a time, Powers had thought those demons would end up killing his little brother.

He grabbed four bottles of beer from the fridge and considered crawling inside the box himself. He'd spent the day in the blistering heat wave roasting the Sacramento summer, and despite a cold shower and his A/C on high in his truck, his bones still felt baked just short of ash. The cooler breeze here at the house Dane and Serena built on a mountainside cliff outside Flynn's Crossing carried a hint of welcomed relief.

"This is what we're eating? Why didn't you get Roxy to make us something?" Self-proclaimed wolf pack head-wolf Vince Cassidy complained loudly as he poked at the deli tray choices. "This looks like it's from some grocery chain."

Powers felt a grumble of anger coming out. Why couldn't someone else organize things? He worked in the hot sun all day, and they got to sit around in their air-conditioned home offices doing intellectual shit for their jobs. He doubted there was a single blister on any of their hands.

"Come on, give the guy a break, okay? He doesn't know the area well – yet." His brother's teasing voice was accompanied by a genial hand slapping Powers' back. "He's still learning."

He turned to look in Dane's face, ready to give in to his anger. The deep white scar on Dane's cheek stood out even more prominently after two weeks in the tropical sun, a visible badge of the challenges he'd overcome. It was the peace and tranquility in his brother's eyes, though, that stopped him. Dane always saw too much, and the tension steaming off Powers was probably visible to anyone's naked eye.

Throwing his own arm across Dane's leaner shoulders, Powers forced joviality into his voice.

"Yeah, sorry guys. I didn't know Roxy's was the only place to go. I thought any old deli would do. But I did bring some great beer."

He'd made a point of stopping at a microbrewery in Sacramento and brought a selection of their seasonal offerings. If it wasn't against the law, he would have given in to the temptation to pop the cap off one of those icy cold bottles for the drive up the hill, but a heavily ingrained sense of right and wrong forced him to be law-abiding. That brew sure tasted good now as he took his first swallow.

"Love this stuff. I may have to drag DK down to the valley and try this place out. It would make a good review for my international column." Vince took an appreciative sip. "Okay, I almost forgive you for the shitty food selection."

It was hard to please a world-famous lifestyle writer.

Beside him, Dane chuckled and slapped Powers on the back one more time. The gesture came just in time to calm a new snarl of frustration.

"…but Dad, I think a dog would be great for us. After all, we have to learn responsibility. There's a fence around the backyard so it can't run away, and between Jeremy and me, we'll take great care of it. We'll feed it and play with it and clean up after it and train it and everything. And it could come here and play with Trina, and it could play with Fusion at DK and Vince's house. It would have its own club, just like we have the wolf pack."

Rick Chagres' lips were set in a single tight line as he entered the great room, trailed by two tall young boys and a puppy currently trying to catch the loose shoelace on one boy's foot.

"Will, you and Jeremy need to lay off the dog thing for a while, okay? Gabby and I are trying to figure out a lot of things, and it's not the best time to bring a dog into the family. Can you understand that?"

Powers noted the boys exchanging a sly glance without saying a word, and two sets of shoulders shrugged as they grinned and winked. As a unit, they dropped to the floor and started wrestling with the mound of yellow fur, punctuated by three sets of happy growls. Rick didn't look back at them, but his face broke into a relaxed smile as if he knew exactly what they were doing, and when he caught Powers watching him, he winked.

"Beer?" Powers extended a bottle, and with a grateful nod, Rick took it and finally turned to look at the boys horsing around with Trina the puppy on the floor.

"Thanks. They've been on this kick for quite a while now, ever since you," he pointed the clear beer bottle accusingly at Dane, "let them play with your new bundle of fur that Saturday night after you adopted her. Before, Jeremy was bothering Gabby about a puppy. Now it's both of them." He shook his head. "More craziness right now is not what we need."

Still, the man smiled, and he didn't look all that put out.

Envy kicked up, and Powers hunched in surprise at the rush of it. To a man, these new friends seemed to be content and fulfilled, with women who loved them no matter how crazy their pasts. First his brother, then the brusque and obnoxious Vince, the stalwart university professor Rick with a ready-made family in his own son Will and his love's boy Jeremy, and finally a new member of the wolf pack, Mac Smythe.

It was Mac's fault that Roxy had nicknamed the guys the wolf pack, responsibility which he accepted with good-natured ribbing. The drool-worthy young actress in his movie had been the cause, and the resulting label now applied to their loosely-knit gang of guys. Rumor had it that Mac was looking at property in the area to be closer to Roxy and had already put his Hollywood home on the market.

Settled and happy. It was something Powers would never be. He knew he was best off alone.

A recurring memory drifted across his thoughts, mesmerizing golden eyes unlike any he'd ever seen and the feel of a spirited woman, powerful in his arms. The trace of intense energy made him shiver in the summer heat.

"So you're coming, right?" Dane stood at his shoulder as all of the men's eyes rested on Powers. He wasn't sure what he was agreeing to, but it was better than explaining his lack of attention. There would be no end of ribbing if he said he was daydreaming of a woman.

"Sure, wouldn't miss it. When is it again?"

The others all laughed, and Powers took a gulp of beer to cover his confusion.

"Yeah, funny Powers. The fourth of July is July the fourth. According to Marguerite, you can see a dozen fireworks displays from the winery." Vince took his own gulp and added, "And she'll be there."

Powers wanted to ignore the emphasis on the word she. He played dumb.

"Which 'she'?"

The men all laughed again, and Rick even punched Powers on the arm and called him a sly dog. "I thought we would need to cover the boys' eyes, you know, before they started asking questions."

"Seriously, the two of you were so hot together at the wedding reception that we thought we were going to have to throw you in the ocean," Vince said with a mischievous smirk.

Only Dane was silent, and Powers could see him, watchful as always, waiting to see how his older brother would take this kidding around. Finally, he turned to a laptop set out on the dining room table and activated the screen. On it, a montage of wedding photos came to life.

"The camera can't lie, you know." He fiddled with the cursor and fast-forwarded through more pictures until he found the one he wanted. "See for yourself. Hot as hot can be." Dane turned the screen towards the group.

It was a photo of the maid of honor and best man, a candid shot taken as they were dancing. Tess was staring into his face, and he was holding her closer than needed. With her hand resting on the back of his neck, she stood slender and dainty in his arms. And his palm was flat on the curve of her hip, his fingers at the base of her spine. The camera captured the intensity of their expressions, as deep as the dark night sky behind them.

Yeah, pretty hot. Damned if he knew what to do with it. His fingers tingled remembering exactly how soft and smooth that bare skin felt, and he wasn't sure the sensation would ever go away.

*****

"Sure you don't want to stay the night? It's a long drive down the hill in the dark, and there are no street lights for miles."

Little brother taking care of big brother, Powers mused. What an interesting shift in priorities.

"Nah, I'll be fine. Besides, I don't want to intrude on the newlyweds."

They both chuckled at that, Dane's tone filled with satisfaction.

Powers cringed. Damn, there it was again. Longing washed over him as quickly as one of those Hawaiian waves, and as soon as he could catch his breath, there she was in the forefront of his mind. It was like he was a laser and his guidance system sought her out, no matter what.

The time in Hawaii had been a test in patience, leading up to Serena and Dane's wedding day. A long punishing swim back and forth across the bay that morning had done little to exhaust his brain, even as it made his muscles feel lax with the burn. Every time he felt her presence, his eyes were drawn to her.

She lounged on a chaise under one of the bright orange umbrellas set in neat rows on the beach. Her sunglasses covered any expression and he wasn't sure if she was looking his way, but as he pulled his body out of the water, it felt like something scorched him. It wasn't the sun at his back, because the power of it ran across his chest and down his torso like a swift caress.

He made a point of staring at her. If she could get an eyeful, he'd take his own in return.

Deliberately raking his gaze down her body, he was immediately sorry he'd done it. The one piece suit fit her curves like the skin she'd been born in. Somehow, it was sexier than a bikini, because while it covered so much, it also left just enough to the imagination to make ripping it off a tempting idea.

When he grabbed his towel, he was grateful it was large enough to casually hold in front and cover the arousal that suddenly made his board shorts seem snug and revealing. He hadn't wanted any woman this badly in a very long time, and there wasn't a single reason why this particular woman triggered his reaction. Finding one of their rooms and slowly peeling off both their suits to explore the longing suddenly seemed like an excellent idea.

He couldn't help his thoughts from wandering further into heated memories. The copper colored dress Tess had chosen to wear for the wedding was a sublime match for the deep olive tone her tan had taken in the Hawaiian sun. From the front, it looked demure enough, a halter that set off her Native American heritage, those high cheekbones, her graceful neck, and strong but delicate shoulders. It ended below the knee, and her bare feet in the sand were sexier than any shoe would have been.

It wasn't until she'd turned to stand next to him as they readied to walk down the makeshift beach aisle that he noticed the rest of the dress, or lack of it. There was no back. The halter met at her neck, and the base of it went oh-so-low down to meet below her waist.

It was barely decent. Fighting the urge to find something to cover all that skin, he had to remind himself that she'd worn less on the beach the day before.

"Ah, Powers? You're daydreaming."

Dane's words snapped him back to the big living room cocooned in dense darkness outside.

"No, not at all, no. Just thinking about a problem – a construction problem. That's all."

He glanced over at Dane to find his brother grinning. With a pointed look at Powers' crotch, the smile got even wider.

"Construction problems getting you that excited these days?"

Powers shifted uncomfortably in his jeans and realized that the zipper was rubbing him exactly the wrong way. Grabbing a pillow from the couch, he covered the evidence in his lap and gave Dane his darkest stare.

His brother laughed.

Getting up to head to the fridge, Dane returned with two beers and a more sober expression. He regarded him thoughtfully.

"The camera didn't lie, did it?" It wasn't so much a question as a statement. "You do feel something for Tess."

Powers shook his head to deny it even as Dane returned the gesture to tell him he was full of shit. Sighing and leaning back against the couch, Powers covered his face in resignation and waited for Dane to say more. He expected some good-natured ribbing, more of the same along the lines of the guys earlier in the evening.

It was quiet for so long, he finally opened his eyes to find Dane watching him with sympathy.

"Oh man you've got it bad, don't you?"

He needed to change the direction of this discussion, and fast.

Waving off the question as he tossed the pillow aside, he got up to pace the length of the living room and stare out at the dark night. It was, as Dane had noted, pitch black. There was no moon tonight and with the interior lights on, few details were obvious outside.

"Yeah, maybe I will stay the night, if you don't mind. Then I can actually finish this beer rather than pour it out. Besides, I have something else to discuss with you."

Not that his brother would welcome this topic. It was one they'd argued about before without any satisfactory conclusion.

"What's up? Dad bugging you again?"

Their father would always be a source of contention, but on this, they were united.

Turning to the room again, Powers dropped back to his place on the sofa and stretched out his legs, toying with the label on his beer bottle.

"Dad's always bugging me. You know how he is. Even though I have legal and financial control over the California branch of Ashland, he wants it run his way. And his way isn't always my way."

Dane chuckled in understanding as he took a swig from his own bottle.

"I'm glad it's you dealing with him and not me, that's all I can say." He paused, mirroring his brother in sudden attention to the paper wrapper. "You know that I invited him to the wedding."

Powers started in surprise. "No, I didn't know that. Why did you do that? Did you really want him there after all of his slights over the years?"

Dane shrugged. "I thought it was appropriate. He is, after all, our father. I thought that it would be right to introduce him to my wife." He huffed out a bitter laugh. "Not that he thought it was important. The bastard said he wouldn't take time off from work. And he invited – though I use the word loosely – Serena and me up to visit him in Portland, at his convenience. I stress the last phrase." Dane paused again, shaking his head. "He said he's a very busy man."

Now, it was Powers' turn to snarl.

Chapter 3

Each whack of the hoe on recalcitrant weeds gave Tess a shot of satisfaction. The sun wasn't up yet, but the heated air already weighed heavily on her shoulders. It was the only time of day during this heat wave when working outside was mildly tolerable.

Weeding was something she usually enjoyed, taking it as a gift of time for meditation, contemplation and centering. Gratification grew in making the beds neat and tidy, and she enjoyed the tumbles of hearty plants, some bound for her kitchen and others for the displays of flowers she designed in her shop. Seeing things grow from tiny seeds and bare earth was always a wonder.

Plants had lessons to teach us, too, though the one about patience was not working for her today. She still had last night's admonitions of the girl tribe ringing in her ears.

"Look at how great the two of you fit together, Tess. Powers is just the right everything for you." Gabby wouldn't stop commenting on this. The shots of the maid of honor and best man, looking first over the photographer's shoulder into the distance, then looking directly at the camera, and finally in candid shots, seemed to be all anyone wanted to view.

Neither one of them was smiling sincerely. In fact, you could see the tension on their faces. They couldn't wait to take two steps away from each other.

Serena added her opinion. "You've never given him a chance, you know. I don't understand why, since you barely know each other. Why did you develop this instant dislike for him?"

Roxy and Marguerite hung back, conferring in the background but not immediately adding their thoughts. When they did, though, she wished they'd stayed quiet.

"We know what it's like to be fixed up, but you have to admit he's a good looking guy. He owns his own business, he's successful, and he's dedicated to his family. What's not to like?"

The weed in front of her didn't stand a chance when she considered this last comment.

She needed to push him away. It wasn't the take-charge attitude, which she'd even appreciated as they fulfilled their wedding party duties to the bride and groom. His gruff demeanor made him an easy target for teasing. And he was handsome in a rugged outdoorsy kind of way.

There was something in his spirit, though, something she felt would be deadly if she allowed him to get too close to her turbulent world. She blamed the sudden flame of heat at the thought on the rising sun at her back.

She'd seen too much evidence of it herself. Most of the time, Powers kept a tight grip on his emotions. He smiled occasionally, laughed rarely, and hid what he was feeling behind a thick cloak that was impenetrable. To say he was intense was like saying the sun currently beating down on her was merely the light from a dim bulb.

But there were times, so few and far between that Tess could count them on her fingers, when his heart peaked through. As he watched Dane and Serena exchange their vows, the cloak magically lifted and she was staggered by the beautiful spirit blazing more brilliantly than the Big Island's setting sun. He seemed to glow with energy and vitality so strong that Tess glanced around to see if anyone noticed. But everyone else watched at the bride and groom.

As her eyes returned to gape in wonder, Powers turned his head slightly and met her gaze. The instant zap of connection had her leaning forward as if he was pulling a rope that bound her. His expression changed from curious to shaken to raw in three heartbeats. He seemed to suck in the humid air, and then turned back abruptly to the ceremony occurring between them.

When the powerful connection cut off with his averted eyes, she wondered how she kept herself from falling forward in the sand. There had been glimpses as they'd supported their friends in preparing for the wedding. But none were as strong as that day.

She felt a bond like this before, at her most vulnerable, but she discounted that. That bond had marked her destiny, the only one who would be her guardian. And she didn't want or need him.

Tess blinked at the ground and realized she was hoeing at the mulched dirt path between her beds. In her reverie, she'd weeded one long row and the sun had risen well into the sky. Sweat ran down her back under her t-shirt and its trickle reminded her of other sensations.

Mixing formal with casual, Serena and Dane chose a celebratory dinner in the open air on the old hotel's stone patio. Tiki torches lit the perimeter and shed small pools of light on the gentle waves lapping in the bay below. Old Hawaiian music drifted over the small group as the ensemble played in a bar on another terrace. At one point, the bandleader could be heard explaining about the wedding party and the dedication of a song for the bride and groom's first dance.

The newlyweds swayed in tightly locked arms, and according to tradition, Tess and Powers joined them next. The gentle strains of Hawaiian slack key were at odds with the stiff way he held her, even as she fought the urge to push as far away as his arms would allow. When she looked up, he didn't need to say it.

God, would she ever get that searing fierce glare he'd given her out of her mind?

"Is something wrong?" She felt compelled to ask the question, because the dislike emanating from him was so strong.

"No, nothing." He shook his head. "You're stunning tonight."

The odd combination of sentiments, angry eyes and compliments from his lips, had her feet faltering, and his hands tightened on her shoulders to keep them both upright. Then his fingers slid to her back and traced her bare spine from neck to waist. And there his hand stayed until the guitar's strumming stopped.

The gentle slide on her skin had been more than enough to set off fires in every nerve in her body. Her reaction was so unwanted that she immediately denied it. It was the magic of the moment, the emotional tides of the day, and the sensuous whisper of tropical night breezes that awoke those feelings.

It couldn't be the man.

His eyes stayed on hers, and after her question, a curtain fell and his face became unreadable in the shifting light. She wasn't sure what hers was saying, but he didn't appear to like it. His lips compressed into grim tightness, which was a shame, given their sensuous fullness during his rare smiles.

Tess heaved a sigh and realized that she'd been standing as still as a tree in her garden for long minutes, remembering his striking features. On Dane, the lines were softer, but for Powers, the planes and valleys were deeply carved jags. Days spent in the weather had hardened him, and no amount of office time dulled the edge.

He reminded her of ancestral warriors, carrying a mantle of responsibility from which others would run. The illusion brought a shiver as sweat burned her eyes. And chants echoed briefly in her mind.

Chapter 4

The bite of chlorine was harsh today, intense enough to stay in his pores past the post-workout shower and his day full of meetings. His skin would still stink of this when he sat with a beautiful woman over cocktails as the sun ditched the city below a smudged horizon.

Except there was no beautiful woman. He would take this lonely perfume to his bed without the benefit of a gentle reproach of flared nostril. It alone would scent his dreams.

Powers pushed for three more laps before pulling himself up on the edge of the pool. Windows lining one wall opened to the building's state of the art gym, empty in the predawn. Those willing to work out this early were probably taking advantage of the only cool hours of the day to hit the city streets for their jog. He preferred the pool. He'd be dry and baking soon enough.

He tried not to linger on his loneliness. This life had been everything he'd known for so long, and he welcomed the lack of distractions. His marriage years ago, right out of college and a mistake before it even started, had lasted only long enough to give him a wonderful son, Chris. Granted, he hadn't seen him as much as he should have over the years, but he tried to make sure he was there for the most important occasions.

At college short miles way, Chris was one reason to move to the region. The fact that he didn't need his father's meddling hadn't completely dissuaded Powers. Not one to shy away from an opportunity, his son shared his opinion on his father's life.

"It's been almost two decades since your divorce, Dad. You're not supposed to be a monk."

There had been plenty of women, Powers assured Chris, distractions who helped pass the time between the pressing concerns of work. What he didn't add was that none of them were willing to stick around once they'd experienced the full force of his personality.

"Why are you so driven?" It was a common question from various dates.

Powers was never sure how to respond, so instead of saying anything, he acted, pushing his intensity into momentary attention to whichever woman was in his arms. His attention never lasted, and neither did they.

He wasn't lonely, he assured himself. He liked being alone.

Toweled off and robed, he headed for the elevator to his penthouse. The more enduring side of his intensity gave him the ability to afford a living space that suited him. Pumping his energy into the family construction business paid off, even if it took everything out of him.

Ashland Inc. had begun as Ashland Construction, a small competitor in the otherwise big industrial and office development market in the Portland area. His father bid on projects that brought the company recognition and always met his deadlines. They delivered fine buildings, and they were now doing it beyond the borders of Oregon and Washington.

It had taken years for his father to acknowledge that Powers was worthy of the mantle of responsibility necessary to expand into new territories.

"Sacramento? Why down there? What's in it for us in California?" His father had quizzed him repeatedly without really listening to the response.

"Dad, the area is ripe for our type of projects. Urban infill is on the political radar, and recovery from the economic downturn means that there are organizations willing to build again. There are more contracts than companies to perform them. And anything we do on spec will be picked up quickly."

Months of arguing did little to change his father's disapproval. But a change of tactics brought immediate agreement.

"Dane's there, Dad, and he's not coming back. He needs me. I have to keep an eye on him." That had been over a year ago.

Of course, Dane no longer needed him, except as a brother and a friend. He'd found his own way back. And with his return, some of the purpose that drove Powers was lost.

*****

"I'm thinking that we could expand the company's horizons, Powers. We've made great inroads in the usual types of projects, but there are some interesting ones that don't fit our standard model."

Powers looked over the top of his reading glasses at his contracts officer. Marty was as bookish as they came, complete with pocket protector and tablet computer running multiple spreadsheet programs. Why he needed the pocket protector was a mystery, since he never seemed to use a pen. The stylus in constant movement on his tablet would never stain anything.

"You don't think we're busy enough?"

Sacramento had been ripe for new development when Ashland Inc. entered the market, and the improving economy was a sign that good investments could be made here. Powers' people had found ideal locations for urban infill projects, converting empty lots or abandoned buildings in and near downtown into new lofts, offices, residential housing and commercial and retail space. The mayor was ecstatic, and the governor, aware of how this would help the state capitol's image, had also expressed her support. The blue and white Ashland logo was now evident at construction sites all over the city. And it had only been a little over a year.

When his father urged him to use an estimator from Portland, Powers refused. Sacramento was a political town, and knowing people, the right people, would go a long way towards being successful in the construction trade. Interviewing candidates for the contracts job had been one of his first priorities a year and a half ago.

The job consisted of the mundane, running numbers to bid on projects and completing the extensive bid packages required. The unsaid but understood part of the job was schmoozing the right people so that Ashland would have the newest and latest information on upcoming opportunities.

Unassuming and unremarkable, Marty still seemed to know everyone and everything important on the region's projects. Not for the first time, Powers was glad he'd trusted his instincts when he hired him. Now he trusted Marty with responsibility way past his job formal description.

Tossing his glasses aside, Powers quizzed him, "What do you have in mind?"

"I'm thinking historical infill projects. You know, old town work, buildings that need to be culturally accurate and fitting with the history in an area. There are a surprising number of projects coming up like this, often sponsored by nonprofits. It might be a good tie-in for Vision Quest too."

Powers sat back and closed his eyes. His foundation, the one he'd originally started in the hope that it could help Dane, had expanded into areas he hadn't even imagined. After their initial disagreement about it, the brothers had joined forces to make it bigger and better, expanding services available to individuals in need. But supporting history? That would be something new.

"I'm not sure about the foundation, but the projects could be rewarding. And most would probably be smaller in scope, so we could use them to keep crews and subcontractors busy at points in the big projects where there's a lull. Of course, it can't become something that stretches us so much that we don't meet our major deadlines."

Marty was already nodding in agreement. "Most are small, like a single building. In almost every project I'm looking at, there's already an architect on board and the designs are detailed and approved. They would be straightforward construction jobs. The crews might appreciate the challenge of the historical aspects too. Something different, you know?"

Different could be good. It kept the guys and gals on their toes to practice their crafts in a way that called to the artisan in them. And the exposure, with the Ashland name supporting these community activities, would be good for networking.

Powers leaned forward and took a long sip out of his soda can. "Let's explore it. Use the same parameters that we established for bottom line potential and ability to schedule the work. I don't see any reason why this would be anything other than a great idea."

Chapter 5

"This is a very bad idea." Tess shot out her conviction to Chase Wolford, the owner of Oil+Vinegar on Main Street, as he smiled across the table.

"Come on, it's a very good idea and you know it. You've been the chair of the redevelopment committee for Main Street for years, and the design of the building is so much yours that we should probably name it after you." Chase chuckled and stirred his coffee.

Tess had her doubts. In fact, she could elevate that to grave concerns. Everything about the project aggravated her to the point where her migraines were becoming a weekly occurrence.

Besides, she knew nothing about construction.

"This isn't my area of expertise. Overseeing the selection of the construction company and being their liaison for general questions isn't what I had in mind when we began the project last fall." She looked around Brew Bank Bakery's half-filled tables and cases of treats for another more likely candidate.

"You are definitely the best choice," confirmed Stuart, one of the co-owners of the bakery, as he delivered Tess's herbal tea. His partner Sarge yelled across the room, "No doubt about it."

She smiled weakly at their voiced support.

"Besides," Chase continued, "you'll have Kevin answering any of their architectural questions, and the mayor is sending someone experienced to help with construction bid review. I'll be in the background too, supporting you in any way I can."

His tone made Tess glance up from her tea quickly to meet his eyes. They were kind eyes behind his glasses, the pain he'd experienced as a widower, realizing that he'd chosen career over family for too long, adding layers of complexity. For the past month, he'd been gently but repeatedly asking her out.

Tess blushed, grateful that the tan her olive skin had acquired in Hawaii had been reinforced by time in her garden. Chase probably wouldn't notice. She didn't want to embarrass him, good friend that he was. The concept of dating him was hard to imagine, since she'd been friends with his wife Marci and still missed the woman's energy on their various downtown business association activities.

"Why don't you head the committee? You'd be thorough, with your management consulting background and your experience in big business and..."

Chase already had his hand up to stop her. "I can't, not while I'm chair of the association too. And with the girls out of school for the summer, I'm trying to be better about allocating my time."

Tess knew his daughters were the center of Chase's universe now. Marci had named them after movie stars she admired, Soph after Sophia Loren, and Bella after Isabella Rossellini. She'd adored anything Italian, which brought her to her business idea of a shop offering olive oils and gourmet vinegars. After her death, Chase quit his fancy consulting gig and become a full time dad and storekeeper.

He'd chosen wisely, in her opinion. Over the past year, Tess had seen her friend struggle to establish a sense of normalcy for his daughters and himself. He threw his extensive energies into the shop, the downtown business association, and the myriad activities of his girls.

Tess realized she hadn't said anything for a couple of minutes, and Chase was staring at her.

"I'm sorry, I was thinking again about how much has changed for my friends here in Flynn's Crossing over the past year."

He smiled indulgently. "They have, haven't they? I heard Mac Smythe visited the old Prescott ranch out near Roxy's restaurant. It's been on the market for years and it's pretty rundown, but I guess when you're a movie star with deep pockets, you can afford to fix up a place like that into anything you want."

Tess chuckled. "Yes, he's in hot pursuit, and Roxy gives him grief for it even though we know she secretly loves every second of his attention. When she agrees to take a day or two away from her businesses, he either flies here or sends a plane to bring her to him. It's kind of cute, actually, to see our men-are-scum girl so smitten."

"Yeah, and Serena, and DK, and Gabby – all off the market. We he-men in the community will need to barricade the streets so that no more outsiders move in on our women." He puffed up his chest in mock bravado.

Her laugh seemed to reward him. Then his face became more serious and he reached across the table to take her hand.

Tess froze. In all of the years she'd known Chase, first distantly as the spouse of a fellow business owner, and then as he'd become the shopkeeper down the street, they rarely ever touched. It wasn't that it bothered her, but it wasn't part of their friendship.

"I have an idea." Chase leaned a little closer across the table, still trapping her hand in his. "Let's go to the Witch Hill Winery fireworks party together."

Blowing out a sigh, Tess relaxed. It wasn't a date. His girls would be there, as they wouldn't miss that for the world. And she'd be going along as a friend. Besides, the girl tribe would be there too. They wouldn't be alone.

"That would be nice, Chase. I haven't had much of a chance to see Soph and Bella in the last couple of months. We can catch up."

Giving her hand a squeeze, he beamed at her. "Oh, that will have to wait. The girls are visiting my mother, so I'm an unattached bachelor for the next two weeks. I'll pack us a picnic and pick you up about five. That gives us plenty of time to find a nice quiet spot away from the winery to watch the fireworks. It's a great idea."

Chapter 6

Sacramento in July was hot, dusty, and golden, with shots of blue from the unfailingly sunny skies and the sparkling ribbons of the rivers running through it. The park around the capitol stood out like a brilliant green emerald among the downtown buildings, with the trees the city was famous for lining the surrounding streets in grid-like precision. There was no denying how flat the valley was, from the low hills to the west, marking the boundary between the valley's heat and the Pacific coast's cooler climate, to the Sierra Nevada mountains to the east, rising up off the valley floor at a steep angle.

From mountains to coastal range, nothing would interrupt the view of numerous fireworks displays in the region. The Independence Day fireworks party at Witch Hill Winery was an event not to be missed, but Powers waffled on committing to Dane. It was only when Chris called with the news that he and his girlfriend were attending that Powers relented. He even tossed off a dismissive laugh when Chris tried to get him to agree to a double date.

But once in his car and pointed towards the mountains, he wasn't so sure he could keep from scowling throughout the evening. Tess would be there, and every time he thought about her, his gut clenched and he had to make a conscious effort to keep his face bland. It wasn't just the wedding and reception that he remembered.

In his memory, it was as clear as if it happened yesterday.

He was already late to a Christmas season dinner at his brother's house, a visit he'd actually been looking forward to as an opportunity to get to know is future sister-in-law better. Serena had been the reason Dane rejoined society. Getting to know her was going to be an honor.

Settling on a gift for the evening had been easy. Dane told him about a flower shop owned by Serena's best friend, a place called Buds and Blooms on Main Street in Flynn's Crossing. He could even order his arrangement online. All he had to do was pick it up and be on his way.

He hadn't counted on the pile-up on the freeway, stopping traffic as the highway patrol sorted out SUVs, cars, and an astounding number of snowboards and skis heading up to the snowy Sierras. The hour-long delay meant he needed to forgo coffee in the unique Brew Bank Bakery up the street and head directly for the flowers instead.

His impatience was already tuned to high as he waited for someone to come to the front display room of Buds and Blooms and give him his arrangement. When no one answered his hello, it moved off the dial to blasting and he went looking for a worker to get his damned flowers.

A search of the downstairs came up empty, and he'd already been there for over five minutes. The upstairs was off-limits according to the sign, but that was the only place left to check. Besides, he was now very late.

In contrast to the airy light of the rest of the old Victorian, the open door at the top of the stairs was dark and forbidding. He couldn't help himself. He had to check it out. And the sound of a woman's voice pulled him forward, dangerous and soothing at the same time.

He stopped abruptly in a doorway, barely making out the form of someone in a rumpled bed. He couldn't see well in the gloom, thought his eyes zeroed in on a remarkable face. The features were Native American and striking, even in the faded light. Her eyes seemed to glow, and when they met his, he'd explained his purpose. He felt like an intruder, and felt compelled to add, "I heard someone talking up here."

"I'll be with you in a moment, if you could just wait in the display room downstairs..." Her tone stroked across his nerves and his impatience suddenly disappeared. He wanted to linger, to hear what else she had to say, and to ask her what was wrong. Her voice held pain and its vulnerability wasn't something he could turn away from.

"Listen, I can come back later..." His voice trailed off as he waited for her to comment. The feeling of impotence, of being a bystander instead of a player, made him antsy. A ripple of energy seemed to thrum through the air between them, heating his skin and making the hairs on the back of his neck stand at attention.

The sudden urge to help in any way he could was not his normal reaction. His slow step into the room decided him. "Are you all right?" If she needed it, he would pick her up and carry her to his truck and find the nearest emergency room.

The voice downstairs distracted them both. Oh yeah, he was here to pick up some flowers.

Turning back to the bed, he could just make out large golden eyes above the bed covers. He wanted to say or do something that mattered, but he wasn't sure what that was. The apology he offered instead felt vague and insincere. Before he realized it, his hand was extended to her in supplication.

When she leaned forward, he hoped – god, he didn't know what he'd hoped. But the longer he stood there, the more unsettled he became. When she didn't answer, he turned again for the door.

The young woman downstairs had apologized profusely for not being there to wait on him immediately. She pulled his arrangement out of a large cooler and set it in a box, and she'd begun her litany of apologies again as he'd turned slowly for the door. On her merry 'Happy

Holidays' as the chimes sounded, he couldn't help but pause and stare up the stairs one last time before shaking his head in disbelief. The connection must have been a figment of his tired brain.

Months later, at Dane's wedding date announcement dinner at a place called Roxy's, Powers wasn't even thinking about that day. He was elated Dane and Serena had set a date, and he was honored to be his brother's best man. Striding into the room off the main hall in the quaint restaurant, his brain was still on a problem with a subcontractor on one of his construction sites, and rush hour traffic had aggravated him. Dinner was not necessarily in the forefront of his mind, but a drink would be nice.

He forgot it all, the drink, the problem, his brother. In fact, he couldn't remember his own name. Golden eyes met his across the room, and any sense of place was lost to him.

Her hair was raven black with a silver streak gleaming down one side. It hung straight and long, out of sight down a back that was perfectly straight without being stiff. Her face in profile belonged to another era. Her Native American roots gave her a regal bearing, any fierceness tempered by the gentleness in her expression.

The voice gave her away. Even across the room, he recognized its husky tone. And as conversation stopped and everyone turned to look at him, her golden eyes widened at their connection.

Chapter 7

"I have to admit that I'm surprised you agreed to a date with him." Marguerite poured two tastes of Sangiovese and handed the glasses to Tess.

"I'm kind of surprised too. I thought his daughters would be here, and it would be like a friend joining a family outing. Once I found out the girls were away, I couldn't think of a graceful way to back out." Tess turned to look over her shoulder at Chase, sitting in a camp chair at the edge of the crowd. He waved, his eyes intent on her discussion with the winemaker.

"*M'amie*, he is quite handsome, a good father, and a good businessman. He is charming and pleasant."

Tess knew that. "He's all of that, and nice and safe."

"That is a problem?" Marguerite's expressive eyebrows went up on the question.

Not really a problem, but not very exciting either.

She was saved from responding when the winemaker's attention was required by other guests. Tess wanted to linger longer, but she was out of reasons to stand at the outdoor bar without anyone around her. Sighing, she picked up the wine glasses and turned back to her chair.

And Chase.

He smiled and stood as she approached. He'd wanted to get the wine himself, but she'd insisted. He was waiting on her, and it was beginning to feel uncomfortable. When Marguerite stepped to this end of the bar, she'd jumped up and grabbed their empty glasses before he had a chance to react.

"You didn't have to do that, you know. I was happy to get it." He took a glass from her and waited until she sat in a low-slung chair before dropping into his own.

"Good turnout, don't you think? Davinia and Marcus must be pleased. And people sure seem to love Marguerite's wines." He took a sip and met Tess's eyes over the rim of the glass. "Luscious."

The remark would have been creepy, except Chase wiggled his eyebrows at her, and she couldn't help herself at his expression. She laughed.

*****

"Dad, this is my girlfriend, Pamela. Honey, this is my father, Powers."

Chris handled the introduction with good humor, an arm around the shy looking young woman at his side. Even behind big glasses and wearing no make-up, Powers could see the reasons for his son's attraction. The girl was pretty in an earnest sort of way, the kind of woman a young man would want to take care of.

"And this is one of our professors, Dr. Melissa Kinkead. Melissa, this is my father, Powers Ashland."

The woman was sleek and polished and austere, someone who knew she was good-looking and expected the world to recognize her allure as well. Her animation was remarkable in its total absence. Powers shook a hand that was too cool in the summer evening and quirked an eyebrow at his son before excusing them both and pulling the boy towards the bar.

"Is this what I think it is?" He all but growled the words in Chris's ear, but the young man didn't seem in the least bit concerned.

"Yes, Dad, I'm trying to fix you up. But it's cool. She's one of our favorite teachers, and despite the way she looks, she's incredible when it comes to being a vet. Give her a chance. I think the two of you have a lot in common."

If he had a lot in common with that iceberg, he'd better check himself for frostbite. It wasn't that he was angry with Chris for trying, but was that the way his son really saw him?

"Is there a problem?" Dane and Serena were standing behind them with questions on their faces.

"Hey, Uncle Dane! And Aunt Serena! I can call you that, right?"

At her laughing assurance, Chris turned to lead them both over to Pamela and the professor for introductions. Dane aligned himself in the small group facing Powers, and when the light bulb went off, he frowned and mouthed 'crap' across the distance.

At least his brother agreed that a blind date to a fireworks party, particularly when at least one of the impacted parties was unaware of it, was a bad idea.

God, he needed that glass of wine. Serena excused herself to fall in next to him and linked an arm through his.

"That's so sweet that he tried to fix you up, Powers." She giggled. "He couldn't know that we all had plans for you tonight, could he?"

Plans? There were more plans? Why didn't anyone feel compelled to check with him first before they planned anything?

She winked at him as she grabbed two glasses and held one out to him. "I'm just teasing you. Come on – we all know Tess will be here, and who knows what influence the stars and the fireworks will have on the two of you?"

The flash of golden eyes in his memory made it hard for him to see the bar under his hands. Powers froze in place, his hand halfway out to his sister-in-law to receive his glass. His fingers itched with the memory of bare skin under his caress.

Serena poked him in the ribs and shoved the wine glass into his hand. Her whisper near his ear had his body on full alert. "And speak of the devil."

He sensed her behind him even as Serena spoke. In fact, he'd have known she was there even if his sister-in-law hadn't said a word. There was something about Tess's energy that reached out to him, running light strokes across the edges of his nerves and making his body tense and predatory in an instant. Straightening to stand taller and filling out his already broad shoulders seemed like the only appropriate thing to do.

"Oh shit." Serena's curse was so low that he thought he hadn't heard her correctly, but when he focused on her face, she was staring over his shoulder with open dismay.

It made him turn too, and when he did, he was captured by the power and calm radiating from Tess's face. She was dressed in a flowing skirt and loose top, and while it might disguise her slender figure now, he remembered how her skin wrapped over tight muscles and how supple curves yielded when crushed to harder planes. Her long hair was gathered up into some sort of flip that made her neck seem even more stately. Her expression when her eyes landed on him was cool and noncommittal.

But it was the arm on her shoulders that threw him off balance. The arm was attached to a reasonably good-looking man about their same age. It was possessive in its arrangement, as if the man was staking his claim.

Serena shuddered once next to him, and he heard her quiet, "Sorry Powers," even as she moved forward to hug Tess. The smile between friends was genuine, in vivid contrast to the polite look he'd been given.

"Powers, it's good to see you again. Have you met Chase Wolford?" Tess assessed him coolly as she stood to the side, allowing the two men to meet face to face. Shaking hands meant this Chase guy had to let go of Tess.

Good.

Formalities aside, the two men sized each other up. Powers found Chase lacking in so many ways that he couldn't count them fast enough. He could read dismissal on the other man's face.

The urge to mark territory of his own rose fast and furious. It was ridiculous, given that he and Tess never seemed to do anything but rub each other raw. But he had been looking forward to seeing her. The rapid recognition of false denial made his disappointment even more bitter.

"Dad, Pamela and I are going to find the four of us a place to park ourselves. Melissa said to tell you that she was going to be in the barrel room, tasting some wine futures, so you can meet up with her there."

Chris missed the implication in his wording, but the rest of the group did not. Tess raised one delicate eyebrow at him and gave the hint of a frown. Dane turned Serena away before she had a chance to say whatever she intended, her mouth open and arguing.

If he pulled himself together, he might be able to carry off the nonchalance that he was nowhere near feeling.

"Thanks Chris. I don't think you've met Tess Willowspring. Tess, this is my son, Chris, and his girlfriend, Pamela."

Introductions completed, he hoped that the man with his arm where it had no right being recognized the slight. Powers noted the hasty glances Chris threw between him and the exotic woman, and then he forgot about his son too.

Energy arced between them as Powers leaned forward. At least he could feel the force of it, and by the sudden tightening of her expression, he thought Tess sensed it too. Thoughts of everyone around them drifted away.

He scowled at the arm around Tess's shoulders, just as the man attached to it began speaking. "I was lucky that my daughters could spend a couple of weeks with their grandmother in Sac. It gives me more time with Tess. It's a wonderful date under the stars."

Chapter 8

The last person Tess wanted to see again was Powers Ashland. In her memory, he was forceful and demanding and too overbearing to be anything but a nuisance.

In the flesh, she was reminded of the steely muscles, the callused hands, and the gentle emotions flowing from him when his guard was down.

Tess told herself it didn't matter that he'd brought a date. After all, she had a date too. The veterinary professor was discussing the finer points of wine maturation with Chase at the moment, and under cover of their debate, she could examine Powers more closely.

His face was tense and worn, no doubt from the long hours Serena said he kept to maintain the success of his construction business. And while he didn't work on the sites on a regular basis, his hard body wasn't a stranger to intense workouts. He made her feel small and delicate in comparison.

The man under her close scrutiny chose that moment to seek her out. His focus was level and precise. The pause before he moved only emphasized the deliberate placement of each careful step he took across the space between them. She felt hunted, choosing to ignore the thrill that ran through her at the idea.

He stopped two feet foot away, the heat of his body closing the last distance and enveloping her. Hands at his sides clenched into light fists as his eyes roamed over her features.

"You look very beautiful tonight, Tess." The raspy quality of his voice added another layer of thickness to the air.

"Thank you, Powers. You look – formidable – as always." She inclined her head in what she hoped was a regal nod. It brought her eyes to the width of his chest, the broad surface rising and falling more quickly than she would have expected.

Choking in air to expand her lungs was a mistake, since it brought the woodsy scent of him inside her. That same magnetic pull she'd experienced before dragged her nearer now. She wasn't sure who moved, but they were now standing toe to toe, his head bent to hers as she inspected the polo shirt's three small buttons. All but one was fastened, providing an enticing glimpse of the sparse sprinkling of dark hairs at the top of his chest.

She remembered what that chest looked like in the sun, glistening with droplets as Powers emerged from his swim in the sea. Hawaiian sun had turned his skin a coppery brown, outlining and defining every curve and cut of his body. Hips that narrowed into the length of his board shorts and long legs that strode out of the waves had dried her mouth and caused her to sigh. She imagined that his bare back would show her bold muscles, as taunt and toned as his chest. When he dropped his towel to pull on a t-shirt and turn away, she barely held her silence in disappointment.

He was dangerous, at least to her. She wanted to shake her head to rid herself of the memories, but they were burned into her brain. He was deadly to her self-respect and hazardous to her well-being, because Powers always wanted to be in control.

"Powers? Excuse me, but I've been paged with an emergency. I have to leave."

The vet professor was standing a few feet away but not watching them, her eyes intent instead on the cell phone in her hand. She typed something into the phone and hit a final button, then gave Powers a distracted smile.

The fact that he was going to be ripped away was suddenly an unexpected disappointment. Powers would leave with his date. That meant she was free to relax again, and out of the corner of her eye, she could see Chase moving towards them with two new wine tastings.

With a potent look of regret for a scant second longer, Powers swiveled abruptly and put a hand under the professor's elbow to steady her over the rugged ground towards the parking area. Her animation in whatever she was saying was vastly different from the stillness of the man. Tess turned away, unwilling to wait for Powers to gently hand the woman into the company truck he always drove.

Expecting to experience a sense of relief at his leaving, instead, she felt only frustration. The anticlimactic buzz of dissatisfaction should have been a clue.

"How are you? Are you cold? Should we head back to our chairs? I brought us a blanket and we could move the chairs closer together and – "

Chase's words halted as his cell phone sounded a bouncy beat. His smile meant only one thing – it was one of his daughters.

Putting up a finger to signal a pause in their discussion, he answered in a jovial tone. "Hey Soph. Having a good time with Grandma?"

The sudden loss of his happy expression and its replacement with panic and concern stopped her more easily than his gesture.

"How bad is it? Let me talk to Grandma. No, you did the right thing to call me." He covered the phone and turned wild eyes to her. "They're at the emergency room at a hospital in Sac. Bella was appendicitis. The doctors want to operate. I need to go."

He was already hurrying towards their remote seating location as he talked with his mother. Grabbing gear and shoving things together with both hands as he tucked the phone against his ear, he coordinated the hospital's location.

"I just need to drop off my friend and I'll be there before you know it."

Tess waved her arms to get his attention. When he told his mother to wait a second, he gave a quizzical look.

"Don't worry about me, Chase. Taking me home will add fifteen minutes to your trip. I can get a ride. There are plenty of people here who go by my place."

The relief on his face spoke volumes about his concern over his little girl.

"Are you sure, because…"

When Tess assured him it would be fine, he grabbed her by the shoulders and gave her a loud smack on the cheek before picking up the last of his picnic things and heading for the parking area at a trot.

She watched him leave, prickling with awareness that she felt like she'd been granted a reprieve. Even as he roared out of the lot, her eyes were searching for the big white truck with the bright blue Ashland logo. But that search was pointless.

This time she couldn't ignore the disheartened feeling.

*****

At least the woman had the foresight to bring her own vehicle. He wouldn't be required to do the gentlemanly thing and drive her home. Even if he'd been unaware that this was supposed to be a blind date, Powers had rules about taking care of a woman.

She'd spent the few minutes weaving through vehicles explaining the emergency, a show horse that had suddenly taken a turn for the worse. When they got to her car, she got in and started the motor before thanking him absentmindedly for a nice evening and roaring off.

She didn't ask for his phone number, and he didn't want hers. If the only thing that caused the iceberg to melt was an animal, they had nothing in common.

Of course, he had no link to Tess either, but that didn't make him any less likely to turn back to the winery. She had a date, and that thought tortured him. At least he could watch over her.

Avoiding the patio and grassy knoll where people were taking up positions for the upcoming fireworks, he covered the ground towards the rear of the winery in long strides and ducked into the back door leading to the barrel room. Marguerite had the wine thief above a barrel, pouring tastes in people's glasses as she discussed something with each guest. She caught his eye across the room and frowned at him.

She was a nice enough woman, though her too-knowing glances annoyed him. She broke her examination and swiveled her head to an opposite corner of the room. Following her gaze, he found his brother and his bride in an intense conversation.

Married only two months and already arguing. That wasn't good. He couldn't do anything to fix his own situation, but he wasn't going to let Dane screw up his.

"What are you two lovebirds up to?" Powers stopped within their personal space and waited for one of them to tell him what was wrong.

They both shut their mouths with audible snaps as they continued to stare at each other. Serena frowned at him first. "I'm sorry Powers, I didn't realize that Tess was bringing a date."

He shrugged, not wanting to make a big deal out of it.

"Come on, this isn't about me. What were you two fighting about? I hate to see you arguing already, so if there's something I can do to help you I – "

"Yeah, there is something you can do, big brother." Dane's words were delivered in a neutral undertone, even if he was throwing daggers with his eyes. Big nasty daggers too.

"You can explain to Serena that you're a big boy and can arrange your own dates. She seems to be intent on matchmaking, and she won't take no for an answer."

"It's just that you and Tess seem to fit together, Powers. I know there's something there. Everyone within a country mile can feel it."

He smiled down at his sister-in-law, even though he was queasy on the inside. He and Tess had nothing to offer one another, other than that strange pull that kept him off his game whenever he was around her.

Or whenever he thought about her.

A wave of energy washed over his back, strong enough to stop his thoughts and compel him to turn around. He knew already what he was turning towards. Or more appropriately, whom.

Tess walked in the door.

"Where's Chase?"

"Who cares? I mean, I like him, but he's not right for Tess."

"Serena, you have to stop…"

Powers blocked them out and stepped away. She was still standing in the doorway, glancing around the room with a resigned expression. Then he lost sight of her as the crowd closed between them.

Chapter 9

She leaned back against him, and his arms wrapped tight across her shoulders as they watched the fireworks overhead. His lips nibbled at the side of her neck and one hand covered her breast possessively. The evidence of his intense arousal pressed to her lower back made her own body wet and achy with longing. He was big in every way and yet she was as powerful as he was.

As the next burst bloomed into a flowering form overhead, he spun her around and…

Buzz-buzz-buzz. Buzz-buzz-buzz. Buzz-

She hit the button on the clock and swore.

Sitting up abruptly did nothing to clear her head. Tess swore again, more mildly this time, and allowed herself to sink back into the covers and examine the remnants of the dream.

It had been like this almost every night since the Fourth of July. She dreamed about Powers and some version of fireworks or a sandy beach.

On the other nights, she had strange visions of darkness and pain that tore her apart, and sudden relief brought by a stranger.

The ones about Powers were based in reality, though they hadn't occurred exactly like she'd dreamed them. The darker ones were, she figured, designed by her over-active imagination.

Fireworks at the winery hadn't gone as she expected in any way. Chase's arm was more than casual over her shoulder. His comment about it being a date made her squirm and feel like pushing him away, but she didn't want to be impolite. They'd been nothing but friends up until now, and there was nothing between them to make her change that.

No spark. No zing. Nada.

Powers, on the other hand, only had to exist somewhere within the same atmosphere she was breathing and it seemed that unknown forces charged the air.

To find him at the party with a date brought both relief and pain. The relief came from her impression that somehow this would keep him away from her. The pain was in the separation.

"What are you doing? Powers is standing by himself. You should be talking to him." DK's fierce whisper had Tess looking around furtively, hoping no one could overhear them.

"He's still here?" The leap in her heart was something she couldn't quell fast enough. She sobered and tried for an impassive expression before continuing.

"Why should I be talking to him? I can't stand him." Her tense reply was met with a knowing smile on her friend's face.

"Go talk to him, for heaven's sake. He's by himself and so are you."

Telling herself she could care less as she glanced around, Tess couldn't find Powers as more and more people filled the barrel room. The fireworks were still an hour away, but the crowd was more than ready to begin the celebrations. Dragged by DK into the tasting room, she couldn't help seeking him out, head and shoulders taller than most of the people there.

"Damn, where did he go?" DK kept a tight grip on her arm as they moved through the throngs. "Why don't you find a seat near us? I'll have Vince find him and bring him over. That way, we'll be close enough by so you don't have to panic and – "

"I'm not panicking!" But the tone in her voice gave her away.

DK giggled. "I disagree, but you'll need to come to your own conclusion, as always. Pretend that this is a difficult plant you're trying to grow. It needs tending and attention and you're not sure you'll like it once it blooms, but you give it a chance anyway. There they are."

She followed DK's raised arm pointing to Powers and Vince standing against the wall of the winery. Vince was delivering a vehement point about something to Powers, who was standing as still as the rock wall behind him. Vince picked that moment to turn, searching the crowd until his eyes roamed to the women. He raised his arm, motioning them over with more excitement than Tess could see a reason for.

"There you are. How's my sweetheart? Good? Good. Listen, we're going to head over there," he gave a vague wave, "and get settled and stuff. We'll see you later." Grabbing DK around the shoulders and turning her away, Tess barely had a moment to see the triumphant wink on her girlfriend's face before they hustled into the increasing darkness.

That left her standing in front of Powers. He was examining the ground at his feet with great interest. If he didn't say something soon, she vowed to leave him standing there.

He picked that moment to look up slowly, his gaze traveling from her toes up her body. His eyes blazed as they met hers. She watched him inhale deeply, which only made his chest seem broader and emphasized the shoulders that appeared to be strong enough to hold up the whole building. His gaze locked on hers, stronger than radar.

And he smiled.

Damn, what a smile did to his face was amazing. The shock of it made it impossible to move. She couldn't help it, she smiled in return.

"Thirsty?"

Oh yes. Her body was making her feel like a traitor to her mind and her resolution. No commanding, domineering men in her life.

The eyebrow he quirked at her in question made her blink and realize that he was holding a wine glass out to her, another one in his other hand.

"Oh, yes thanks." She commanded her hand to stop shaking as she reached for it, with almost perfect results.

"So, I hear Chase's little girl got sick?" His eyes skipped around her face as he posed the question.

She nodded.

"What happened to the vet?" She almost bit her tongue off for even asking.

"She was my son's idea. Luckily, she brought her own car, so I didn't need to play chauffeur."

They sipped. She was usually very good at small talk, since being a shop owner meant she had to chat up her customers as part of her business. At this moment, though, she couldn't think of a single thing to say. It didn't seem to matter. He stood by quietly, observing the crowd and lingering every once in a while on someone who caught his attention. As she did the same, she realized she was relaxing.

"This brings out an interesting group, doesn't it?" His low question reverberated through every cell in her body.

She nodded, not willing to trust her voice. She felt him examining her and she turned her head to give him a warning look.

Something was different about him tonight. He was watching her with an air that bristled despite his quiet words, almost as harsh as the emotion she'd first seen on his face the night they'd celebrated Serena and Dane's engagement. Curiosity and awareness tinged the edges. The sudden pull of attraction crested in a wave over her, making her gasp in surprised recognition.

She almost boggled her wine.

"Hey, you okay?" His voiced concern was pitched so low that she was surprised she could hear it over the people around them.

It was him. That day before Christmas, in her bedroom, playing havoc with her emotions and calming the voices in her head. Her destiny, one that she couldn't avoid if the spirits were correct.

She blinked at him, confusion meeting his concern. "Uh, fine. I must have lost my balance for a moment."

He looked down at her feet and frowned.

"It's nine o'clock, everyone. The fireworks should be starting. Look!" Marguerite perched on a large rock and pointed to the west.

On cue, fireworks began to light up the horizon. From the vantage point of the winery, you could see displays across the Sacramento valley floor. People ooh'ed and aah'ed as heads swiveled to track the sprays of light.

Tess shifted from foot to foot, suddenly aware that the ground under her made for treacherous movement. What possessed her to wear these strappy sandals tonight she wasn't sure.

"Why don't you come over here and lean? It would be safer." Powers' low voice twitched against her nerves.

It never made sense why only the sound of his voice could shake her. Each inch she moved closer to him intensified the sensations. Trouble could only come from being near him.

She shook herself free of new feelings of uncertainty and lifted her chin. They were only going to lean against a wall and watch some explosions, nothing more. It was no life-changing event. Meeting his gaze, she nodded and replied, "Good idea."

When she walked next to him and turned, ready to lean back, his arm suddenly stopped her.

"The rocks are rough. You'll snag the material on your outfit."

She glanced back at the wall, then down at her skirt and blouse, before sighing in frustration.

"Here, lean against me."

Gentle pressure as an arm snaked around her shoulder astonished her. Before she could figure out what to do, he had her in front of him, leaning back against his hard body and anchored in place with his arm under her chin.

It didn't feel anything like the irritating possessiveness of Chase's arm earlier in the evening. In fact, it was steadying.

She stared at the hairbrush in her hand, suddenly confused about how it had gotten there. In her contemplation about that evening, she'd made her way through shower and make-up and dressing and was all the way to brushing her hair before she'd even noticed she was out of bed.

Powers held her like that as they watched the rest of the fireworks, neither of them speaking. He shifted her slightly to the side once, seeming to shiver when he did so. She wasn't sure, but she thought she detected a bulge in an important part of his anatomy. Rather than embarrassing her, it made her blush in the darkness and wish he'd shift her back to nestle against that fullness.

Once the fireworks were done, they lingered in that same position. A couple of his fingers were lightly stroking her shoulder through the fabric of her blouse, and she wasn't sure he was even conscious of his movement. As the crowd thinned, he set her away from him and reached for her glass.

"Come on, let's get us both home. It's a school night after all."

She blinked around at her kitchen, marveling again that she could accomplish so much of her morning routine on autopilot while her mind and her memories were tied up in a man she had no business being interested in. Dunking her teabag, her thoughts drifted back.

The car he'd led her to was completely unexpected.

"A Mercedes?"

He smiled in the dim light of the dashboard, the vivid gleam of white teeth highlighting his unmistakable boyish glee.

"Yeah, it's a classic convertible too – 1978. They don't make 'em like they did back then." And he revved the engine.

The pure pleasure in his voice vibrated in her bones, leaving her shaking.

Chapter 10

Powers scanned the bid documents one last time. As always, Marty had done a thorough job of making Ashland Inc. look good. This construction project would be a new direction, one that would further their reputation and expand their domain.

His hand hesitated, though, when it came to signing the proposal. Flynn's Crossing. This historical project was on the same street that Tess lived on. That Tess worked on.

And he could be there too, almost every day.

That night nearly a month ago had challenged everything he believed in. Dane's words still rang in his ears.

"Take the same advice you gave me last year. Get back into the mainstream of society." His brother had raised an arresting hand when Powers tried to argue. "You isolating yourself in your work is no different from me isolating myself on my land."

On that night, he'd thought maybe his brother was right. When Vince came over to add his words of support and encouragement, it was harder to ignore the feeling.

"Chemistry, I'm telling you. You can't ignore it. You know it when you feel it and you can't do anything about it." Vince waved his arms around for emphasis. "It's karma, man."

Yeah, he felt it alright. Doing something about it was a different story.

Then she stood in front of him, looking as uncomfortable and uncertain as he felt. He couldn't help it. Every protective cell in his body made him do it.

Pulling her into his body was the hardest thing he'd ever done, and the easiest. She fit perfectly, her shorter frame settling the top of her head just under his chin. His arm reached across her body easily, and the delicate bones under his hand made touching her a priority.

He hadn't counted on what the feel of her like this would do to his libido. He was hard, not instantly, but with a growing awareness that his world had changed forever. Shifting her slightly so he didn't embarrass them both, he tried to hold still to avoid making his condition worse. Reciting building codes in his head to kill his desire had no effect, as people left the winery around them.

Her prissiness about his choice in a car had been cute. She'd shifted around in her seat, one hand holding the mass of her hair in a tight tail to keep it from whipping around in the wind.

He has a sudden vision of her hair wrapped around that uncooperative part of his body, like the best of all caresses, and he dropped two wheels off the road onto the soft shoulder.

"Are you okay?" She'd asked the question sharply without a hit of fear in her voice. Strong and powerful, like the woman herself.

"Yeah, fine. Thought I saw something in the road." Or in his mind's eye.

The ride passed too quickly. There was something magical about the darkness, the top down and the stars overhead, and most of all, the woman beside him.

He parked on Main Street in front of her shop and came around to open her door. By the time he did, she'd finger-combed her hair into its usual glossy curtain and straightened her top and skirt. When he held out his hand to help her up from the low-slung car, she only hesitated a beat before putting her tapered fingers in his.

He'd found he didn't want to let go. Ignoring her slight tug, he started them walking towards the front door, hands still locked. She pulled with more determination but he refused to release her.

"Are you always this domineering?" Her question wasn't delivered with anger so much as resigned curiosity.

He wasn't sure how to answer that. Instead, he stopped and looked down at their joined hands. She wasn't fighting to pull away anymore.

The rightness of what he saw scared the hell out of him.

When she tugged again, he let go.

The heels of her sandals clicked softly against the walkway and the second step of her porch creaked more than it should under her light weight.

He was still staring at his now-empty hand when he heard her put a key in a lock and pause. When he turned to see what was keeping her, he found her staring at him, her expression hidden in the shadow of the alcove.

"Powers, thank you." And she slipped inside.

He found himself staring at that same empty hand now. In the month since, he'd tactfully avoided all of his brother's attempts to set up a group event of some kind to lure him up the hill. They were trying to bring them together in any kind of informal setting, he could tell. But he'd had time to think about it.

Being alone was a better idea. It was better than causing a fine woman pain by becoming too involved in his work to realize what was happening around him. Ask his ex or any of the girlfriends he'd tried to have in the past few years. Work was his only passion.

His brother's words about isolation came back to him often. He had few friends in the area, surrounded instead by work associates and employees. His life was fairly rigid, days and most evenings spent on construction projects or his nonprofit foundation. Even his weekends were filled with work.

Most nights, or if he was honest, all nights, were filled with Tess. In the darkest parts of those hours, she was a warrior princess, surging forward to save the weak. He'd be trying to pull her back, worried for her safety, but she was unrelenting and determined.

Those nightmares had him waking up drenched in icy fearful sweat, though why they seemed so real to him he wasn't sure. This wasn't the raw country of centuries past, and there was no battle for her to fight. The uneasiness that he would lose her stayed with him for days afterward.

It was the other kinds of dreams, though, that left him hurting even more. She was under him, over him, wrapped around him. He was so deep inside her that they were one body and one spirit. When they both came in his dreams, she screamed his name.

He woke up from these hard as steel with a body heated to burning. Nothing would stop the ache, and he tried to visualize throwing himself on an iceberg to ease it. The only thing that would contribute to was an increase in global warming. It did nothing for his hard-on.

The pen in his hand was standing at attention, and the analogy to his current thoughts had him smiling grimly. He couldn't get her out of his head. There was no middle ground. This wasn't a woman he could date idly and then just as easily set aside.

He set pen to paper and signed his name. They would submit their bid. When they were selected, because he had no doubt that they were the best company for the job, he'd use his time in Flynn's Crossing to inoculate himself against the woman who kept him up at night.

Maybe then, her haunting quality would work out of his system.

Chapter 11

"You seem tired."

Tess grumbled before responding. "I haven't been sleeping well."

Chase's hum of concern sounded from a far corner as he advanced through the flower shop's front room. Winding through the tastefully decorated space with vases of every color, size and shape, old wire bird cages, bric-a-brac and all sorts of pieces that could be used in floral displays took time. When he was standing in front of her, he quizzed her. "What's wrong? Is there anything I can do? You need your rest."

Tess continued creating her current work of art at her large bench near the back of the room, close to her coolers full of flowers kept in what was once the connecting dining room.

What was wrong was nothing she could discuss with him.

"Hey, why don't you come over to the house tonight? The girls would love to see you. I can cook us dinner and we can all watch a movie together."

He'd been urging some version of this for the past month. Bella had bounced back easily after her surgery in the way that only kids can, but he was still protective and hovering. Every date he'd asked her on – and she hesitated to call it that because she didn't want to use the word – included the girls.

They were sweet kids, and he was a nice man and a good friend. He was harmless. She could probably wind him around her finger and still be able to build another flower arrangement at the same time. The only commands he seemed to be familiar with were the ones on a computer.

He was perfect in so many ways.

She'd been thinking a lot about the whole settling-down thing in the past month. Maybe it was those thoughts of Powers as Mr. Wrong in contrast, but Chase was looking more and more like Mr. Right, at least on paper.

And the girl tribe members were falling like rose petals around her.

DK and Vince decided on a wedding venue, though they hadn't yet discussed it publicly. Gabby carried an air of settled satisfaction, and when they asked her about wedding plans, she giggled but declined to comment. According to Roxy, Mac was due back from the movie promo trip next month, and he planned to stay indefinitely. When she got all huffy about it and said it didn't mean anything, everyone laughed at her.

Even Marguerite met someone.

"He is a neighbor of the winery. This family has been on that land for generations. He is…intriguing." Her French accent on the last word made it sound sexy.

Maybe it was time she too let someone in.

"Tess? Tess, it's time to go. The bid opening."

Chase stood next to her worktable and stared at her. She let go of the flower in her fingers, realizing that she'd been holding it so tightly that the poor stem probably never would recover. She tried out a smile and was rewarded when he gave an uncertain one in return.

Penelope the cat chose that moment to jump up and stand in front of Tess. She turned on her paws delicately and eyed the man across the table.

"Nice kitty, do you want a scratch?"

As Chase reached out a hand, Penelope arched and hissed, swiping menacingly for good measure. Jumping back, Chase swore, even though no claws made contact.

"I'm sorry Chase. She never does that. Penelope, what's gotten in to you?" Tess scooped her up and headed for the stairs to her quarters.

"I'll get my things and be right back. Sorry Chase, really."

His hesitant reassurances followed her up the stairs, cut off finally by the closing door to the house's upper stories. She held the cat out in front of her and looked her square in the face.

"What's gotten into you? You like everyone. The only one you ever growl at is the vet, and that's because he gives you shots and I know you feel threatened. What's wrong?"

The cat's green eyes regarded her solemnly. Then she picked up a paw to lick it carefully before rubbing it over an ear. When she returned to staring at Tess, the woman swore she could hear what the cat was thinking.

Beware the threats ahead.

*****

Tess let her eyes roam over the room full of construction company representatives and other interested parties. She'd scanned the room several times now and didn't see anyone wearing an Ashland logo. Powers himself wasn't in sight.

It was not disappointment she was feeling, she kept repeating silently. It was relief. If he was here on a regular basis…

"I said, Tess, can you please explain again why the proposals are in two parts?"

Realizing that she'd been asked the question and it seemed like it was more than once, she narrowed her focus down to the proceedings in front of her.

"We didn't want big names or flashy marketing to distract us from our review. And we all know that the lowest bid isn't necessarily the best, because you get what you pay for." The audience chuckled at that. "Jess from the city will be reading out the names of the companies that submitted complete bids. The packets will be divided into the parts that identify the bidding company – the cost and qualifications section – and the job approach section – which does not."

She turned to smile encouragingly at Jess. "Why don't you begin reading those names?"

Tuning out the crackle of envelopes opening and drone of names gave her a moment to herself. The occasional clap of applause signaled a familiar company. There were eight bids in all, and as each one passed and the one name she didn't want to hear was avoided, she rested a little easier.

It was too small a job for Powers to consider. Big man that he was, his company was probably too busy on important projects to deign to consider their little building to be of consequence.

"...and our final bidder is," Jess paused, "Ashland Inc."

Her heart stopped. Forcing herself to draw in air, Tess struggled to keep her face neutral as her eyes darted around the room again.

A mousy looking man half-stood and gave a wave to the surrounding crowd. Chase leaned over from her right and whispered, "Hey, I recognize that guy. He came into my shop a while back, asking all sorts of good questions about the town. I'm impressed. He must have been checking things out. Isn't that the company that belongs to

Dane's brother? Gives us a chance to keep things in the family."

Her heart started beating again, too fast this time, as she remembered too. The nondescript looking man had come into Buds and Blooms as well.

"This is a great looking town. You all have kept everything so historical. Too bad there's that empty lot at the other end of the street. Stands out like a missing tooth in a great smile." And he'd grinned winningly at her, all teeth intact.

It would be just like Powers to send a spy to check things out. But she assured herself it didn't matter. An architect prepared the drawings and plans pro bono. The bids were to be based strictly on those plans, no changes accepted. It was a simple, straightforward project.

And if Ashland had a good bid, they might be selected. It really didn't matter to her. Powers would send a flunky to oversee this little project, she was sure.

An icy finger of doubt snaked up her spine and embedded itself in her mind, deeply enough to make her gasp out loud.

Chapter 12

Powers drove slowly down the quaint length of Main Street of Flynn's Crossing, anticipating coffee and a pastry and a casual stroll looking in shop windows. And, he admitted, delaying the inevitable. Tess wouldn't be happy to see him, of that he was sure. Things had become even more strained. Parking halfway between Buds and Blooms and Brew Bank Bakery, he wondered how that was even possible as he delayed the inevitable for a few minutes more.

"What can I get for you?" The short baker he now knew as Sarge – and baker he undoubtedly was based on the look of his apron – stood looking at Powers expectantly, wax paper in hand, ready to dive for a selection in the case. Blinking twice at the choices, his mouth watered and he pointed at a huge Danish bloated with fruit filling.

"One of those, and a large coffee please."

"Hey, you're Powers, right? Ashland Construction?" Sarge handed over the pastry and gestured Powers down towards the register.

"Yes, I am." Digging in his jeans pocket for money, he looked up at the cashier, Stuart, standing in front of him with a friendly hand outstretched.

"Welcome to the neighborhood. We're glad you won the bid to fill the vacant lot. It's been an eyesore for quite a while."

Oh yeah, Marty had told him that Stuart, Sarge's partner in every sense of the word, had been on the committee. He, along with other business association members and representatives of city and county government, had made the construction company selection. Chase Wolford had been on the sidelines.

And Tess had been the committee chair.

Powers was surprised that they'd won, given that circumstances. It wasn't that he thought she'd be unfair and influence the committee unduly, but he was sure she had reservations about using Ashland.

Or maybe she didn't care. That thought speared through him and he chose to ignore it.

Still, when his assistant set up today's meeting, he'd asked her to be deliberately vague about who would be attending. All Tess knew was that the Ashland project manager was coming to discuss timing, design issues, and construction planning.

The fact that it was him and not one of his people wasn't of any consequence.

"Wait, boss, why are you taking this on? You don't do project management anymore." Marty had voiced the question that was undoubtedly on everyone's mind at the company's Monday afternoon planning meeting.

"It's a small, straightforward job. No surprises, not complications. I won't need to be onsite that often. The idea of supervising a historical infill project appeals to me. I'm the boss, so I get first dibs." He forced a smile to his puzzled leadership team even as his mind raced over the real reason.

He had to get her out of his system.

Of course, now that seeing her was minutes away, he dawdled. Taking in the ambiance of Main Street seemed to be a good way to get grounded in the project. At least that's what he told himself as he stared into shops and restaurants.

Crumbs of the pastry covering his shirt, Powers had to sigh in appreciation. Sarge and Stuart were definitely baking geniuses. As he stared in the window of a cheese shop and its neighbor, a place selling cured and fresh meats, he anticipated other treats in the upcoming months. Flynn's Crossing had become a foodie's dream destination.

Too soon, though, he walked the short blocks to the base of the residential hill. The tall Victorian that served as the Buds and Bloom haven was nestled in lush greenery and flowers. Three stories tall with a tower reaching an additional level overhead and what appeared to be a cellar below the wrap-around porch, it was painted a rainbow of shades. He wondered how much it cost to color the damn thing, because there must be seventeen different shades on the gables and cut-outs and fish scale shingle siding.

Sipping his coffee, he considered the style. The engineer in him appreciated the fact that it looked old, and if it was as old as he thought it might be, the original architect was a genius. It was aging as gracefully as a dowager queen herself, with a few wrinkles that only added to her charm.

It also looked vaguely familiar, like he'd seen the design work somewhere before.

The tower of bells on Main sounded the hour behind him. Ten o'clock, and no way to avoid the inevitable any longer. Tess was expecting him.

*****

Trying as hard as she could, Tess couldn't get anyone else to stand in for her on this meeting. She knew it would be some flunky sent to manage this minor construction, but that person would have only one degree of separation from Powers.

And that was about a million degrees too close to where she wanted to be.

Her office had been the informal visiting parlor in the old house. It wasn't particularly large, but it was adequate for a desk, a small conference table, and the various filing cabinets and other administrative requirements for a small business. She didn't spend more time here than she had to, preferring to meet with customers in the display room or with suppliers in the garden.

Today, though, she wanted to go over the basics and end the meeting as quickly as possible. She felt as nervous as if Powers himself was going to walk through the door, even though she knew differently.

Powering the computer to screensaver mode and taking a last look around the neat space, she considered offering the Ashland project manager a bottle of water. The idea of making coffee sounded too welcoming. Water didn't invite anyone to linger, and she reached for coasters as the door chimes sang out.

"Just a minute. I'll be right with you." She took a final quick look in the mirror behind the door. Professional, distant, and quick to get on with things. She smiled her satisfaction at her reflection.

Pulling open the door, she came face to face with a broad chest clad in an Ashland Inc. logoed dress shirt. The cuffs were rolled up and muscular tanned forearms extended from the sleeves. One hand clutched a Brew Bank cup, the knuckles oddly white against the paper. Looking up, she bit her lip just before gasping.

Powers. Damn, didn't the man have anything better to do?

"I'm sorry. I thought you might be waiting for me to come to you." He paused, his expression indecipherable. "Hello, Tess."

His deep voice did the same nasty things to her insides that it had before. And even though she hadn't heard it for a month and a half, it was exactly as she remembered it. Evidently, her body remembered it too, because spots that shouldn't have been suddenly grew hot, flowering under his gaze alone. And the magnetism of the man pulled her forward.

Remembering her manners and the reason for their meeting, she shook her head to clear it and turned away from the intensity of his stare and his outstretched hand.

"Powers, I didn't expect you to be in attendance. Are you here to introduce me to the project manager? You didn't have to do that. I know our project isn't the highest priority for your company."

When he didn't respond, she forced herself to turn around again, trying to look around his body.

Of course, that just made her look at his body instead and the heat amped up to scorching.

"I don't see anyone behind you. Did you lose someone?" She met his eyes again, shooting for cool and distant and hoping that she was able to pull it off.

He seemed to shake himself free of some kind of spell too, and he lost the stiffness of his stance in the doorway to lounge against the jamb.

"No, it's just me today. Just me you'll be dealing with every day." He paused, and she wasn't sure if his mouth changed to a grimace or a smirk when he added, "Only me."

Chapter 13

"What do you mean he's doing it himself?"

Chase glanced at her with puzzlement as he picked up bottles of olive oil and dusted them, replacing them on the shelf once they were spotless. When he fussed with the alignment of two in the row, moving them back and forth even though they looked perfectly straight to her, she wondered if he was OCD.

Tess turned away, too anxious to stand by while he fiddled.

"He's going to be the project manager. He said something about being intrigued by the historical design and wanting to work on it because it was different. He also said that he wanted to make sure his subcontractors – subs he called them – would understand and respect the artisan quality of work that was required."

Chase hummed quietly as she finished. It was getting on her nerves, this humming thing. Had he always been doing that?

"I think it's terrific that he's taken a personal interest in the project. After all, we kept the project in the Flynn's Crossing family. I don't know why you fought it so hard when we were deciding."

Tess knew exactly why. It brought the domineering idiot one step too close to her home and her livelihood.

Not to mention her spirit and her heart.

She paced the length of Oil+Vinegar and came back to stand at the front of the shop, staring with blind eyes out at Main Street. The big man filling her office door and towering over her only an hour before shocked her. Despite being large enough, the space was too small to contain the energy radiating from him, and the responding waves of intensity coming from her. His declaration that he would be her primary contact had her heart leaping unsteadily. She barely managed to stay polite as they got down to discussing business.

"Tess? Did you hear me?" She turned back to Chase, who was holding a duster in one hand and a large bottle of flavored vinegar in the other. "Are you feeling okay? You seem kind, I don't know, upset."

Hell yes she was upset, because now she was stuck working with the one man she wanted nothing to do with.

"I'm sorry Chase, I was thinking about my garden and this heat. What did you say?"

He smiled at her warmly and went back to his cleaning. "I said that I think it's terrific we have Dane's brother working on the project. Who knows, maybe he'll decide to move up here permanently too."

Tess thought she'd have to bury herself six feet under in her garden if that happened.

*****

The girl tribe settled into the chairs and settees on the covered rear porch of the old Victorian. The heat destroyed their energy to the point of lethargy, and everyone was hoping for cooling late afternoon breezes.

"I'm so happy Powers got the job. Dane's alternately happy, though he doesn't say much about that, and bugged because he's convinced Powers will use this as an opportunity to poke his nose in our business." Serena laughed. "He can poke away. We're boring married people now."

Roxy, seated across from her with her feet up on a low table, harrumphed. "I'm glad that you're happy being married. Me, I don't see it. Mac keeps making little noises about settling down, but it's not for me."

The others laughed at this, because while Roxy made a lot of noise herself about staying single and free, as she put it, she got a certain radiance whenever she said her boyfriend's name.

Tess had that feeling of the earth shifting under her foundation again. Things were changing with more than her friends. Danger was on the horizon, and she was dreaming about it every night.

DK's teasing and Marguerite's debating on the virtues of married life fell into the background as she stared out into the garden. The dream early this morning was set here, except it wasn't here. Her house and the others around hers weren't in the picture. Trees and bushes dotted the edges of the open clearing, and her ancestors were arguing. One pointed towards the river that flowed around the town. Another pointed away from it, down into the valley.

Then a loud wet roar sounded, and she woke with a shriek, the sweat coating her skin causing her to shiver sharply in the air conditioned room. Wheezing in and out noisily, she started again when Tigger, still no better mannered than when she adopted him a year ago, jumped up on her chest and knocked her back. He meowed loudly and batted at the silver stripe of hair over her ear like it was a toy.

"Tigger, you never will learn to behave yourself, will you?" Still, she picked up the cat and snuggled his warm purring body against her chest, willing her heart to slow down.

She'd had the dream before, and each time, it was right after she'd seen Powers. This time, it was newly vivid.

"Tess? See a weed you don't like?"

Blinking away her fear, she focused on Gabby's face. She blinked again at the rosy glow her friend was wearing. She'd been uncharacteristically quiet as everyone had been teasing this evening.

"I'm sorry, I got distracted." She smoothed her hair with a hand that shook only a little and focused in on her friends.

"As I was saying," Gabby seemed to be continuing, "I have news."

Tess joined the others in leaning forward. Gabby's first book had been sold to a publisher within two months of signing with her agent. Things looked promising for her second being a winner as well.

DK piped up, "Your new book's been sold."

Gabby smiled and shook her head no.

"You and Rick are buying a bigger house," guessed Marguerite. The little bungalow that Gabby bought from Serena could hardly contain the four members of her family.

Again Gabby shook her head, though her smile faded a little. "But I guess that should be on the table."

The twenty questions game was wearing on Tess.

Gabby seemed to be bursting with her news. Waving off the rest of their questions, she nearly shouted, "I'm pregnant, and we got married!"

The screams of happiness that followed could probably heard throughout the small town. And Tess felt another rumble from the earth beneath her feet.

Chapter 14

Mother Nature did nothing to allow the heat to abate in late August. After an energetic start, last winter had turned warm and dry, a fact that only made the discussions about drought more real, especially months after grasses and tress were baked to brown.

Powers cringed at the sweat as it ran down his neck, drying almost before it hit his shirt collar in the midday sun. If they were lucky, any rain would hold off until they had the underground work finished and the foundation poured. They'd estimated two months, given the issues with the site. Of course, almost everyone else wished the wet stuff would start sooner.

The site had been sitting abandoned for so long that it had taken on a flora all its own. Tree trunks as big around as his arm set deep roots. Weeds and debris tangled in ugly piles in each corner against the broken chain link fence. An old sewer system lurked just below the surface. And the water table level was questionable, given the plot's proximity to the river.

The first step was clean-up before they could begin the real work.

Though he didn't discuss it with his crew, he was looking forward to this project. There was something innately appealing in building an architecturally accurate replica of something that fit with the rest of the old buildings on the street. Other than the Victorian and a couple of other older structures, most of the rest dated back to the early 1900's or younger.

His meeting with the architect had been enlightening.

"The original town was built of wood, as most mining era villages were. Sure, there was a rare stone building thrown in by people who had an eye towards permanency. Problem was, there was a big fire in Flynn's Crossing in 1900. Most of the town went up like tinder. But that old Queen Anne Victorian at the end, the one that holds the flower shop now, was a bordello. The miners and workers and professional men of the area couldn't bear the idea that their fancy ladies would be without their trademark gowns or their place of business, so they stopped the fire before it consumed the place."

The man chuckled then. "Amazing that the one structure they saved had history behind it. It was designed by Newsom and Newsom, the famous architects that brought the Queen Anne style to California. Built by them in 1885 for a gentleman who made money off the mining trades, and it took 'em two years. Cost a pretty penny back in the day, I'd imagine."

Powers now realized why he recognized the style. Up and down the west coast, evidence of those famous builder/architects could be found in many older settlements. His thoughts about lending Tess a hand by fixing a few things in need of repair suddenly had a whole new appeal.

He glanced down the short city blocks to the house in his thoughts. In addition to the front steps, he'd seem some dry rot in the detail work, and in a few places, the shingles on the sides were loose. It wouldn't be a big effort to get those repaired before winter set in and did more damage.

It was no trouble at all – as long as Tess let him do it.

*****

She told herself she was cleaning the display areas and straightening up the bric-a-brac, but in reality, she was watching the activity at the other end of Main. Today was the day they were beginning the real work on the lot, and despite the distance, she could pick Powers out of the crowd milling around the site in hard hats.

He'd already removed and replaced the fencing, setting the barrier in the street and covering parking spaces, along with blockading the courtyard in between the lot and the next building and taking part of an alley as well. That had been their first negotiating skirmish.

"The subs need a place to park their trucks while they're working." He'd looked at her as if this was the most obvious point in the world.

"You'll be keeping people from parking and shopping, and the whole lot will look unsightly. Isn't there another way to do things so that you don't take up so much – space?" She had been thinking of adding, like you do right now in my office?

He'd finally agreed to move the chain link closer into the site for the weekends, to allow for a few of the parking slots to return to use. When she'd given him a gracious smile of thanks, he examined her strangely.

"The first step will be to strip off the debris and overgrowth so that we can begin the process of digging out the old pipes and god knows what else that's underground."

She'd put up a hand to stop him when he would have continued.

"Were will the debris go?"

He got that look again, the one that said he was working with a construction newbie with no sense. "To the dump, of course."

She was shaking her head to disagree before he even finished. "The trash should be picked up by hand. There are a lot of recyclables in there. That can all be sorted and taken to the recycling center and the rest can go to the dump. And the green waste should be segregated too."

Powers tilted his head to the side at this point and squinted his eyes, as if he was observing an unusual insect in its native habitat.

"What kind of car do you drive?"

Tess pulled back and wondered why this suddenly matter. "A hybrid, of course."

Powers' quietly voiced 'ah' sounded like this explained it all to him.

Duster in hand, she watched with satisfaction as the workers moved through the site with large trash bags. Glass and cans seemed to be headed for trash cans placed in the center of the site, and the true trash was tossed into the back of one of the pick-ups. One of the workers shook his head with apparent disbelief as he threw in his load.

At least Powers kept his promises.

In the early morning hours before Main was hustling, a bulldozer had arrived on the back of a large flatbed truck. To anyone living close by, its deposit on the street sounded like major work had already begun, but it had been sitting idle all morning. Soon, she suspected, it would begin the time-consuming process of scraping away the top layers until the crew knew what it was dealing with.

"For old city lots like this, there aren't always complete drawings of where pipes were placed and how things were built. Your architect Kevin did as good a job as he could to identify where things might be, but no one will know for sure until we scrape things down. Because we'll go down layer by layer, and because we don't want to upset commerce," he'd emphasized the word, "by having the dump trucks waiting in line for their loads, it will take us about a week to get that cleared out."

She'd thanked him again for the consideration, and he'd opened his mouth to say something in response, clamped it shut rapidly, and shook his head from side to side, smiling.

"What?" She suspected her naiveté was showing again.

He looked at her with real humor in his eyes. "I can tell that this job is going to cost me." And he chuckled.

The sound was like a smooth petal feathering over her skin. He budgeted his humor so tightly that she was surprised he was sharing it now. But she didn't like being the cause of it.

"Things worth doing – "

He cut her off and finished, " – are worth doing right. I know. It's just that my crew was skeptical that anything interesting would happen on this job. To them, it's just a simple little project."

He leaned across the table. His eyes bore into hers with sudden intensity as his voice dropped a few notes and added, "But then, nothing is ever going to be simple between you and me, will it, Tess?"

The premonition of danger fluttered through her now as it had with his words. All pretense of cleaning up the shop was gone. She stared at the bulldozer as it backed up with a trademark beep-beep-beep, then started forward and scraped the first few inches of dirt.

The sudden stab of pain in her head and a shrieking in her mind was almost enough to bring her to her knees. She put a hand out to a large column to hang on, hoping the sensations would pass. But with each bite of the bucket, a new voice screamed.

It was worse this time. She'd felt ghosts of this when she and Powers met. She'd had echoes of these feelings at each meeting about the site and each planning session for the building design.

Shivering in the sunny front window, she raised her eyes back to the site in time to see Powers turn and stare in her direction.

Chapter 15

"Honestly, I'm kind of surprised she didn't come down the street to make sure I was complying with all of her conditions."

Powers clinked his brother's glass with his own and looked around the stonework in the bar.

"Oh, she wasn't feeling all that well, according to Serena. Something about a migraine." Dane frowned as he shared the news. "My wife is worried. She says that Tess rarely gets sick, and she never takes a day off. But since late last fall, she's been getting these killer headaches. When Serena asks about them, Tess waves them off as no big deal."

She was ill, that was why he hadn't seen her. He wish he'd known. He would have taken her flowers or something.

Hah, funny one. Taking flowers to a florist.

"What are you smiling at?" Dane stared at him in fascination.

"Nothing, just thought that maybe I should take something by, to cheer Tess up."

Dane now openly laughed. "Man, what has gotten into you? You've been the picture of congeniality ever since you won the project in town. The fact that you wanted to get together tonight – "

"Now wait a minute. Is there a law against having a beer with my little brother at the end of the week when I'm working only a few miles away? I mean, just – "

Powers cut off whatever he was going to say next when his tirade had no effect on stopping Dane's laughter.

What was he doing here? A normal Friday night for him was a visit to the office from whatever project job site he ended at that day to wrap up any last minute details from the week, and a stop at one of the restaurants near his condo for take-out dinner. Sometimes he sat at a bar and had a beer by himself while he waited. He'd head home, take a shower, reheat dinner and eat it alone, watching something on a sports channel or the news.

Damn, this was almost social. And normal.

If Dane could make an effort, so could he. "So, what do you and Serena have on for the weekend?"

"She's busy planning a wedding reception for Gabby and Rick. Roxy's doing the food, Marguerite's bringing the wine, and Tess is preparing flowers and centerpieces. According to Vince, DK's working on some hush-hush piece of art for them. I didn't think there would be much left to do, but Serena, being the master organizer that she is, is finding plenty of tasks for herself." He smirked as he took another sip of beer. "For me, too. Want to help?"

It was Powers' turn to smirk. "Nope, I have plenty to keep me busy. I have plans to review for a new project in Stockton, and there are a couple of bids that Marty wants me to consider. And there's a grant application cycle coming up for the foundation, so I need to sign off on those docs too."

Powers trailed off as he realized his brother was watching him with sympathy. There it was, pure and simple. Dane felt sorry for him.

"What do you do for fun, Powers?"

Fun? This was fun. He opened his mouth to reply, and closed it just as fast when he realized he couldn't lie to himself.

It wasn't fun. It was his existence.

"This is how I pass my time. I'm better off working. It's what I do best."

Eying him carefully, Dane seemed to consider his next words carefully.

"The boys think you're scary."

"The boys? Which boys?"

"Jeremy and Will, Gabby and Rick's kids. They're going to be staying with us during the honeymoon cruise, and the only thing they wanted to know was if my brother was going to be there too." Dane shook his head. "They called you one scary dude. Their words."

Dane signaled the waitress and circled the glasses with a finger to indicate another round. When he turned back, he started in once more.

"So, scary dude, I say you need to lighten up and get a little fun in your life."

Powers had a sudden vision of flashing golden eyes and fingers like talons digging into his shoulders as a woman with fluid grace danced under him. Her long hair wrapped around them as one more sweet caress. Her spirit joined his as sound shrieked around them, and it felt – inevitable.

Chapter 16

The ruffle of a breeze in her hair was a pleasant contrast to the on-and-off sweltering heat of the last two months. Finally, there were signs that fall would be around the corner, and hopefully with it, much needed rain.

Tess eyed the wilted flowerbed next to the back of her house. It appeared that once again, a valve on her irrigation system had gone on the fritz and this area had been lacking any watering for the past few days. It only took a couple of hot days of exposure in the western sun to fry the poor plants.

Penelope and Tigger played in the shade of a wisteria covering the small patio at the edge of the garden. Pods were already hanging thick and dense from the underside of the vines, and before long, she knew they'd be dropping seeds everywhere. That brought the squirrels to visit, much to the cats' happiness. Today, though, they were content to toy with long grass fronds that overflowed a couple of pots.

She frowned at the sprinklers again, not having included this in her outdoor plan today. With Jan covering the shop, she planned on deadheading and pruning and the myriad other tasks necessary to keep her garden looking its best.

When the migraine finally left her completely last night, she'd exhaled fully for the first time since she watched the project activity last Monday. The pain abetted each evening, but her dreams were haunted by angry shouting voices or moans of pain. Each time she awoke, she couldn't remember any details other than those desolate sounds.

Feeling more herself last night, she'd expected a full night of deep sleep.

Instead, she got dreams of Powers.

In her dream, he was carrying her over his shoulder, caveman style, and they were walking through tall grasses at the edge of denser woods. Even as she'd argued that he needed to put her down, he'd remained silent. Gradually, the cadence of his tread lulled her. When they'd reached a river, she'd roused enough to argue with him again. This time, he put her down only long enough to wrap her in a crushing embrace.

She'd woken up with her sheet twisted around her legs and her heart pounding too hard. But at least her head didn't ache. The wisps of the dream refused to clear completely, and finally too frustrated with their renewed energy pulsing in her head, she began reciting her meditation chants aloud.

It had been a couple of months since she'd last used her chants to calm herself. Frankly, she usually didn't need them. But the recent events culminating in the ground breaking on the new building seemed to be adding up to trouble. She was rusty and tripped over some of the words, but the calm that finally settled over her allowed her to fall back into a deep and dreamless sleep.

Feeling more refreshed this morning, and heartened by the gentle breeze and cooler temperature, she was ready to face the priority projects outside.

Evidently, this would begin with a check of her watering system. She grabbed the toolbox of irrigation supplies and rounded the south side of the house to inspect the problem. And stopped with a hand on her gate when she saw a tall man squinting up at the side of her house, pencil in the air and counting.

"What do you think you're doing?"

It came out with more bite than she'd intended.

He held up a finger and continued his inspection, mouthing an addition to the count every once in a while. Finally finished, he made a note on the small pad in his big hand and turned to her.

"Good morning, Tess. I'm glad to see you up and around. I heard you weren't feeling well this week."

There was no smile on his face, and if the words hadn't been so polite, she'd have thought he was angry with her. As it was, he stood waiting, obviously expecting her to respond with something in turn.

Recovering her cool took longer than anticipated. Today he was wearing longer shorts with plenty of pockets, work boots, and a thin white t-shirt that molded to every muscle. The image flashed her back to the vision of him climbing out of the waves in Hawaii. And it did seriously hot things to her libido.

What the hell was this strange attraction? It was as if he'd invaded her mind, the thoughts of him almost constant, humming in the background if not in the forefront of her brain. And it had to stop.

He was still waiting, his face unreadable behind wraparound sunglasses and standing as motionless as grasses on a windless day.

Fighting to find a reserve of her earlier calm, she sighed. That cost her dearly. Even standing ten feet away, she could smell his soap and the earthy aroma of a man used to working outdoors.

"Powers." She tried for a regal nod and was pleased when she thought she pulled it off. "I didn't expect to see you here today. And by here, I mean here, on my property. Did I forget a meeting we were going to have?"

*****

He hadn't expected the punch to his gut that seeing her would bring. Her miles of long raven hair were piled up under a big floppy hat. She looked pale, he guessed from being inside as she was fighting off the migraine. Even at this distance, he could see the residual strain it left behind on her face.

It was that vulnerability that nearly did him in. An overwhelming urge to protect her and care for her overtook him faster than an explosive collapse. Her expression, however, said it loud and clear.

Stay away from me.

How could he? The shorts she wore had seen better days, and the tank top only highlighted the toned arms and sleek skin that here and there was already speckled with dirt. Her knees bore matching sets of soil stains on silky skin.

He knew it was silky skin all over her body. His fingers twitched, and the rest of his body remembered too.

He shifted on his feet in sudden discomfort. Heat and a surge of physical shock replaced the protective instinct. He wanted to carry her inside, pull her into his lap, and ravage her mouth for a few hours.

Staring at those lips, the ones that were now set in a grim line in a face that was frowning at him, brought ideas of deeper tangles. Limbs, hair, his body over hers.

"Is there some reason you're here?"

Her question startled him. Taking a moment to tuck the notepad in his pocket gave him an excuse to adjust his shorts, maneuvering so that his hardening arousal was less obvious if no less uncomfortable.

"When I dropped you off on the Fourth of July, I noticed that you needed to have a couple of the front steps replaced. Then when we met here for the project kick-off, I saw some shingles and cut-outs that were loose. I thought

I'd fix things for you, so you won't have any problems come winter."

"I take care of things myself."

The snap in her tone as she raised the tote full of piping and valves almost made him smile.

"This may be more than you want to tackle."

She frowned outright now, coming through the garden gate and staring up at the side of the house intently. What she saw had her frowning even harder. Setting her lips together in a tight grimace, she scanned back and forth across the scalloped siding. When she bit her lower lip, his erection twitched in response.

Shit.

Turning away and pulling out the notebook again, he examined the prop without seeing anything he'd written on the page. He had to get himself under control. The last thing he needed was Tess getting mad at him because of his body's undue excitement.

*****

He lounged in a big wicker chair across the porch from her, their spot shaded from the sun and cooled by the lazy movements of the ceiling fan overhead. Appearances were deceptive, though. He felt anything but relaxed.

And she was uptight enough for both of them.

"I don't expect you to be doing anything for me." She pushed at her hair with marked impatience. Once the hat was gone, it was everywhere, falling now in a cascade down her back. Much as he wanted to ignore the feeling, Powers found it incredibly sexy.

"I'm not giving you anything elaborate, Tess. I'm only offering to repair the shingling and steps, and any other loose boards I find, like the ones at the end of the porch. Call it a tribute to this wonderful old architecture. I can't see a monument like this falling into ruin."

She made a rude noise, one that he'd never have expected her to utter.

He'd walked her around the house once, pointing out loose wood that was warped or cracked. While he was at it, he couldn't help telling her about the history of the architects. The structure was a beauty, with all of the fabled features of the American Queen Anne style. It deserved to be restored it to its full luster.

Their journey brought them eventually to the backyard. Her garden stretched towards the hillside of residences above them, and on either side, it extended past the width of Main Street's buildings. The grand dame was seated with Flynn's Crossing stretched out at her feet.

"How much land do you have?"

Tess turned slowly, her eyes hidden behind sunglasses as her face tracked from one end of the garden to the other.

"The lot is over an acre. I know, a big size for being in town. The madam who ran the bordello at the time of the fire bought up the land on either side before the cinders were cool, according to the city's records. Maybe she had thoughts of expanding. The property passed to her son, and it was just before the Second World War that he changed it over to a rooming house. The town's reputation by then was a little less – wild, I guess you could say. Respectable people didn't want the fancy ladies here anymore."

Powers chuckled at that. He could imagine the gowned inhabitants parading up and down Main, at about the same time that many of the stone and brick buildings were changing over from their less savory pasts to decent businesses. No doubt those shopkeepers would want nothing to do with that longstanding neighbor.

"How much do you think it will cost?"

Her question, delivered as she waved him up the back steps – two needed repair here too – to the porch, took him by surprise. He didn't think she was going to let him anywhere near the place based on her previous arguments.

He took this as a good sign.

"I'd need to run the numbers to give you a solid estimate. The material needs to be high quality hardwood. I think that was the problem. Did you renovate once before?"

She stared at him, curiosity and frustration warring on her features. When she discarded the sunglasses, he had a clear view of the troubled look in those golden eyes.

It was her eyes that always got to him faster than anything else. They held a depth of wisdom that he'd never noticed in anyone else. Staring into them for too long raised swirling mists at the edges of his vision. They pierced his soul and left him drained, feeling like only she could fill him up again.

Shaking her head, she opened a small cooler set next to the house and pulled out two bottles of water, pointing one at Powers in question. When he nodded, she placed it on a low table and gestured to the chair he now occupied.

"The work was done before I bought the house eight years ago. It needed paint immediately, and at the time, the painter suggested I have someone take a look at the wood to see if anything should be fixed. I didn't have the money back then to do any more than paint, so I ignored it." She shrugged and looked out over the garden. "You do what you have to do. I didn't understand the full nature of the history of this place or its value. No one really did."

His protectiveness roared up once more, only this time, he didn't even have a place to direct it. She must have been, what, twenty-four when she bought this house? Even back then and without a complete historical reckoning of its worth, it would have run quite a few dollars.

He hunched forward, forgetting his desire to seem nonchalant and indifferent.

"That must have been a stretch for you, even before anyone realized the gem this place is. Did your family help you get started?"

When a cloud passed over her face and all animation disappeared, he knew he'd asked a very wrong question.

"No, I did it on my own. I worked and saved and received a small inheritance from my maternal grandmother. My family and I aren't – close."

The pause wasn't lost on him. Neither was the fact that he was now making her distinctly uncomfortable.

Chapter 17

"Glad you decided to stop in, Powers. You're just in time for the big unveiling. I got one for you too."

Vince waved him over to a large corner table in Mallory's. Part sports bar with blaring flat screens and part restaurant complete with stuffed animal heads and a large unlit stone fireplace, the cavernous rooms were filled to the ceiling with old California history. It was also the place the wolf pack now claimed as its den.

Dane lifted a bottle of beer and saluted him. "And here's to many future days spent in your happy presence."

The men around him alternately shook his hand, slapped him on the back, or congratulated him on becoming part of the Flynn's Crossing community.

Powers wasn't sure what the big deal was. He was only building a building.

"Anyway, this design is the combined effort of Dane," Vince tipped his bottle towards the man, "for the photo, and Dave," another tip, "who helped us find someone to make them up, for a very reasonable price, I might add."

"Don't forget your highly esteemed organizational skills, Vince." Steve smirked at him across the table and Deke, standing silent until now, leaned over and asked, "What are we doing with these things, exactly?"

The men all laughed, and Powers didn't get the joke.

Seeing his confusion, Deke filled in the blanks. "Roxy thought up the name when we were all watching the starlet in the movie Mac was filming. Evidently, according to her, every man in the place, present company included, was drooling. She thought we looked like a pack of rabid wolves. Ergo the name."

"So now, we have t-shirts!" Vince pulled something out of bag at his feet and displayed it with a flourish. "Ta-da!"

The image of the wolf was powerful, teeth bared and appearing to jump off the shirt into anyone's face. Its eyes were fierce, the brown tinged with yellow to make them appear to glow. With one large paw extended, the whole effect was one of three dimensional power.

"So? What do you think? Awesome, right?" Vince held up the shirt and glanced around at the men for confirmation.

The strangest sensation came over Powers. His hair, cut so short it was almost a buzz, felt like it was standing on end. He heard a rush of noise and something knocked against his solar plexus. Rage and fury and tremendous power surged through him. Just as quickly, it vanished, and left him staring at the shirt with intense misgivings.

*****

"I still can't believe you went to Tahoe and got married without any of us there. I mean, Gabby, really?" DK continued to pout as Tess passed her a bowl of nuts and the bottle of wine.

Of course, since Roxy was at the restaurant tonight and Marguerite was at a winery event, only Tess, Serena and DK were drinking. Gabby sat with a Cheshire cat smile on her face, enjoying a tall glass of milk.

"It was spur of the moment. The boys were going back to school last Monday, and we took a day off and had a midweek getaway, just the four of us. We passed the wedding chapels, and Jeremy asked why we didn't get married right away. By the time Will took up the chant, it seemed like the perfect celebration. Besides, it gives us all some much-needed stability in our lives." She smiled again, the picture of serenity.

The good-natured kidding continued, with DK the most vocal and Serena coming in a close second. Only Tess sat silent, lost in her thoughts.

He'd been so damn nice today, it was annoying.

"Can I tell you more about your house?" He'd spent a good half hour on that topic alone. Then he dragged her off the porch again and around to the front, pointing out the noteworthy detailing. Finally, he pushed open the door to her shop and continued inside while still talking.

"These pocket doors? One of their features. And look at this wainscoting and the detail around the fireplaces. How much has changed?"

"I think the rooms down here are original. The house was built for a man who had grown wealthy, not on the Gold Rush, but on goods for the stores and trades that miners and then later settlers needed. It was a home first. Then he lost his money in a stock market gamble, and the madam bought it. Clarisse was her name. According to the previous owners, she divided the rooms upstairs to make additional private spaces for the working girls. That suited her son fine too, when he wanted to use it as a rooming house. The people before me tore those walls out, and upgraded the plumbing and electrical."

He nodded with an excited air even as she was still speaking.

"I'm so glad no one decided to tear it apart and remodel. At least the first and second stories are intact. What about the third?"

It took her a minute to realize what he'd said. He could see the public first floor for himself. But the second floor?

"What do you mean, the second floor's intact?" She eyed him carefully, afraid of his answer.

The backpedaling was only visible for a few seconds before his face became a smooth palate of interest. "I mean, the original floor plans for the second and third floor are still intact, right? No one altered them." And he waited, unreadable and unwavering.

She was sure now.

"You've seen it."

He covered his surprise well, nodding negatively first, then halting and staring at her. Then he changed his nod, as if it cost him plenty to admit it.

"Yes, I've seen it."

"It was you, last Christmas, wasn't it?"

She felt the vibration of sensations echo off him and back onto her. He was fighting it, as disturbed by the memory as she was, and he didn't even know the half of it.

"Tess? Is something wrong?"

The question came from a woman's voice, and it took her a minute to focus on the body attached to it. Serena was watching her with interest, DK and Gabby looking at each other and then at her with almost matching grins.

"What's got you so hot and bothered?" DK delivered her question with only a slight hint of teasing.

Tess shook her head and forced a laugh. "Nothing, only thinking about what a weird day it was."

Serena sat back and continued to stare. When Tess didn't say anything more, she tsk-tsked and gave her friend a knowing look.

"It was Powers, wasn't it? I overheard Dane talking to him. It sounded like he'd been over here today, for more than a business visit, I'm guessing."

Sighing, because it was next to impossible to keep secrets around here even if you tried, Tess took her time munching on a few nuts, one at a time. Then she sipped her wine, and when the silence was unbearable, she answered.

"Yes, he was here today. I was working in the garden, and when I rounded the corner by the gate, he was standing there, counting."

"Counting?" Gabby's face was puzzled.

"Counting. Shingles to be replaced, to be exact. And measuring for boards needed to fix the front and back steps and a few floorboards here on the porch. He's going to give me an estimate of the costs of some necessary repairs."

"You asked him for help – that's wonderful. I'm so glad the two of you are getting along." Serena leaned forward and smiled broadly.

Tess felt compelled to clarify the situation. "No, I didn't ask him. He took it upon himself to look for things that need fixing. I think he's trying to get on my good side."

She was pissed about that part.

"I knew it! You wouldn't be this upset about something as simple as a gentleman giving you a helping hand if it didn't mean something to you." DK was almost dancing in her seat with glee.

"Tess, it's easy to deny what the rest of us already see. You have a thing for him, and he has a thing for you." Gabby had stars in her eyes again.

"Honey, I think the two of you are perfect for each other. I couldn't think of a better match. Two spirited souls, two powerful personalities, one explosive relationship. It's destiny."

Shivering on Serena's final word, Tess had that rending feeling again, the one where something tore her spirit out of her, and pain flooded back in its place.

Chapter 18

Shifting the blue neon safety vest that all Ashland employees wore and shoving the hard hat further back on his head, he nodded towards the two coffee cups in Dane's hands. "One of those for me?"

Camera slung over one shoulder and vest bulging with alternative lenses, the characteristic watchfulness on Dane's face gave way to a trace of a grin. "It depends on whether or not you're going to let me take pictures."

It was Powers' turn to share a brief smile. "You want to take pictures of us digging? There isn't anything exciting to watch here. We've already taken up the old sewer line, a real treat, and found two sets of water lines, only one of which was on the plans. Then there was a phone line that even the telephone company had misplaced. Cutting that meant this side of the block was out of business until repairs could be made. At my expense, of course."

Shaking his head, he thought about how the contingency budget, something they included in all projects because you just never knew, was already shrinking. And they weren't even halfway done with the trenches for the foundation's footings.

Dane put his coffee on the ground and pulled the camera up, sighting and shooting as he moved a few feet in either direction. Scanning the pictures he'd taken, he gave a satisfied nod and walked back to Powers, stooping to pick up the cup again.

"So that's why you're going so slowly now?" Dane nodded towards the trenching equipment and two men standing on either side of the bucket as it dug through the earth.

"I can't afford to hit anything else and delay things further, not to mention incur more costly repairs. It's better to go slow and see what we have, shovelful by damned shovelful."

Powers took a big gulp of coffee and considered. He was already four days behind schedule and only three weeks into the project. The phone company's re-routing and repair to the severed line had taken three days, and the extra water line had taken an additional day. They kept running into problems.

The unease he felt was more than money, though. There was something inherently spooky about this site. More than once, he thought someone touched him in passing, on his shoulder or his knee, but no one was anywhere close. He couldn't explain these sensations, of the whispers of conversations, even when no one was near. Something pulled at him, the same kind of feeling he'd had last Christmas, standing over Tess in her bedroom.

He'd felt eyes more than once too, or so he thought. And he thought they belonged to someone in the Victorian. Involuntarily, he glanced to the western end of the street and wondered if Tess was standing behind the thin curtains of her shop, examining them.

These weird superstitious feelings were getting the better of him. First the golden eyes. Those were Tess's eyes, right?

Then the rushing sensation and voices. But he put that down to being tired.

Finally, there was his reaction to the wolf on that stupid t-shirt.

He shook it off. "I'm imagining things. I have to be."

Dane shook his head, and Powers wondered who he was trying to convince, his brother or himself.

A commotion on the site distracted him, and he and Dane turned as one to see one of the men at the side of the trench bend over and examine something on the top of a discarded dirt pile. Then he looked in the bucket of the trencher. He took off his hardhat and swiped at his forehead with a worried gesture.

Powers was already moving, Dane at his side, when the shout came.

"Boss, you're going to need to see this."

*****

"They're bones. And I think they're human bones."

Powers had his cell phone to his ear and the architect on the other end.

"Kevin, you did check that this wasn't a protected site, right? Like an old cemetery or something?"

When the man confirmed this, Powers put his head back and tried to crack the sudden tension out of his neck.

"You'll need to call the county coroner, Powers. And the city cops. I'm sure the sheriff's got some kind of jurisdiction too. I've never run into bones on any project before, so I'm guiding you blind at this point."

"The cops already arrived, because the crowd got big so fast you'd think we'd found gold. Now they're showing great interest in the bones, though they say they'll need the county to help them with the crime scene, because this is outside their expertise. At first, they were worried it was a current missing person. But that dirt hasn't been moved in decades, if even that. Maybe a couple of centuries."

Hearing this, the other man sighed at his end of the phone. "I know you didn't expect this to be a problematic project, Powers. I'm sorry. There was no way to tell what we'd find once we started."

Bystanders were now gawking at the construction zone, lining the sidewalk on the opposite side of the street and craning their necks to look over cars and trucks that slowed to see what was happening. Murmurs and louder discussions could be heard blanketing the crowd, with each new arrival treated to a full rundown of why everyone was standing there and staring at a hole in the ground.

Bones. Goddamned bones.

A sheriff's deputy shook loose from the group around the mound of dirt and headed for Powers. He recognized Deke's brother, Jake, a man who'd appeared a time or two when the guys invited Powers to join them for a beer. Except now he was part of their pack, he supposed.

That brought a shiver once more.

"Powers, hell of a thing. Good that your guys were watching so carefully, or we'd have a bigger mess on our hands." Jake surveyed the watchful crowd. "How did the word get out so fast?"

Shaking his head, Powers explained. "That woman who works at the art gallery, Bettie, came running over when we stopped. She wanted to know if we hit another line that would cause them a problem. Then she looked down and saw the bones, backed up, and bustled away."

Jake chuckled. "Yeah, that would explain it. Telling something to Bettie is more efficient than activating the reverse 911 system. She probably had all the shop owners notified within minutes."

Sudden quiet from the crowd had them both looking up as the city cops standing at the edge of the site parted for the black and white county coroner's van. They watched in continued silence as two men exited the front, a young Hispanic from the driver's side and an older African American from the passenger seat. The older man paused and took a slow inventory of the construction site and the people milling around the dirt mound, and when his eyes finally settled on Powers and Jake, he shook his head.

"You'll like Ben. He's a character." Jake had dropped his voice low so that only Powers could hear. Then he stepped forward with his hand outstretched in greeting.

"Jake, this sounds very interesting. I love a puzzle." The man looked Powers up and down and took his hand in turn. "Dr. Ben Petry. I'd say a pleasure, but by the look on your face, I don't think you're having a good day."

Powers shrugged.

"Don't worry too much about it, young man. It's probably animal bones. People find 'em all the time up here. I'm getting pretty good at recognizing horses and cows and mules and all sorts of creatures on sight." When he chuckled, Jake joined in.

Powers did not.

"Okay, boys, let's see what we have," and he moved towards the trench, rubbing his hands together.

Short hairs stood up on the back of his neck and Powers felt a set of lasers pointed at him. He stopped, letting the other men drift on, and waited for the feeling to pass. But it didn't. The eyes felt like sharp stabs of pain, echoing old hurts.

It was ridiculous. There were a couple of hundred people staring this in his direction right now. But this sensation was specific and wrenching, and he couldn't help his shudder at the feeling.

Chapter 19

When the phone started ringing nonstop, she was working on a large display of early season mums and fall colors. Bettie's excited voice pitched to near hysteria.

"Tess, it's Bettie. They dug up bones at the construction site. Bones! Can you imagine? Anyway, I'm calling everyone." And she hung up without even saying goodbye.

The phone rang again almost immediately. Delilah at the cheese shop shared the same message, then Larry at the meat place.

Finally, Chase got through on a brief second when the line wasn't engaged.

"Tess, have you heard? They found bones when they were digging. Maybe human bones. Gosh, who would have thought? Good thing our contract with Ashland is fixed price. Anyway, I'll come down and get you and we can walk up together and see what's happening. You're the project coordinator after all, so you should be there."

When he hung up without signing off, she cringed. His shop was halfway to the site already, and there was no reason for him to come collect her except as an excuse to see her.

She'd been avoiding him, but that wasn't the worst of her current problems.

Not long before the phone calls started, head pain gripped her. There weren't any of the usual warning signs – no flashes of bright light or sudden retched smells or pounding pulse. One minute she was fine, and the next minute, her head felt like it would explode.

Shrieks and moans echoed inside her brain. The pain turned physical, which was why she was still sitting at her table, her head down on her arms while she willed it back. She didn't want Chase to find her like this, because he'd insist she go to the emergency room. And she had a suspicion that this wasn't a medical problem.

Pulling out her phone, she called Chase on his cell and assured him she'd meet him at the site eventually.

"You sound funny. Are you okay?"

She managed to assure him she was in the middle of something that she needed to finish and was preoccupied. He didn't sound convinced, but he talked himself into heading over the site alone to represent the business association.

As if every shop owner on these blocks wasn't already standing in the crowd.

Stretching out on the table seemed like a good idea, and she crawled up and laid down among the branches and flowers, hoping that the noise and pain would fade to something manageable.

When she next looked at the clock, she was surprised to find that two hours had passed. The voices were chanting now, an angry chant and one she recognized.

A chant of curses.

*****

"They're definitely human. Old too." Dr. Petry stood up and placed a gentle gloved hand on the bones already collected in a body bag. "Did you do a historical survey before you started the project?"

The architect Kevin nodded his head in the affirmative. Trying to release the steely clutch of tension in his neck, Powers shifted and swiveled, using the opportunity to scan the crowd.

Chase stood with a few of the other business owners off to the side, in deep discussion and pointing at the trench several times. Powers didn't see Tess, though Chase had told him she was coming as soon as she could.

He didn't see her, but he felt her. He couldn't explain that. Tension tightened his own bones, making him feel brittle and unusually vulnerable. Glancing around the site once more, he knew he was missing something, something very important. But he had no clue what it was.

Jake might have been standing in front of him for seconds or minutes, he wasn't sure. When the deputy frowned, Powers just shook his head. "Don't ask."

Sympathy crossed the other man's face as he delivered his news.

"We have to shut the site down for the time being, at least anything related to construction. Ben's going to confirm the bones first, and assuming they're human, date them too. And if they're human, we need to dig them up, but carefully. I doubt it's a crime scene, but it might be a historical site."

He looked back at the trench thoughtfully, then scanned the surrounding buildings and the hillsides. "I don't recall any stories about a cemetery set here, or anything about graves within a few blocks of Main, at least not since the Gold Rush."

Powers didn't want to ask how he knew this, but he had a feeling it was going to bring him more grief.

"And what does that mean?"

The deputy's next words made him consider finding the nearest bar and asking for a bottle.

"It means that this could be a Native American burial site. And if that's the case, nothing will happen until we bring in the elders."

*****

It was after seven when the group agreed to disperse and return whenever the coroner called with his findings. He appeared to be certain these were human bones. Powers had a gut feeling that he was right, but for completely different reasons.

With yellow crime scene tape circling the chain link fence and a city cop settled in for guard duty tonight, there was nothing else to do but make the drive home and find that much-needed drink.

Over the last few hours, Tess still hadn't appeared. Chase and the other business owners finally trickled back to their shops. The crowds on the sidewalks dispersed with some gentle persuasion from the cops and sheriff's deputies. Cars and trucks still slowed in the street though, pointing at the site and having animated conversations until equally enthusiastic drivers behind them honked to get them to move on for the next group's better viewing.

At the west end of Main, Tess's Victorian was dark. In fact, he hadn't noticed any activity there all afternoon. And he'd been watching, though he didn't realize it until Dane had remarked on it.

"Your eyes don't lie any more than the camera does, my brother," Dane teased.

It didn't look like Tess was home, but even so, he could talk himself into walking the short blocks to her house and ringing the bell. He had a good reason to see her. Her Native American roots were from the area, according to Dane. Maybe she knew some of the history and could shed light on this fiasco.

A small voice that he wanted to ignore coaxed a different response. Maybe he just wanted to see her.

Chapter 20

Peering in the window felt like an intrusion, but Powers was curious why Tess had never shown up at the site today. Everyone else on the street had been by, usually for long visits and intense discussion, sometimes behind the shield of a raised hand. He felt her presence, though, like a tight clutch of claws at the base of his neck exerting pressure that bordered on pain.

He knocked, but received no response. When he turned the knob, the door swung open, and he frowned at the welcoming flute music. Closing time was an hour ago, and it wouldn't be like Tess to forget to lock the front door on her way out. He already knew too many of her habits from the wedding work and their construction discussions. She was careful and precise and paid attention to details.

"Tess? Are you here?" His voice sounded like an echo returning to him. Even though he heard no response, he sensed she was lurking somewhere in the big building.

Listening brought only the creaks of old wood cooling as the sun lowered in the sky. Outside noises were muted since the windows were shut to hold the air conditioning hostage. But maybe that's why she didn't hear him. Maybe she was working in her garden.

Banging out the front door again, he rounded the side of the house where the back gate stood latched as it usually was. He pushed it open on a small squeak of hinges, and scanned the yard for any sign of her. There was no woman bending over her flower beds or vegetables. No sign of tools or cans or other equipment indicated that she had been working. All was pristine and perfectly still.

A prickle of worry wedged its way into his busy mind. This was so un-Tess-like that his concern for her grew stronger. He didn't have any right to worry about her, but she was the best friend of his sister-in-law, and that alone should be reason enough.

He rounded to the front once more, eyes lighting on the hybrid car she drove still parked on the opposite side of the Victorian. Next to it was the delivery van, another hybrid, with the merry Buds and Blooms logo painted across the side. Wherever she was, she hadn't driven there.

Hands on hips, he turned to examine the windows again. No sign of life stirred behind any of the curtains. Where the hell was she, and why was her store still unlocked?

He'd programmed her phone number into his cell, because he had to reach the construction liaison with the business association upon occasion. There wasn't any other reason, he had assured himself at the time.

Scrolling to her number, he hit the call button and waited through the rings until the phone answered. Her voicemail message started its recitation and he hit the end button with more viciousness than needed.

Maybe she hadn't heard him come in before.

Taking the front steps two at a time and opening the door within seconds, he tried again, louder this time. "Tess? Are you in here?"

There was no response, but this time he ventured further into the space. There had to be a reason why she wasn't home but the door was unlocked.

The old parlor to one side was dark, but he could smell fresh greenery and flowers from her work area behind the display room. Something raced by his legs and disappeared back in that direction, setting his heart racing with surprise.

One of her cats. There was another one someplace and he didn't want to step on it and go flying himself. He was intent on the placement of his feet in the semi-darkness, and it wasn't until he was almost next to the work table that he looked up and gasped.

Flowers and leaves littered the table, strewn around like they'd been wiped from side to side by a giant hand. A vase lay on the floor next to the table, shattered into fine shards of pottery. The green clay she'd been using as a foundation of the arrangement was against the wall near the corner. And her stool, the one she customarily sat on while she built her masterpieces, was on its side in front of the cooler doors.

Every protective instinct Powers had went into overdrive. Tess would never leave things like this, at least not voluntarily. The claws tightened on his neck once more, and he almost yelped at the sudden surge of pain. He didn't know why he felt it was a link to Tess. He just knew it was, even though he couldn't explain it with any logic. His brain said that he should walk out the door and leave her a voicemail.

His soul told him to keep going until he found her.

He backed up and tried the other side of the building, the small front parlor that housed Tess's office. The lights were dark here too, but when he flipped on the switch, the tension in his neck transmitted to fear twisting his gut.

Her desk drawer stood open, and her purse was in the drawer, also open. Keys sat on the desk blotter next to a cell phone, and in the center, a half-finished cup of tea, the bag still in place, waited for someone to take the next sip.

Now he was terrified.

*****

Sitting with her legs pulled up tightly did little to ease her pain, but it was the only position that brought any other comfort. She pushed into the chair, taking deep breaths and blowing them out slowly in hope of defeating the pounding. Her fingers gripped into tight balls, clutching empty air. It was the only way she could hold on.

She hadn't anticipated that she'd still be crippled like this, unable to move and long past calling for help. The voices in her head made her believe she was losing her sanity. Who would you call and admit that to?

Serena would understand, but Tess left her cell behind when she tried to find refuge. It was stupid, but she wanted some air and thought that it would help ease the burden. She recognized it for what it was, her ancestors' revenge.

She wasn't a true believer, not like her father or uncle or many of the other relatives who said that you can't escape the path laid down for you before time began. The past chased her down an ever-narrowing track until there was no veering away and no going back.

The harsh chant in her mind chided her. There is no escaping your destiny.

*****

Thoughts of her private quarters had him taking the central stairs two at a time, but when he reached the door, it was unexpectedly locked. The keys were on her desk, and she could have entered and locked it behind her, but then why was the downstairs still standing open to anyone who wanted to enter? Pounding on the door and calling her name proved to be a useless exercise.

He considered running up the street for one of the city cops, but that might be an over-reaction. After all, there might be a legitimate reason why the place looked like a crime scene and Tess was missing, leaving behind all of her personal belongings.

He thumbed his phone and tried Tess again, hearing the cell ring on her desk. The crunch of pottery shards underfoot brought a cat streaking across the space again.

"Tess! Damn it, where the hell are you?" He was yelling, but if others heard him, he didn't care. The talons in his neck urged him forward.

Shoving past the work table and upended stool, he crossed into the back of the house. The large kitchen was empty, holding none of the damage evident in other parts of the house.

But the door to the back stood unlocked and gaped open. Stepping out on the porch brought an immediate sense of danger. His guts turned to jelly and he was suddenly afraid of what he would find. The fear quieted his footsteps until he was creeping over the old boards and praying nothing would creak underfoot.

Chapter 21

Mocking words filled her head. This was no migraine. It was the ancients, taunting her, urging her to accept what she couldn't change.

Over their voices, she thought she heard her name called. First, it was angry. Then there was fear in the tone. Finally, this last time, the voice sounded close and lowered with pleading anguish.

"Tess? Where are you?"

She vaguely recognized it, and as she did, her hands gripped tighter until her nails dug into her palms. The pain of it steadied her and allowed her to suck in enough air to fill her lungs. She held it, willing the self-control to order her pain away on her next breath. When it whooshed out of her, she couldn't help a moan as the pain remained.

Boots stamped in quick succession across the porch and down the steps.

"Tess? My god, Tess! Are you hurt? What happened?"

It was Powers, she confirmed with a start. He was the last person she wanted finding her like this, defenseless against him.

With gentle hands, he tipped her head back from its position buried in her knees. Keeping her eyes closed seemed the safest guard against what she was sure would be demands for information. That was beyond her right now.

When his fingers simply caressed her cheek and he didn't say a word, she forced herself to open her eyes.

They locked on his, and at this close range, she could see terror that hadn't faded, mixed with relief only now growing. A shaking hand pushed back her hair, and he examined her features carefully as if taking inventory to see what was wrong.

How long she stared at him, she wasn't sure. It became too much, and she closed her eyes again, willing him to leave her alone.

Instead, he picked her up in his arms as easily as if she was a child, and taking the seat she'd been curled in, he put her head on his shoulder and wrapped tight arms around her.

*****

Her skin was too pale, the color of ash bleached in the sun for months. In her face, her golden eyes glowed too brightly, and he wondered if she was ill.

Strangely, though, the tight claws of tension in his neck eased as soon as he picked her up. Relief flooded through him. He hadn't realized how scared he'd been that something very bad had happened to her.

They'd been sitting like this for at least an hour, he estimated. Her breathing, which had been harsh and uneven when he found her, gentled to an even ebb and flow. When she shifted against him and pushed back to look into his face, he released her only that far.

She was still too pale, but some of the pain etching her features was now gone. Her eyes were half-lidded, and exhaustion was evident in the slump of her shoulders. Still, she tried to push further away and swing around as if she planned to stand up.

He wasn't ready for her to leave, not yet.

"Tess, can you tell me what happened in there?" He tossed his head to the side to indicate her store. "Did someone try to break in or steal something?"

His linked hands at her back made her escape impossible. He wanted answers before he let her move away. And he wanted to reassure himself that she was unhurt.

She stared at him now, regaining some of the solemn composure he was used to seeing. She frowned, then looked down at her hands, examining half circles cut into her palms.

"I, ah, got a migraine. Around midday, just before everyone started calling me about the bones you found today. It came on so fast, I wasn't prepared. I crawled up on the table to stretch out."

He wasn't convinced she was telling him everything.

"Your purse is sitting in plain view in your open desk drawer. There's broken stuff in the work room. Your chair's on the floor." He waited.

She shook her head before replying. "I keep migraine medicine in my purse, and I took a pill before I came out here. I must have pushed the arrangement over when I rolled off the table. I don't remember much about getting from the table to my office, or out here."

He held her loosely, unwilling to allow her to move away. Under her muscles, he traced bones as finely shaped as any bird's. The image stayed with him, and when she turned her golden eyes on him again, a tremor of premonition shot through him.

*****

The voices all but disappeared, leaving in their wake a bone deep weariness that made her want to find her bed and collapse. She suspected she'd be hearing them again soon enough.

Powers still examined her face as if he wasn't sure she was unharmed. When she pushed against him, he only let her get an arm's length away. Sitting on his lap was too personal, and she wanted to insist that she be allowed to stand and put distance between them.

At his hip, a cell phone chirped. He held her eyes while he fished for it between his body and the side of the chair. When he picked it up, he glanced only briefly at the display before putting it to his ear.

"Powers Ashland. Yes, Dr. Petry. You're sure? But surely – no, I understand." He paused, his frown deepening as he listened. "Yes, my crew can help with that. Tomorrow at seven will be fine. Thanks for the call."

She was fascinated with the expressions that chased across his face. The vulnerability he'd worn an hour ago was long gone, and in its place he carried determination like a shield. In the scant seconds of the phone call, this had changed to uncertainty, frustration and finally, resignation.

"That was the coroner, Dr. Petry."

All she could do was nod.

"The bones are human." At her nod again, he finished. "And they're old."

She bit her lip to keep from blurting out what she knew.

"And Tess? He believes that the bones are Indian."

Unable to meet his eyes any longer and maintain her mask of composure, she turned away to scan her dark garden. Night had fallen while they sat here, and lights now shown in the houses up the hill.

He put a finger under her chin and turned her back to him. His stern expression held puzzlement as he watched her.

"Did you know we'd find Native American bones on that site?"

She hesitated, and he seemed to grow impatient as the silence lengthened.

"Tess?" The demand for a response was evident in his tone.

"I, ah – I mean, no. Or rather no, but yes."

When she pushed away this time, he let her go. Standing was shaky after being so overwhelmed, but she managed to cross to another chair and drop to its edge without mishap. Powers stayed where he was, though he leaned forward, clasping his hands and kneading tense fingers as he rested his elbows on his knees.

"I don't understand. You knew there were bones on the site and agreed to the project anyway?"

Tess realized that this was going to be even more difficult to explain than she thought.

"No, I didn't know there were bones buried there. There's no record of them that I know of. But once you found them, I knew they were ancestral."

He was shaking his head before she even finished.

"How do you know that?"

When she shrugged dismissively, he reached across the space between them and ran a finger down her cheek before grasping her chin. His fingers grew more insistent.

"Tess, what aren't you telling me?"

Watching his face so closely, his breath mixing with hers as both their pulses increased, was not the way she wanted to end the day. She'd been through too much and her hold on fragile emotions was tenuous at best. Not knowing how to answer him, at least not in such a way that he wouldn't believe she was crazy, she just shook her head again, refusing to say more.

"Damn it, Tess, you owe me an explanation!"

That pushed one too many buttons.

"What the hell do you mean I owe you? I don't owe you anything, Powers nothing at all." She didn't need to raise her voice. The vehemence of her words, delivered the message easily enough.

His gaze darkened further, and he opened his mouth once before closing it again and setting his sensuous lips in a grim tight line. Fingers left her face as if he was suddenly burned, and he stood to his full height and looked down at her searchingly.

In a tone as low as hers and just as forceful, Powers finally said, "You're right, you don't owe me anything. We're business associates, tied together by a contract of what should have been a simple project. It's no longer simple. Just because I found you in pain and tried to help you doesn't mean you owe me. But damn it all to hell, Tess, we're connected over this in some way. I don't understand how or why, but until we get this resolved, you're stuck with me."

Halfway through his speech, she closed her eyes. There was an echo of laughter in her mind, the voices taking gleeful revenge at the situation of their human counterparts. She knew why they were laughing.

Like it or not, she and Powers were connected, and stuck was only one way of describing it.

Chapter 22

"What happened today? No, you can wait to tell me. You look awful. What can I get for you?"

Tess sank into the corner of couches on Serena's back porch and stared out over the canyon. The balmy afternoon breeze rustled across her face as the murmur of voices whispered in her mind.

The voices were multiplying. The two or three adults of yesterday still chanted, joined now by the playful sounds of children. And more adults, young and old, men and women. At times today the chants were war-like, and at other times, they were mournful and bereaved moans.

Pushing a steaming cup of tea into Tess's hands, Serena sat next to her on the couch and waited. She could sit like this, silent and patient, and out-wait almost anyone when she was in counselor mode.

Tess felt as fragile as a crazy person today. Maybe tiptoeing around her was a good idea.

Sipping her tea, she watched a buzzard turn in a lazy circle above them over the canyon, catching the updrafts so efficiently that it barely needed to move a feather to maintain position. Maybe she should have been a buzzard. It was less a prowler and more intent on cleaning up the mess others left behind on its own terms.

But she was meant to be a warrior, a carnivore, a predator. It was part of her destiny.

"Today was difficult," she started, her voice scratchy and unlike her. She cleared her throat and began again.

"I watched them dig, you know."

Next to her, she saw Serena nod in her peripheral vision.

Suddenly too nervous to stay in one place, Tess rose to pace the distance to the railing. A hawk screeched as it was chased by two smaller birds at the tops of pines down the slope. It settled on a tree top, perching on the needles alone, and the other birds retreated. Then it turned and seemed to look at her.

"The thing is, Serena, I think I'm going a little crazy. That's why I needed to see you today."

Serena made a rude noise and Tess turned to find her best friend and confidante regarding her with disbelief.

"You are the sanest and most stable person I think I know. You are certainly not going crazy. Maybe you're just tired. You certainly look exhausted."

Now it was Tess's turn to make a harsh sound, one that wasn't too different from the hawk's screech from moments before.

She knew how she looked. She'd examined her face closely in the mirror this afternoon, because she knew she looked different. Her cheekbones were more fiercely pronounced and the lack of sleep had taken a toll. Overnight, she'd become more like the thing she wanted to deny.

"You're staying for dinner. I'm not taking no for an answer. Dane will be home whenever they finish on the site today. Powers asked him to come down and take pictures, particularly after they started finding – other things."

Tess already knew what they were finding. The news traveled fast up and down the six blocks of Main Street, and if every customer coming into Buds and Blooms today hadn't mentioned it, the frequent update phone calls from one shop owner or another would fill in the blanks.

More bones. A lot of bones. Multiple bodies' worth of bones, young and old.

Chase dropped by around opening time. Pacing the display area front to back and stopping at Tess's work table, he ran a frustrated hand through his blond hair.

"The coroner said that the bones they found yesterday were a femur, a tibia, and some smaller leg bones. When they dug around the area on the sides this morning, they already noted that there seems to be a pelvis next to the leg bones. So there's more of a skeleton still resting there."

A high wail crossed her mind, and Tess knew they'd find the bones that belonged to a young woman.

Shaking his head in disbelief, Chase continued, "So now they're going to ask that the surrounding area be dug out. The surface scraping will happen with machinery, and then they'll move to shovels and finally to hand trowels. Dr. Petry is going to oversee it."

He put out his hands to Tess as if entreating her to find an answer to his next question. "How long is this all going to take? We can't have Main Street messed up for longer than our original plan. The holidays are coming up."

While she didn't say anything to respond, only shrugging as he continued to rant, she suspected that the true answer was far longer than he wanted to contemplate.

When he called a couple of hours later to tell her they'd found more of the skeleton, and it was a woman's body according to Petry, she only murmured inconsequential words. Mid-afternoon, he let her know about parts of a second body. And finally, just before closing, a third call notified her of the first child.

*****

"No, Marty, I don't know what we can do right now other than agree to help. The county will pay us for the additional excavation work. They decided it was cheaper to use us since we already had equipment on the site."

"How long will the project be delayed?" Marty's question came through Powers' Bluetooth, the hint of worry beginning to grow.

Wiping a hand across his face and setting his sunglasses back in place, Powers shrugged, and realized that Marty wouldn't know what he was thinking unless he spoke the words out loud.

"Indefinitely. That's all they could tell me at the moment."

Clicking off without bothering to say goodbye, Powers put both hands on the wheel of his truck with a death grip. Dane drove in front of him, taking the country two-lane road more sedately than Powers wanted. Putting his foot down might give him a place to put his frustration and anger.

His brother had spent the day with him, watching as the earth surrounding the original trench was dragged and dug to a depth above that where they'd found the first bones. The coroner supervised the work, telling Powers when it was time to switch to shovels gently spaded into the earth. By the time they needed hand trowels and brushes, the crew wore out their nervous jokes about digging in a cemetery and worked silently in the early afternoon's sun.

It was then that the second adult was found, followed by the child. When the little one was uncovered, a couple of guys moved away for a bit and looked anywhere but at the hole.

Dane moved around the work, shooting with two different cameras and multiple lenses, sometimes set on a tripod and sometimes crouched at unusual angles. The coroner at first fussed at the intrusion, but as the site yielded more bones, he began directing Dane on shots that he needed before moving anything else.

The bones were staying in the ground for the time being.

And they were digging a wider hole tomorrow.

Pulling up to Dane and Serena's house, Powers flashed again on his stilted conversation with Tess last night. She had known that the bones belonged to Native Americans, but she denied knowing they were there before. He believed her, though he had no facts to back that up.

He knew, just as he knew somehow that they were tied up in this thing together.

His feeling persisted throughout his late drive to his condo in Sacramento last night, during his almost sleepless night, and through his hour-long drive back up the hill this morning. He couldn't shake it. And again, there was no rational reason why.

When Dane insisted that he come for dinner and stay the night, Powers relented. It was better to be close by, and easier and safer to make a shorter drive if he was visited by demons as he had been during the scant sleep of the past twenty four hours.

He was stalking something in his dream, something dangerous and deadly that needed to be killed. Powerful though he was, he was encircled by the danger and its frightening intentions increased his desperation. The circle surrounding him grew tighter and tighter until he thought he was going to die.

Suddenly a flash above him broke the spell, and the circle expanded once again, taking the danger with it. A screech that rose and fell made him pivot as he drove the danger further away. Then a sharp cry sounded and he was racing towards it, needing to help in some way.

And that was how he'd woken, with the cry of pain still ringing in his ears and his hands clutching the sheet in a knot. Twitchy and uneasy, he gave up trying to get back to sleep and paced his living room, as early morning lights begin to spark the city into activity. When the horizon lightened, he showered and threw his gear together, heading east before the sun broke over the horizon.

He was the subject of everyone's scrutiny and the target of their questions as he made his stops in Flynn's Crossing. Buying gas at the local station on the west end of town, the clerk at the counter inside eyed his truck's logo and asked if he'd been there when they dug up the graves. Powers made a noncommittal sound that clearly disappointed the young man.

At Brew Bank Bakery, his breakfast choices were delayed as an older man with a dog questioned him on what parts of the body the bones had come from. When Powers said he honestly didn't know, the man began a lengthy and uninformed monologue about his assumptions and conjectures about the bones.

No one yet said anything about them being Native American bones. At least for now, that part of the story appeared to be kept quiet.

It wasn't until the hubbub in the coffee shop died down that Sarge and Stuart regarded Powers carefully and let him know that they'd heard the rest of the story.

"Indian bones. That's pretty unusual for the middle of town, don't you think?"

When he agreed that yes, it was an unexpected find, they asked him a few more pointed questions. But he couldn't tell them what it meant, or why the bones were there.

Rounding his truck and Dane's, he tried to shake the day's activities free and think instead about how a cold beer was going to taste. Bitter. Maybe staying as company was a bad idea tonight.

His work boots ground to an abrupt halt where he spied the vehicle parked between the truck and an SUV. A hybrid, one he knew.

Suddenly any desire for escape disappeared.

Chapter 23

Tess felt fragile. No other term described it. She ached for no specific reason and the sadness blanketing her was almost suffocating. And she hated it. She needed to be strong.

"So you had a very bad migraine. You've told me before that when you get a bad one, it seems like you're particularly susceptible to loud noises or strong odors or bright lights. Couldn't this be more of the same?"

Serena had been attempting to use logic and reason. Tess knew she meant well with that intervention. But the rationale was weak.

Shaking her head, she replied, "No, it couldn't. The pain was wrenching yesterday. And it's still there today. I tell you, Serena, the voices in my head are related to the bones."

"How can they be related?"

The sharp male voice held skepticism and anger.

Powers.

"Powers! What a pleasant surprise." Serena jumped up and hugged her brother-in-law, a move that clearly surprised the man. It momentarily distracted him and gave Tess a chance to select an indifferent expression for her features.

Now if she could just pull it off.

He was unfailing gentle as he hugged Serena back, pushing her away from him towards his brother's welcome home kiss. His features softened for a few brief seconds as he watched them before swinging back to Tess. When his eyes lighted on her, his face tightened into a grimace once more.

"You're hearing voices?" The incredulity in his question was matching by the mocking expression in his eyes.

Tess attempted to make light of the situation, giving a nonchalant shrug. But when his expression didn't change, she turned away to hide how much that hurt her.

Much as she wanted to deny it, she was still drawn to him. His worry that something hurt her last night and his gentleness in caring for her had opened a door into her heart. And as hard as she tried to slam it shut again, she couldn't find the strength.

"Tess was talking about her migraines, that's all." Serena turned from the kitchen alcove with two beers in her hand, popping the metal caps and handing one to each of the men.

Dane frowned at Tess. "Your migraines are getting worse? Since when?"

She waved away his concern.

"It's not worse, and it's nothing at all. Nothing I can't handle." Moving towards the kitchen to find the glass of wine she found she suddenly craved forced her to walk too close to Powers. She kept her eyes on anything but his face as she crossed the room with more bravado than she was feeling.

"That's not the way it was last night."

His words stopped her faster than the large strong hand on her arm. She looked up at him, pleading with her eyes for him to keep his mouth shut.

For a moment, he seemed uncertain. That changed to questioning intensity as their eyes held. Tess swore she felt that same protective mantle that had fallen around her shoulders last night the minute Powers picked her up and nestled her in his arms. It made her feel weak.

And it made her feel stronger.

Confused, she shook off his hand and moved towards a cabinet. Hidden by the open door, she shut her eyes and tried to block out the mocking voices in her head.

"I was just under the weather last night, and Powers happened to come by and find me like that." She wanted to cross her fingers that he would go along with her fib.

Glancing across the room at him, she found his eyes hooded and his expression unreadable. Watching her for more heartbeats than she cared to count, the sudden heat in his look shocked her more than his next words did.

"Yes, she wasn't feeling that well last night. I intruded, and I apologized for it. But at least we established that we have a bond, didn't we, Tess?"

She couldn't look away from the dare in his eyes.

*****

"I'm glad that Powers is going to follow you home." Serena's words were filled with worry. "You're not yourself. And you look even more tense than you did when you arrived."

Dinner, a simple meal of pasta and sauce and salad, had taken an eternity. Why Tess agreed to stay for it, she wasn't sure. When Powers took her hand and pulled her towards the table, she didn't resist him. Long minutes passed before he relinquished his hold.

The message was obvious. Stay. And when you go, I'm coming with you.

It was everything she was trying to fight, everything she had been trying to fight for years. Yet another domineering man who thought he knew what was best for her.

"I don't need him to follow me home. I've been on these roads my whole life. I know this route to town well enough to drive almost blindfolded. It's Powers you should be concerned about. He's not used to dark nights without city lights."

But as much as she stated the obvious, here she was, cruising into town in her little hybrid with the tall headlights of the big pick-up close in her rear view mirror.

And the voices had become louder with each passing mile. She detoured on side streets to avoid driving past the site itself. It didn't seem to matter to the screaming in her brain.

She pulled into her driveway and gave a vague wave out the back window, hoping that he'd see it and drive on, turning for the canyon house again. But of course, he didn't. In fact, he pulled into the driveway behind her, cut the engine, and climbed down from the cab.

Staying in her seat and watching him in the side mirror did nothing for her peace of mind. His gait was deliberate, stalking to her car door and wrenching it open before she had a chance to open it herself. Without saying a word, he took the key ring from her hand and put a palm out towards her, waiting to help her out. She hesitated as her fingers curled into an unlikely fist.

She took his hand, and the electricity shot up her arm into her body, making her suddenly aware that it was late and the street was otherwise empty. For all intents and purposes, they were completely alone in the town.

The anger she felt vibrating from him was in sharp contrast with the gentleness he used to tuck her against his side. It was as if he thought she would crumple taking the few steps to her front door. At the bottom of the steps, she forced him to pause.

"Please, Powers, there's no need to treat me like an invalid. I'm fine. See?"

She held out an almost steady hand as proof, hoping that he couldn't discern the slight tremble in the darkness. Ducking out from under his arm was harder, since he didn't seem to want to let her go.

"I'm worried about you." His gruff frustrated tone seemed to say that he wished he wasn't. "You haven't been yourself."

She gave a mirthless laugh. "How would you know? You don't know me, not at all." Her wave of dismissal seemed to anger him more as she turned towards her door and the few steps up to refuge.

A piercing shriek echoed in her head, the keening cry of women mixing with angry shouts of men. Its sharpness made her stumble and land hard on the second stair, and with her impromptu crash, the wood splintered beneath her.

"Shit!" The pain was jarring, an edge of rough board poking her in the back and another set against her hip. The instant tears brought on by the shock of it were just one more embarrassment in an already disgusting evening.

"Tess! Don't move."

Powers was by her side before she fully processed what happened. The sudden ashen cast to his tanned face told her it was worse than she thought.

"I can't believe you swore. I don't think I've ever heard you swear, even at me when I deserved it." The gentle tone in her ear made her look into his eyes, his face now inches away as he surveyed the damage.

"I was surprised, that's all. And I do swear, just not often and then only in front of people I – trust."

He didn't overlook the hesitation. His frown, at her and not the situation, was telling.

She shifted to move away from him, his nearness letting her feel his heat and smell his woodsy aroma. She could see concern in his eyes, the pupils large enough to swallow her whole at this range.

"Don't move that way. Roll towards me. Otherwise, you're going to get stabbed. I'll help you."

And effortlessly once more, he lifted her into his arms, taking the stairs two at a time to avoid the break. He still had her keys and she reached out to take them, but he already had the key inserted in the lock and turned.

"You can put me down here – I'm fine."

But he ignored her, hitting the light switch for the small fixture over the stairs as he turned sideways and continued to carry her up the stairs. Again he used her keys, and after only one try, found the correct one and pushed that door open. And without turning on the light, he unerringly found her bedroom and placed her gently on the bed.

"Are you going to be okay for a minute? I want to put something around that hole on the steps so no one accidently falls in." He waited for her answer.

She couldn't see his face, backlit as he was by the fixture over the stairs. When she hesitated, he started to move towards her. Raising a hand was enough to stop him.

"Really, Powers, I'm fine. You can go now."

The impression of anger hit her hard. His face remained in darkness, but she could see his hands close into fists. One still held her keys.

He turned without another word and his footfalls down the stairs were tame compared to the wildness she felt emanating from him.

Chapter 24

Damn woman couldn't allow herself to be taken care of even when she was hurt. He raged at her while he found yellow caution tape in his truck and blocked off an area around the broken wood. In the morning, he'd do a better job of creating a barrier, but it would be enough for now. He doubted anyone else would be stumbling up her steps in the nighttime.

Another part of his rage was completely self-directed. Why did he keep putting himself in her path when she kept telling him she didn't want him around? Was he that stubborn?

Hell yes, but that wasn't the point.

She needed him. And she wanted him, even if she was trying to argue against it. He could feel it as strongly as he felt his own need for her.

It wasn't as if he was completely happy about the situation either.

But he felt it in his bones.

The sneering chuckle he allowed himself for that thought was followed by a sudden chill. What if the bones did connect them somehow? Ever since they'd start working on that cursed construction site, things had been happening that were out of his control.

He still had her keys, now transferred to his pocket to make the emergency repairs. Closing the front door and locking it behind him, he doused the outside light and stood for a moment inside the stillness of the house. She wasn't making any noise upstairs. And the door stood open at the top of the stairs.

Decisions. He needed to make at least one, whether he would climb those stairs. After that, they might be out of his hands. Once he saw her lying in that bed, he knew he wasn't going to leave unless she demanded it.

When had he fallen so deeply into this hole of emotions? It wasn't today, or even this summer when they'd watched the fireworks. Or the wedding in Hawaii, for that matter.

It was the first time he'd stood in the doorway of her bedroom and looked at her fragile features in the shaded light.

Protective and scared, just as he was then, he wasn't even aware he'd climbed the steps until he turned towards her bedroom door. A small light now shown from a bedside lamp, but other than that, she hadn't moved.

Tess regarded him with wide eyes in a face that was paler than it should have been. Nerves, he decided, because he had them too.

"I locked up."

She nodded at his words.

"Do you need anything?" He waited, hoping that she wouldn't tell him to go.

Turning on her side away from him, she rubbed an unsteady hand at her temple as if to quell the voices she'd talked about before. That was when he noticed it.

"You're bleeding." He inhaled a sudden gasp of air to settle himself.

She turned to look at him, uncomprehending. When he sank to the side of the bed and reached out a hand, it seemed like she would push him away. Then she looked down to where his hand now rested at her waist and her eyes got wider.

"How did that happen?" She sounded confused.

"Probably from the broken wood. I was worried that it had punctured you. Let me take a look at it." He willed his hand not to shake as he began to pull the shirt from her jeans.

"Powers, it's nothing. Just a scratch I'm sure. You don't need to do anything." But at least she didn't tell him to go.

"Let me make sure it's not worse than it seems, okay? You don't want to get an infection, do you?" He raised his gaze to hers and locked on to the myriad emotions racing across her face.

Her hand still rested on his where she'd tried to stop him. She bit her lower lip, and the sight had his blood racing faster than it should have. The attraction always seething right below the surface stormed up and boiled over.

Gentling his touch further cost him. Letting the backs of his fingers trace like a breeze over the skin he'd exposed cost him even more. Each touch burned him. If her breathing was an indication, it was doing the same to her.

"Powers, I don't think – "

He didn't let her finish the thought. He lowered his head to take her lips, suddenly knowing that whatever the cost, he wasn't going to walk down those steps again until morning.

*****

He tasted like the finest feast, and she was gluttonous and starving. And she hated herself for that.

His lips were persuasive and just as sensuous as she feared. He was swamping her with a kiss alone, and they hadn't even deepened it yet. If she wasn't enjoying herself so much, she would have recognized the fear for what it was.

A spell was falling and there wasn't a damned thing she could do about it.

One of them turned, or maybe they both did. His tongued traced her lips as his hand cupped her head, and she opened for him and returned the favor. Her fingers trailed the corded muscles of his neck, the strength obvious from his years working heavy labor jobs. It brought back memories of dancing in the sand and the sight of his toned body dripping from the sea.

"Ow – damn!"

The sharp sting in her side brought her back from dreamland. Powers halted on her exclamation but didn't move right away. His eyes were glazed as he continued to stare into her face for seconds before he focused and frowned.

"Let me see how bad it is," and he turned her towards the light, allowing no argument this time.

"You've cut yourself up pretty well. Do you have a first aid kit?" He brought bloodied fingers up for her inspection.

She felt a little lightheaded at the sight.

"In the bathroom down the hall, under the sink."

His lips compressed as he rose. "Can you take your shirt off?"

She nodded, not thinking about the consequences. Sitting in her bra around a man who's ardor seemed to have cooled at the sight of her blood didn't seem like as big a deal now. Besides, he'd seen her in much less.

The multiple stings in her side told her she'd probably accumulated a few splinters in the fall too. "You might want to bring the tweezers as well – top drawer on the right." Along with all sorts of girlie stuff that would probably be better than pepper spray at chasing him away.

Powers reappeared in her bedroom door, his hands full of the kit, tweezers, tissues, and a towel and washcloth.

"Thanks, I can take it from here." He didn't move. "Powers, I said I can take care of myself."

His grunt of disagreement had her anger rising. "I said, I'll take care of it myself, thank you very much." She didn't mean to yell, but it came out that way.

When he grunted again and moved forward, she wanted to stop him. He sank to his knees next to the bed and assessed her side.

"Unless you've had a past as a circus performer, the kind who can tie themselves up like a pretzel and then do tricks, I doubt you'll be able to pull out the splinters, clean this, and bandage it up, all by yourself. Relax, Tess. I've never ravaged a bleeding woman in my life, at least not yet." And he smiled.

It was the smile that did her in. It was that same tender, gentle expression he'd had on the beach as his brother got married. The same one he'd used on her only twice before and then fleetingly, as if he couldn't help himself. It made her heart stumble and restart in a staccato beat.

She didn't resist when he turned her so that he could see her cut more easily. Moving the bedside light forward, his eyes flickered over her body before concentrating on the wound. She saw a small tick at the corner of his mouth, the same twitch of tension she'd seen from him in other completely different circumstances.

Heat burned through her body at his first touch, even though his fingers were cool and comforting. The damp of the washcloth stung, and she didn't try to hide the small sound of pain. When he glanced up, his eyes locked on hers and he moved forward to give her a small kiss.

"I'm sorry. I have to clean this. It won't hurt for long."

His kiss must have made it all feel better, because she didn't flinch again when he moved back to his work. She was too distracted by his harsh features softening in the glowing lamp, the intensity of his attention in getting the cut cleaned, and the occasional pinch of the tweezers as he picked out pieces of the wooden step.

He'd taken over, and she'd allowed it. A whole-body shiver shook her as she realized she was falling under his spell. Just what did that say about her?

Chapter 25

Standing beside his truck at the construction site, Powers lifted his arms to pull off yesterday's shirt. The spare he kept in the back of the cab was a duplicate, the logoed polo shirt fresh and cool in the morning air. His jeans would just have to do for another day.

As he folded the used shirt, he spotted a dark stain on the front near the bottom. Blood. Dried blood. Tess's blood.

Blanching at the sight, he couldn't help it when his mind wandered back to last evening. Nothing had turned out as he'd expected.

It took him over twenty minutes to clean the gash and pull out a number of splinters, the dark green paint of her broken stair still visible on some of the pieces. She'd gasped softly when he doused the cut with peroxide, and by the time he used gauze and tape to cover it, her eyes were closed.

He thought she might be dozing, but when he finished and was cleaning up the supplies in the adjoining bathroom, he heard her quiet voice.

"Thank you, Powers."

When he returned to her bedroom, she rolled on her back and watched him. He didn't think she was aware of the tears in her eyes, because he was sure she'd never let him see her vulnerability.

It cracked something open inside him. That protective instinct took over and he wasn't surprised when he found himself sitting on the edge of her bed and pulling her unresisting body into his arms.

She was weeping silently, the barest shakes of her shoulders giving her away. Wrapping his arms around her and settled against her pillows felt natural. He smoothed her hair back and rocked her, remembering hurts that his mother had rocked away decades before. It had been a long time since he'd thought about those times.

When Tess became still and quiet, he thought she'd fallen asleep. He didn't want to move, though. He couldn't resist dropping a light kiss to her lips before shifting her, intending to stand and let her rest.

"We don't have any choice, you know."

Her words stopped him mid-movement, an arm around her shoulders and the other hand propped on the bed beside her hip.

"What are you talking about?" But even as he said the words, he was afraid that he knew.

"We're predestined to be in this together."

He shook his head to deny it even as his soul chided him.

"There is no such thing as predestination. We have free will. We can and will do whatever we want."

She watched him steadily, a tired smile on her face, one that matched the resignation in her eyes. Shaking her head slowly, she put a hand on his.

"Don't go." She looked up at him, her eyes glowing golden in the single light. "The voices are quiet when you're here."

She moved over, giving him more space on the bed, and tucked herself back into his arms. When he tightened his hold, he swore that he would try to leave again as soon as she fell asleep. But it was so comfortable to nestle back into the mound of pillows, pull her closer against his side, and let his eyes drowse.

*****

"You're in early this morning," Sarge greeted him as he walked through the door of Brew Bank, the bells jingling merrily. "But then, I noticed that you didn't have far to travel today." And he winked at him.

Yeah, and he wondered how Tess felt today about having their night together broadcast all over the small town.

Deciding to ignore the comment seemed like the best way to deal with it. If he didn't make anything out of it, maybe Sarge and Stuart wouldn't either.

"I have to say that it's about time Tess found someone who cares for her like she deserves. You do care for her, right, man?" Stuart stood watch over the cash register as he delivered this message with a stern face.

So much for passing it off as nothing.

Besides, it was something. He just didn't know what that something was yet.

"Listen, I'd appreciate it – Tess would really appreciate it – if you didn't say anything to anyone about that. Okay?" Powers didn't want to embarrass Tess any more than he might have already. Because it would be wrong for the town to think they had something going on when nothing happened – nothing at all.

Which was probably why he felt a little surly this morning himself.

Sarge ran an imaginary zipper across his lips, but did nothing to hide his knowing wink. A few feet away, Stuart now wore a beatific smile, nodding sagely.

"You know that we all love Tess. We're just – protective."

Powers had a moment to take in the big muscles bulging below Sarge's bakery t-shirt before turning to Stuart, who looked no less intimidating even though his bulk wasn't showing. And he got the protective part. Hell, he felt protective himself.

"Thanks – and I can relate, believe me." He tried for a chuckle that fell a little flat, pointed at a loaded croissant for breakfast, and motioned for his usual coffee.

When Stuart opened his mouth as if to continue the topic, Powers took the proverbial bull by the horns and changed the subject so quickly that he blinked.

"Do you two know anything about why there might have been someone buried under the old town?"

After the two other men watched him, not in the least bit confused by his change of topic and probably recognizing it for what it was, they shook their heads and picked up the new conversational thread.

"I never heard any stories about a burial area within the town's limits, at least not dating back to the Gold Rush. Before that, this wasn't a town so much as a river crossing. The name came from that originally. A man by the name of Flynn fashioned a barge of sorts, and when the river was high, he'd run people back and forth across it, tied to a rope on either side. When the river was low, you could cross it on horseback or walking, depending."

When the bells rang to indicate more business, Powers didn't even bother turning to see who was behind him. This was news the whole town was buzzing about anyway.

Stuart nodded at his partner and added, "When Flynn was getting on in years and didn't want to work the crossing anymore, he built a bridge – only wide enough to carry an oxcart or wagon. People had to pay a toll to cross it. Early mail carriers even used it, though they didn't have to pay."

Powers shook his head. "So there was no town before then?"

When both men shook their heads, he frowned at his coffee and took a hot sip.

"Do they know where the bones came from?" Sarge asked the question even as he loaded some pastries into a bag.

Powers was already shaking his head again, when a voice piped up behind him.

"There are some pretty strong indications where they came from, and probably who they belong to."

Powers spun around to see Jake, the sheriff's deputy, standing behind him. Sarge was passing a bag down the counter to Stuart even as Jake was heading for the cash register, a to-go mug open and outstretched in his hand.

"Deputy, I didn't see you there. You have news about the bones?" Powers decided that it probably wasn't good news, considering the way the deputy was frowning as his mug was filled. He reached into his pocket and pulled out his wallet, laying bills and change on the counter. Stuart passed the mug and bag over and counted the exact change back into the till.

"First, it's Jake. We're part of the same pack, so to speak." He smiled, though it wasn't something that reached his eyes.

Confusion was all that Powers felt at the moment. "Pack?"

"Your brother, my brother, and that damned wolf pack that they've got their heads wrapped around." He walked over to the cream and sugar and added both to his mug before snapping on the lid. Then he motioned with it towards the door. "Walk with me."

The morning was cooler today, and while it still promised to be warm, the blistering heat seemed to have abated. Jake didn't seem to be in a hurry to say anything as they strolled up the sidewalk towards the construction site. The only truck on the site belonged to Powers, and now he could see the sheriff's patrol car parked behind it outside the chain link fence.

"So you know how this goes, right?"

Taking a moment to sip his coffee to process the question, Powers wasn't sure what Jake was referring to. Tess? The bones? That pack thing? In any of those cases, he had no idea how to respond.

Playing dumb seemed like the best alternative.

"Why don't you lay it out for me?" Trying for a neutral tone didn't work. He knew he bristled. Based on the look he got back, Jake did too.

"The construction site. Petry confirmed that the bones are old and Native American. There are multiple bodies. And there are no records of an official burial site, according to what Kevin researched since the first bone turned up. That means you have to wait." Taking a sip of his coffee, Jake regarded him with a much more effective bland expression.

Wait for what? Tension spread from the base of his skull to the top of his head, and he wondered why he'd ever thought this project would be simple.

"Wait for...?" Powers left the question hanging.

Taking another sip of his coffee, Jake regarded him thoughtfully. "You don't know what comes next, do you?"

Feeling more than stupid, Powers shook his head. He'd never run into bones on an excavation before, and that alone had him feeling on edge. Taken together with Tess's belief that she was hearing voices from the bones and their strange personal connection, he wasn't at his best.

"I had this happen twice before up here, once when someone was building a new strip mall, and another time when someone with a lot of money was building a gigantic home out in the South County area. Until the burial site is identified, it's treated as sacred ground."

Realizing that this was sounding less like progress with each passing word, Powers was almost afraid to ask. "What happened in those cases?"

Jake chuckled and shook his head. "The flatlanders – that's what we call people who come up from the valley with no clue how to handle being in rural mountain country – got spooked when the bones turned up on their mega-mansion grounds. They were convinced it was cursed or something. Abandoned the property and let it go into foreclosure, and didn't pay their property taxes when the bank took it back. Bank still has it, I think." He paused before adding, "And nothing's moved on it since. The bones were covered up and left, though I doubt they're still there. People still do grave rob sometimes, though what they expected to find I'm not sure."

"And the strip mall?"

Jake put a booted foot up on the bumper of his patrol car and opened his bag, poking a hand inside and pulled out a bagel covered with seeds. Taking a bite out of it, he surveyed the street with a look that could have passed for casual attention. After chewing and swallowing for what seemed to Powers like minutes, he carried on his explanation.

"That case is more relevant to you, actually. The mall had to be completed, so the builder had to put a guard on the lot until the consultant could come out, do the proper rituals, and determine if there was any history on the site. Turns out, there was. It was an old Indian burial ground, but one that wasn't on any of the official maps." He took another slow bite, almost smiling, though if it was at the memory or the bagel, Powers wasn't sure.

His impatience was rising. He had a building to finish, and the basics had to be done before the winter rains started or they'd be delayed with significant money tied up until spring when the ground dried out again.

"So how long did it take?" Powers forgot about his coffee and wasn't hungry any longer for the pastry in his own bag.

"Oh, to find out it was a burial site? About a month."

A month. Not great, but he could live with a month. His stomach eased enough for him to open the Brew Bank bag and pull out his croissant, taking a big bite.

"Of course, then the tribes needed to agree on what to do with the bones, since it wasn't clear who, exactly, the buried members belonged to. Then they had to be excavated, with the appropriate rituals. Then the ground needed to be blessed and laid to rest, so to speak. Yeah, it was quite a to-do."

The pastry was bone dry in his mouth, and Powers was sorry he'd taken a bite in the first place. Feeling like he could choke, he stared hard at Jake, unable to ask his next question around the food sitting in his mouth.

Jake nodded as if he understood. "About five months after, as I remember it. Six whole months from the time the bones were originally uncovered until the construction could proceed."

The acid in his stomach roared to life and Powers wondered if there was a local law against spitting unchewed pastry into the street. He doubted he could swallow it.

Jake put his boot to the ground and crumpled up the bakery bag, tossing it one-handed into a nearby city trashcan. Turning back to Powers, there was a hint of mercy in his eyes, as if he knew how bad this news was.

"In the mean time, you have to put that guard on the site, twenty-four/seven. Can't risk having someone – grave robbers or collectors or kids needing a prank – digging up any of them."

Choking down the pastry was more difficult than swallowing sawdust, and Powers coughed at the end of the process with the lump lodged in his chest. Taking a fast sip of coffee to find his voice, he felt the hairs on his neck stand on end.

They were there again, angry whispers and eyes on him. He turned on his heel and looked down the street towards the flower shop. The blocks were getting busier now, and Powers' own men and women were arriving at the site, unaware that there would be nothing for them to do today.

Swiveling again to look in the other direction, he ran head on into Jake's considering gaze. "Powers? Something you want to tell me?"

Frowning, Powers shook his head, the feeling of being watched, and not in a friendly way, now overwhelming. He couldn't pick out anyone specifically among the people on the street who were staring openly. A few stood still, but that could be for any reason.

"Powers?" Jake dropped his casual air and he set his mug down on the hood of his vehicle, already in a slow scan of the street.

It would sound lame. All this talk about bones and burials was getting him as nervous as Tess with her supposed voices.

"Something I need to know, man?" Jake's voice was soft but firm.

"I think someone's watching me."

Expecting a laugh, Powers was surprised when Jake began a detailed visual examination of the buildings and sidewalks and passing cars and trucks. He was on the balls of his feet and checked every face a couple of times before moving on. His head seemed to barely move.

"Since when?"

Shocked to be taken seriously, Powers couldn't help letting out a brief guffaw. Then he thought about it, and sobered in an instant.

"Since the first day we scraped ground."

Jake nodded, still watching the goings-on.

"And since then?"

"A couple of times since. Nothing major, no particular time of day."

Frowning, Jake finally turned back to him. "I don't see anything obviously suspicious, but I'll let the police chief know. Maybe it's someone wanting to get at the bones."

Already shaking his head, Powers didn't believe that was the case. "No, this felt – personal."

Jake watched his face carefully, and Powers stood still and met his eyes.

"Anyone after you for anything?"

Shaking his head, Powers now felt the puzzlement of it all. He didn't have any reason to believe that he was a threat to anyone.

Chapter 26

"What do you mean, the voices belong to the bones?" Roxy stood with a metal spoon the size of a small bowl in one hand. In the other, she balanced an enormous pot. Both looked a little precarious right now.

Tess put a fist to her forehead, the residual exhaustion of long days of the chanting voices strangling her. And it wasn't going to end any time soon.

At least they were quiet for now. In fact, they'd become silent as soon as Powers held her last night. She didn't want to think about the ramifications of that, at least not yet.

"You have to tell us, Tess. This is like oh-my-god spooky stuff. Is this part of your native rituals or something?" Gabby had forgotten the chopping she promised Roxy she'd do and sat unmoving, knife in one hand and carrot clutched in the other.

Restless and unwilling to explain it since she didn't understand it well herself, Tess leaped off the couch and paced to stand in front of one of the prints that decorated Roxy's living room walls. This one was of Lake Tahoe, and Tess was familiar with the vantage point. It was ancestral too. Used for rituals and blessings, it had long since been desecrated by the addition of a highway and many trampling feet.

When Serena laid a hand on her shoulder, she jumped.

"Tess! This is so unlike you. We're worried." Serena gently turned her friend around to face them.

She felt lucky that DK wasn't here tonight too. It would give her time to come up with a dodge. Already, Vince was bugging her about Native American burial customs for a story he wanted to do for his column. He said it would add even more reasons for people to come visit their town.

This would be a very wrong reason, though. It would be more of that same desecration.

She tried smiling, though she didn't think it was convincing. "Really, between all of you and the sheriff's deputy and Chase and Powers…"

"Chase?" Gabby's voice held interest.

"Sheriff's deputy?" Roxy was more shocked.

"Powers?" Serena nearly purred.

If Marguerite had been here, she would have purred too, Tess mused.

"What is Chase doing, other than chasing you?" Gabby leaned forward, now all avid curiosity.

Tess waved the question away, wishing she'd kept her mouth shut. "He came by today, asking me out again, that's all. And he was very persistent. He said that he wanted us to have an opportunity to develop a more serious relationship."

Gabby clapped her hands, realizing suddenly that she still held a knife and a carrot. She went back to chopping, but not before adding, "It's about damn time."

Roxy set the pot on her commercial-sized stove and shifted her grip on the big spoon. Then she turned and frowned. "Is the deputy after you too?"

That was more complicated. At least this time when her head started to pound, she could tell it was the tension of these crazy stories and not the voices returning.

"No, he wanted to ask if anything unusual had been happening recently around the shop, or if anyone was bothering me."

"Bothering you? Is someone bothering you?" Roxy looked like she would willingly beat any attacker off with the spoon.

Only the voices, she wanted to say. Them, and Powers. But Powers was for a totaling different reason.

"He said that there had been a report of a potential stalking on Main Street. He didn't give me any details, other than a friendly warning."

"But Tess, you need to be careful! You have that big place and no one's around at night on the street and – "

Tess waved Gabby's worries off with a more forceful hand. Elation at the possibility of Tess having a real date morphed into concern with an edge of anger to it. Roxy looked like she was ready to skewer someone.

"And Powers?" Serena's quiet question had everyone's gaze shifting.

That answer would be much more complicated, even more so because Tess had no idea how she herself felt about it.

"He's just being Powers. You know, over-protective and controlling and so damned domineering."

Once the words were out, she realized how they sounded. There was more heat in her voice than the situation called for. After all, it was just Powers. It wasn't like he meant anything to her.

Serena smiled knowingly and turned to face the others. "Looks like Powers has gotten himself involved in something." She didn't bother to hide the glee in her voice.

"There is nothing going on between Powers and me. He's only around because I'm the liaison for this construction project. If he stays on my good side, he'll have an easier time when he needs something."

She was protesting too much. And even as she did so, she knew that it was a lie. She was involved too, and the reason went much deeper than representing the other business owners.

"So let's get back to the voices for a minute," Roxy redirected. "When do they start, and how long do they talk, or whatever the hell they do?" She watched Tess like her friend was mildly crazy but she was willing to humor her – for a while.

Hesitating about how much to explain, Tess used the moment to find a glass and pour some water. Taking a sip bought her another few seconds. No one was talking to fill the silence, so she was going to stay wiggling on that hook for as long as it took her.

"They don't talk, exactly. They chant, or they're saying angry things but I can't understand the words. Sometimes there are children too, being noisy."

Everyone was watching her now with varying degrees of confusion and amazement. Tess pulled in a gulp of air and decided that coming clean about all of it might make her sound less – crazy.

"They've made noise inside my head off and on since the association decided to develop that lot last fall. When things were active on the project, they would pop up, usually just for a day or so. They were bad around the holidays last year when we were putting together the design specs." She stopped, considering other times she'd heard them. "When we were making the decision about the builder, they were always in the background. The day before I met with Powers to discuss the final timing of the work, they were angry. Then they got quiet again until the day the bones were found."

Gabby had dropped any pretense of chopping, setting the knife and vegetables down so that she could lean forward. Roxy was frowning, ladle still in hand. And Serena was eying her speculatively.

"So what does Powers have to do with it?"

Tess knew that this would be the first question Serena would ask.

"He's always around when they get to be their noisiest, and when he appears, they back down." Tess shook her head, unwilling to say the rest.

Serena had no such compulsion. "He can chase away the voices, is that what you're saying?"

"Maybe," Tess replied, drawing the word out into individual letters.

"But that's a good thing, right?" Gabby nearly fell off the stool she was seated on in her growing excitement. "It means there's something between the two of you."

Shaking her head in denial would do no good, not when her friends were already convinced that she and Powers had something going on.

But Roxy was shaking her head from side to side as well. "No, it could mean that Powers is the cause of the tension – and I'm just calling it that, because, well, you know." She looked vaguely embarrassed. "I don't believe in that mumbo jumbo about ghosts and stuff."

Tess cracked a smile at that. At least Roxy wasn't calling her crazy.

"But Tess, you said that the voices go away when Powers comes around, not that he brings them. Or did I misunderstand?" Serena leaned forward on the words.

Sighing heavily, she realized that there was no way out of this.

"The voices go away when Powers arrives on the scene. It's like they're – I don't know – afraid of him."

All three of the others now grinned at her with varying degrees of enthusiasm. It was Roxy, though, who finally put their thoughts into words.

"But that's just it, isn't it? You and Powers – you're meant to be together. Now, what the hell are you going to do about it?"

Chapter 27

"What the fuck can we do about it?"

Powers boomed the words, even though Marty was sitting next to him in the office conference room. The Sacramento skyline filled the distant view outside, but neither of them noticed. Their eyes were glued instead to the words on piles of contract documentation in front of them.

"As nearly as I can tell, there isn't much we can do. We're responsible for the site until the work is complete, which means we have to post full time security on it now. And we have to wait until it's released by the Native American Heritage Commission and in accordance with that, and I quote, 'the historical resources must be handled in accordance with the California Environmental Quality Act'. There's shit we can do for the work to continue until the site is released back to us."

Powers glared at Marty. He should probably be grateful the man had balls enough to stand up to him.

Pounding a fist on the table, he shot out of his chair and stood at the window, unseeing as he stared out at the street below. "This is going to take a long time to resolve. And once the site is ours for work again, it will probably be the middle of rainy season."

Marty made a harsh noise behind him, and Powers wanted to echo the sentiment. There would be no winner in this, unless you counted the tribe whose bones were discovered. They were bound to be grateful.

Sighing and running a hand through his hair, Powers swung back to his contracts officer. "Dr. Petry, the coroner, is in touch with the state university's archeology department, and they will have a crew working by Thursday at the latest. And the monitor who'll be assigned is coming next Tuesday. Someone will have to be onsite with the crew until then."

He watched Marty open his mouth, close it again, and frown in disappointment. When he started to speak, he was already pulling the papers together in neat piles.

"I'll call Nancy and let her know that I won't be able to go camping this weekend. Amy and Dave – "

But he stopped abruptly when Powers raised his hand.

"There's no need for that, Marty. I know you and Nancy and the kids have been looking forward to this last trip of the season. I'll work onsite for the weekend. I didn't have anything else planned."

When Marty stared at him, uncertain, he added a smile to his voice. "I can stay with my brother, which will give us time together." He didn't add that it would give him more time with Tess too. No one needed to know how much he wanted to dig deeper into this impossible attraction she held for him.

"It will be no problem, I promise."

*****

He paced the length of his penthouse living room, the windows letting in the dusky light as the sun sank well below the horizon. Restless and uneasy, he had a feeling he was going to make a mistake, a big one.

He wanted to call Tess. Fingering his phone's list of numbers, he stared at her name on the screen for long minutes before pressing the button to darken it and try to distract himself again.

Working out hadn't helped. After his swim did nothing to tire him enough to feel settled, Powers rounded the weight room circuit three times. Then he took a run on the downtown sidewalks. Only a few short blocks away from his building, he encountered crowds of couples and groups of singles circling the restaurants and bars of the downtown area. Midweek or not, people were hooking up to enjoy each other and themselves.

He wanted to hook up too, with Tess.

He wasn't sure when he'd made this decision, because it wasn't a conscious one. Or maybe his body had made it for him, perhaps during the night she'd slept in his arms and he'd been a complete gentleman about it.

A hot shower eased the workout muscles but a cold one did nothing to quell his rising interest in a woman who gave every impression that she wanted nothing to do with him, beyond his ability to mysteriously relieve her headaches.

Voices? He doubted that entirely. And predestined to be together? No way.

After nine, activity built on the streets below. As he turned his gaze up the hill, Powers knew that the opposite would be happening in Flynn's Crossing. The security company he hired to guard the site confirmed it. They rolled up the sidewalks and turned out the lights pretty early up the hill.

That didn't mean she wouldn't be awake, though, he reasoned. He wondered if she'd be curled up in the middle of her big bed, reading a book or watching something on the small flat screen TV. Or maybe she was drinking her favorite tea and working on the books or something for her business.

He shouldn't bother her.

But what if her migraine was back? Despite the lack of activity around the construction site today, she hadn't been by. Everyone else seemed to have stopped what they were doing at some point or another and visited. That too-smooth Chase Wolford was nosier than all the others put together.

"Do you think they'll find anything of value?" His question struck Powers as odd at the time.

"Value? I'm not sure. I suppose they could." When Powers turned to look at the other man, he met a speculative gaze.

"If they do, it belongs to us, you know. The business association, I mean. We own the land, so we own – whatever." Chase almost seemed to rub his hands over that prospect, staring at the pile of dirt and unfinished trenches.

Powers shook his head. "I don't know anything about that. I've been given to understand that whatever they find is turned over to the tribe that has a claim to the bones. Any artifacts have to be treated with cultural dignity, that's what I was told."

Chase frowned at this, then turned to look up the street in the direction of the flower shop. "Well, Tess can take care of any of those concerns. She's Native American and she's part of us. They can turn anything they find over to her."

Powers didn't like it. He didn't want her any more involved than she was already. The charge of concern at the thought of someone pushing Tess to do anything uncomfortable made every protective instinct rise to the surface.

Chase was already walking down the block, and Powers would have followed if his cell phone hadn't rung with his foreman from another construction site on the other end, asking him a detailed question.

Shaking his head now at the memory, he wondered if the presumptuous man had pushed his ideas on Tess. Did she get angry? Did she agree? Was she feeling okay?

Sinking into a leather couch, Powers activated the phone screen again and hit the send button as soon as Tess's name appeared.

It rang once, and he thought about hanging up. At two rings, he knew his name and number would be captured and she'd wonder why he called only to hang up before she answered. At three rings, he was kicking himself for making more out of this than it needed to be.

"Hello? Powers?"

Her voice sounded breathless and tired, with an undercurrent of edginess that matched his own.

"Tess, hello. I just wanted to check in, to see if you need anything."

Silence greeted his statement.

"Are you feeling alright?" He paused on every word.

Still silent, he thought her heard a brief sob on an inhale. Then nothing again.

"Tess? You're scaring me. Are you okay?" He didn't realize until he was by his front door, fingering his keys, that he was on his feet and pushing them into shoes.

Her voice was faint. "I'm okay, Powers. Sorry. Just another nasty headache and a long day fraught with arguments." She sighed on that.

"What kinds of arguments?" He still held his keys, but now he rested a shoulder against the wall as he waited for her response.

She sighed again, her voice stronger when she continued. "Chase, wanting to figure out how the association can profit from any finds on the site. I honestly don't think he understands the implications of this being an ancestral burial site, if that's what it is."

Intrigued now, Powers dropped to the edge of his couch again. "What do you mean, if that's what it is?"

He could hear her hesitate, probably wondering if he'd come back with some retort about her so-called voices again. But she continued, which gave him some hope.

"I don't think it's an intentional burial site. In fact, I know it's not."

His heart suddenly picking up its pace for unknown reasons, Powers leaned into the phone.

"How do you know?"

She paused again, as if considering. When she continued, he couldn't hide his gasp.

"The voices told me."

Chapter 28

Tess joined Serena on the front porch of the flower shop, watching Gabby and Rick say goodbye to their boys. The admonitions to behave were obvious, as was the difficulty each of them had in parting ways, even for a couple of weeks.

She'd wanted a few minutes with her friends, but time got away from them all as Gabby and the boys went through the checklist of everything they brought one last time. Tess tried to pull Serena aside for a brief discussion, but Gabby needed her for a review of the boys' long lists of do's and don'ts.

She needed to talk to someone about Powers. Something had happened between them last night, and she wasn't even sure what it was. It sounded like maybe he finally believed her.

Gabby broke away from the group as Rick crouched down, having a few serious words with the boys as they all nodded solemnly. She swiped at a tear before putting on a big smile for her friends.

"Okay, I think you have everything. Doctor's number, dentist's number, all of our contact information for the trip. Remember, if anything happens, we can fly home almost any day. And if they get to be – "

" – too much trouble," Serena supplied, "Dane will just tie them up and leave them in the photo workroom until you get back. Honestly, Gabby, we have it covered."

Tess poked Serena in the ribs at Gabby's mildly shocked expression, one that quickly faded into the grin they knew so well. "I know, I'm over-thinking this. It's not like you and Dane haven't had them over at your place so many times before. But just remember that they'll feed the dog their vegetables, and – "

"Gabby, don't worry! We'll take care of everything. Your only concern right now is making that flight and having the wonderful honeymoon the two of you deserve. Enjoy yourselves! Skype us whenever you feel the need."

Rick stood at the curb when the big dark blue truck pulled up and Dane climbed out of it. "Okay, who's turn is it to get strapped on the hood and who gets the top this time?" He and Rick slapped hands, and then he did the same with the boys. Then he turned and grinned at the women on the porch.

"Dane, don't let them get away with anything. And don't let them talk you into taking them to the pound for a dog, okay? Don't let them do anything too risky. Promise me!"

His grin widened at Gabby before he turned to the two boys, who were now looking less sad about their parents leaving and more intrigued with whatever Dane had in mind. "Well men," he addressed them solemnly, "I guess we can't try out those new explosives then either, huh?"

When the boys started climbing all over him, Serena put an arm around Gabby and squeezed. "Don't worry, sweetie, Tess is coming over a lot for the next couple of weeks, and between us, we'll keep all of them in line."

Putting a hand out to his new wife, Rick called out his thanks once more, adding, "Come on, Gabby. We don't want to miss our flight. Paradise awaits, my love."

Tess gave her a hug and a shove as everyone started waving them off.

"You are going to come and give me some relief from all of that testosterone, aren't you?" Serena whispered the tense words behind a big smile.

Tess's grin widened. "Of course I am. I promised, didn't I? Jan will be watching the shop this weekend and I'm going to be with you every day, as much as I can. And after that, we'll work out a schedule."

The sedan pulled away and the boys were already climbing up into the truck cab. Dane sent them to the small back seat and dug around for the seatbelts as the two women walked around the broken stairs and down the walkway.

"Good, particularly this weekend." She turned to give Tess a quick hug before climbing up herself. Dane revved the engine while Serena hung out the door for a last word. "Because with Powers coming to stay too, I'll be surrounded."

Before Tess could get her mouth to form the words, Serena smiled slyly at her and slammed the door shut, and the truck was in gear and moving.

Being around Powers for the long holiday weekend was not what she had in mind when she agreed to hang out at the house on the cliff. Her heart rate picked up and she felt the sheen of sweat on her forehead. It matched other dampness she didn't want to think about. His strong arms holding her while keeping terror at bay came racing in on a hot memory.

They'd be chaperoned by two active boys and his brother and her best friend. What did she have to be nervous about?

The staccato rhythm that beat through her nerves to make every cell in her body throb told her the answer.

*****

It should have been a dream, but it wasn't. It was too real and his voice was saying things she couldn't believe.

Tess stirred her tea, more for a reason to do something with her hands than any real need. The shop was quiet today, and she had too much time on her hands to remember ever nuance and tone of their late night call.

"The voices told me."

She expected to hear him laugh with derision, or maybe tell her she was nuts and hang up on her.

Instead, he'd gasped into the phone. Then all she heard was the rasp of his breathing, accelerated and as loud as hers.

"I believe you."

It was her turn to gasp now. The warmth that suffused her at his statement made her skin heat and tingle as if he was touching her.

He sighed deeply, a sound that almost ended on a moan. "I don't know why I believe you, but I do."

She smiled at that. Even her girl tribe wasn't completely sure they believed her. But this odd man did.

"There's something about you I can't explain. I feel the need to protect you, even though I know you don't need it."

Ah, but that's where he was wrong, she realized. And she hadn't even realized it herself until a moment before.

"You do protect me." Her voice was husky when she said it. She thought she heard him hum on his end of the line.

"You have the power to make the voices go away. They run from you. I don't know why. But when you put your arms around me, they leave."

That sounded so incredibly stupid as the words left her mouth, she considered disconnecting. Any minute now, he'd be laughing his ass off at her expense.

When he remained silent, she waited too.

He cleared his throat, his voice suddenly deeper when he took up the thread of their discussion. "I feel it too, the power flowing between us. There's something about you that I can't shake, and I don't understand it. But that's also why I have to protect you." He gave a harsh laugh. "I'm probably as crazy as you are."

She felt her temper rise before she considered what he'd said. Whatever he felt, it was as strong and overpowering as her senses.

"So let me up the ante. When I held you in my arms that night, you felt powerful but weak. Does that make any sense? Your hair, when it brushed my arm, was like the touch of a feather. And I got lost in your golden eyes."

Her blood heated. Thinking of her head laid on his shoulder, then his chest, she thought she'd been imagining things. The brush of his hair as thick as any pelt of fir under her cheek, even when she knew she'd been leaning again his polo shirt instead.

When she told him of that sensation, he sat quiet on the other end. She could almost picture his face, the frown of consideration pulling his thick brows together and the hand he'd brush across his hair when he was frustrated. She could easily feel the rise and fall of his chest, up and down, with each deep breath.

"When I kiss you, Tess, I almost feel like we're breaking a sacred taboo."

The sudden clench of her fist surprised her, and she looked down at her nails biting into the palm of her hand.

He hissed on the other end of the line. "What the hell?"

"Powers, are you okay?"

He was quiet for so long she worried that he'd dropped off, except she could still hear his labored breathing.

"It's like I can't escape it. I can feel your nails on me, digging into my shoulders as if you're holding on. And I'm surging over you." He stopped and pulled in air again. "As if we're making love."

Chapter 29

"This is Dr. Shakiff and a few of his students, Mr. Ashland. They'll be documenting the finds on the site. You can now safely leave the digging to them."

As the coroner made the introductions around the group, Powers did his best to sound gracious. What he wanted to ask but didn't was how long the good doctor thought this would take.

Assigning the students preliminary tasks, the archeologist turned back to where Powers stood, watching the activity. He smiled and nodded at the site.

"You probably want to know how long this will take. Do I assume correctly, Mr. Ashland?"

Taken aback at being read so easily, Powers nodded curtly.

"It will take as long as it takes, is all I can tell you at this time, I'm afraid. Give us a few days, and once we find the perimeter of the burial area, I can provide you with a better estimate. At least initially, it will be good to have you nearby in case any questions about what we might be digging around or into come up."

The man turned to the coroner who still stood a few feet away. "Ben, when did you say the monitor is arriving?"

The older man moved forward. "On Tuesday, Ari. That gives you time to learn something of what we're dealing with, eh?"

With an affirmative nod, Ari pulled out his cell phone and looked at Powers expectantly.

"If I could please have your cell phone number, Mr. Ashland. It would be very helpful in case we need to reach you."

Rattling off the numbers, Powers was torn. He wanted to stay, looming over the students to encourage them to move faster. But he wasn't of any use here.

His eyes traveled up the street to the old Victorian. There, at least, he could do something useful. There were steps to mend, and a board or two on that old porch that could stand replacing. At least he'd be accomplishing something.

Besides, he needed to see her. She was all he dreamed about last night, when he finally managed to sleep. Her hair was streaming over him as she rose above him, and then he was holding her close and running as fast as he could, loping through dense woods with hell chasing them.

Turning back, he found both men eying him questioningly. The archeologist smiled and nodded to the coroner, who slapped Powers on the shoulder.

"Best to find something else to occupy your time, Powers. A watched pot and all that."

*****

Drums beat at the base of her skull and wrenching screams wafted across her consciousness. Tess tried hard to ignore them, pushing the stem of a rose into clay in the vase's base with more force than was necessary. When it snapped, she did too.

"Damn!"

Jan popped her head out of the small office and asked what was wrong.

"Nothing, I just broke a stem. I'm a little off today, that's all."

It didn't help that today of all days, Powers was on her mind, in her dreams, and the subject of her unusually distracted attention.

Waking more than once during the night with the sheet wrapped tight around her and her pillows thrown to the floor, Tess wondered what kind of strange magic they'd now engaged. This was more than native tales.

This was the way of the healer.

Damn again.

When the drumbeat escalated into rapid loud pounds, the weight of something thrown behind it to add even more force, she wondered if her head would explode. But the voices inside her mind were easing, even while the percussion in her world picked up in pace.

"Um, Tess? There's a guy outside ripping the steps apart." Jan crossed the display room to stand in the front window, staring in the direction of the front entrance. Her mouth made a small 'oh' of surprise before she started to grin.

Tess didn't want to stand beside her and examine the sight, but she found herself joining Jan with a rose in her hand. When she reached the window, pulling the curtain back further only revealed a well-muscled back attached to a tall male frame, currently on its knees on the third from the top step. The top step already gaped open like a missing tooth, and the man was attacking the second step's removal with ferocity and purpose.

Powers, replacing her steps as promised. She shouldn't feel a wave of pleasure at his caring gesture. But they'd come to no agreement on price and she wasn't going to enter into any deal without knowing what it would cost her in the end. No smart business person would.

Her snort of frustration must have surprised Jan, for the young woman almost tripped over a column with a wire bird cage set on top of it when Tess pushed by. When the flute music marking the front door's opening was drowned out by the slam of her shoving through it, the man on the steps – or what was now left of the steps – looked up.

"Powers! What in the world do you think you're doing?" She all but screamed it at him before she pulled in a deep breath and tried to regain her composure.

"Why hello Tess. It's a lovely day, don't you think? And yes, it's a pleasure to see you too."

He regarded her calmly. Sunglasses hid the true expression in his eyes, but she had the distinct feeling he was laughing.

Shaking his head, he started to whistle as he turned back to the fourth and final step. One good yank of the cat's claw and he had it freed from its nails. And as he yanked it to the side, it broke in half, the rot of the wood showing clearly in the pieces he held in each big gloved hand.

His hair was stuck in odd directions like he'd been running his hands through it and didn't care how it ended up. Even as she watched, a single bead of sweat ran down the back of his neck and disappeared into the collar of his shirt. From her vantage point on the porch, she could clearly see the strong muscles in his legs supporting him as he crouched over the steps to work. The position did miraculous things to his jeans and his butt.

Fanning herself against the sudden heat, Tess knew she should look away. She had planned to call her usual handyman as soon as she was able to think clearly.

"It's amazing no one has gone through these boards before you did the other night."

He was ignoring her, or at least not looking at her. With a humph and a frown, he slammed the hammer into the right side support for the stairs, and it too crumpled into broken pieces.

"These steps are filled with rot, Tess. The frame's going to need to be replaced along with the top boards."

She blinked at the mass of destruction that had been the entry to her business. It would have made sense to have everything ready to replace before he'd torn up what was left of it. Damn the man for taking over as if he owned the place.

"I still don't understand why you're here doing this. We didn't agree that I would hire you to fix the stairs. In fact, don't you have a big business to run? Aren't there construction projects all over the region with the big Ashland logo hanging on chain link fences, announcing your presence? Powers, are you listening to me?"

The desire to stamp her foot astonished her. She rarely ever lost her temper, and when she did, she tried to do it in a responsible manner. But he pushed all of her wrong buttons.

"I can fix this, Tess. I can fix – anything."

When his eyes wandered up her figure slowly, finally stopping on her face, she inhaled gulps of air. She didn't need him to fix the steps, and she certainly didn't need him to fix her.

Striving for her lost calm, Tess lowered her voice and slowed the pace of her words. He was still staring at her, and part of her wanted to rip the sunglasses off his face to see what he was really thinking.

"I can hire someone locally to fix this. You don't have to do it. I haven't hired you, and you haven't told me how much this is going to cost. I don't have to pay big city rates for something I can get locally for a more reasonable price."

Shaking his head as she spoke, he finally pulled off the heavy gloves. His hands were finely shaped but hard-working, the kinds with rough edges and scars and marks that time would never erase. Kind of like his heart, she supposed, though why she thought she knew this, she wasn't sure. He was too much of a bully to give away anything about how he felt.

When he stood and took off the sunglasses, he looked up at Tess with a friendly smile. "Oh, you can afford it. My price is very reasonable. Have dinner with me, Tess."

Flustered by his direct eyes, which were busy missing nothing about her usual working clothes of skinny jeans and tank top, her mind fumbled on the idea.

"Dinner? You want to have dinner so that we can discuss your price?"

The resonant chuckle he let out was enticing. If the steps weren't missing, she would have walked closer on those notes alone.

"No, that's my price."

She faltered again, pulled towards him like a magnet with the low hum of desire starting to chime in the background. The lack of drums, chants or angry voices screeching in her head stopped her. He was here, and again, he chased away the ancestors.

Maybe he could fix almost anything.

"You want dinner in exchange for doing all of this work on the steps."

He nodded, turning back to his tool bag and tossing the hammer inside. "Yes, materials and labor. You can't get a better deal than that. All you have to do is spend a few hours in my company, having a meal. Which I'll also pay for, by the way."

And he grinned at her.

Chapter 30

"This is fuckin' amazing, man. Native American bones, right here on Main Street. When do you learn more about 'em?"

Vince stood on one side of Powers, and his delight in having a cutting-edge story to write about here in his new hometown was obvious.

Deke and Jake, currently off duty, were on the other side, shaking their heads.

"Come on, Vince. We don't want this to turn into a three ring circus. Give it some time, and maybe once we have the full story, you can write about it. But until then, the less press, the better." Jake's words had Deke nodding in agreement, and Powers frowned at the ever-growing hole in the middle of the vacant lot.

The trench to support the footing had now been expanded into a ledge about seven feet across and five feet wide. At the bottom of it, bones lay in what appeared to his untrained eye to be random patterns that didn't represent normal bodies. The archeologist stood at the edge of the area, camera in hand and tablet computer hanging from a strap on his shoulder. He alternated between taking photos of what they were uncovering, making notes in his tablet, and giving directions to the students who were swarming over the site with small picks and brushes.

It would be hell to rebuild the supportive soil structure that they had counted on as part of the foundation of the building. Cha-ching. This project was costing him more by the second, and there wasn't a damn thing he could do about it.

"Hey, what're you building?" While Powers ruminated on the additional overruns, Vince had wandered over to the chop saw and worktable set up near the back of the Ashland pick-up. When the professor asked Powers to hang around today to discuss the soil composition in the layer that held the bones, he'd decided to make use of his Saturday rather than sit and stare.

Staring wasn't getting him anywhere.

"They're stairs for Tess. Her front steps were rotted and she fell through them the other night. I'm replacing them for her."

When he snapped his tape measure for something to do with his hands, no one said a word. And when he looked up, Powers found all three of the other men staring at him with varying degrees of interest.

Vince broke into a sly grin. "Why you dog. You and Tess – we knew it!" And he slapped Powers on the back and put up his hand for a high five. "Does Dane know?"

Powers held on to his tape measure like an insignificant shield.

Dropping his hand eventually, Vince glanced over at Deke.

"Ah, that's very nice of you to do that, Powers. Tess would have had to hire someone to get them done sooner or later. I'm glad that she hired you." Continuing to watch him carefully, Deke added, "You have told Dane and Serena this, right?"

The shield felt smaller by the second.

Deciding that a partial truth might be better than saying nothing, he turned away from the three and mumbled, "She didn't hire me. I decided to fix them, and that's what I'm doing."

When no one responded, Powers huffed out a bark of frustration and spun around one more time.

Deke was eying him with sympathy. Jake was frowning. And Vince – well, Vince looked like he'd been given the best gossip in the county to spread around.

Since no one was saying anything, he released the tape measure with a crack, the rasp of metal on metal zinging with too much force, and marked his next two cuts on the big piece of wood.

"Powers, far be it from me to tell you how to do things. But Tess is a proud woman, as she has every right to be. She wouldn't want you to do something this big and not expect to pay you for it. You have to make an effort, at least giving her a chance to offer you something in return."

The rasp was louder this time, and Powers could feel the metal heat in his hand as he snapped the tape back into its case. The clang of the end hitting home broke his resolve about saying as little as possible.

"Damn it, she is offering me something in return. I told her all I wanted was for her to go to dinner with me. And she agreed."

Now it seemed that even the professor and his students had picked up on the tension in the air, for all sounds around them stopped. In fact, traffic on the street was still for a moment too. Knowing that Vince had the tact of a bulldozer, Powers was sorry that his temper had allowed his mouth to say so much.

When sound didn't return, he waited three more beats before looking up once again. The shield of his tape measure was now miniscule in proportion to what he'd blurted out.

Surprisingly, Vince wasn't laughing at him or even smiling. He walked over to Powers and gave him a knowing pat on the shoulder, like he felt his pain. Then he opened his mouth.

"Man, you have got to tell Dane and Serena about this, and you better do it soon."

*****

"Tess agreed to go to dinner with you?" Dane's question wasn't so much amazed as probing.

Powers shifted on the balls of his feet, ready for a fight. He was positive that Dane would guard his wife's best friend. After all, while it might amuse everyone to see the desire he couldn't hide in those wedding pictures, dating someone they all cared about was a completely different story.

Glancing around Mallory's, Powers was grateful that their upcoming argument wouldn't have a huge audience. He wasn't sure why he allowed Vince to drag him along when he and Deke and Jake decided it was time to adjourn the construction site in favor of a beer. The sports bar half of the building wasn't as busy as the restaurant, but at least no one could see them from those darker reaches.

The audience was big enough already, though, consisting of all of Vince's so-called wolf pack with the exception of Rick. How he'd gotten involved with this group, he wasn't exactly sure.

Dane punched him on the shoulder, then threw a companionable arm around his brother's shoulders. "That's great, man. Really great. Tess is an incredible person, and it would be nice to see you happy."

Powers blinked.

"Ah, come on. I was hoping for some blood and guts. You know, you telling him he's not worthy and all that shit. Maybe a couple of punches." Vince snorted in disgust, breaking a laugh out of Dave and Steve. Even Deke and Jake, reticent as always, smiled.

"But he is worthy. He just thinks he isn't." Dane dropped his arm and looked at his big brother closely.

Powers shifted under the scrutiny. He wasn't worthy. He was too much like their father. It was a struggle to be friendly and affable. Even his current truce with Dane was tenuous.

"It's probably a very bad idea. It popped out of my mouth when she asked me how much it was going to cost."

Dave leaned forward, fascination on his face. "How much what was going to cost?"

He didn't blush, though he wanted to. Powers took a sip of his beer to buy himself some time. Fortified, he responded. "I'm fixing her steps. They were full of rot and she fell through them the other day. So I'm fixing them for her."

Dane simply beamed. "You were trying to fix something, Powers. It's what you try to do best."

*****

"When are you going to dinner with him?" Serena stirred the large bowl of pasta salad and turned back to Tess on her perch at the kitchen's large island.

"We haven't set a date." She cringed at the word.

She didn't date. She didn't date Chase even though he was much more appropriate for her and much nicer to her, and she wasn't going to date Powers.

"It's not a date – I didn't mean that. We just haven't picked a day on the calendar to go, you know, for me to keep my end of the bargain."

A bargain with the devil.

Serena reached across the counter and squeezed Tess's hand. "Well I think it's wonderful, whatever you want to call it. Powers isolates himself too much, just as much as Dane did, except he hides behind his work rather than on a cliff. Dane tells me that way back when, Powers used to be a friendly social animal who couldn't be around family enough. But there are parts of the story he won't discuss."

Intrigued by the prospect of learning more about this mysterious man despite her misgivings, Tess leaned forward.

"You mean Dane hasn't told you everything?"

Serena picked up a glass of wine and sipped, stirring unconsciously. She shook her head.

"I know bits and pieces. All of the kids were close to their mother, Dane most of all. According to him, Powers is most like their father, but neither one of them have a good relationship with the man."

"He didn't come to your wedding." Tess had never been clear about why that subject had been considered taboo in all of the wedding preparations.

Serena smiled sadly and shook her head. "Dane invited him. He refused. It's like he ignores his sons altogether."

"And Dane never told you why they don't get along?"

Again shaking her head, Serena turned her attention back to the pasta. "He's said that he'll explain it – someday, and when he's ready. Even as close as he and I are, Tess, I still don't know everything about the man I married."

Shifting on the stool, Tess fought the urge to blurt out her own little family secret, the one that she had promised herself she would never share with anyone. Everyone was entitled to a little privacy, right?

"Anyway, at least Dane and Powers are getting along better now. Powers still pushes Dane's buttons sometimes, but they seem more united than divided these days. Maybe Powers has found something else he can use as an outlet for all of his control needs." Dumping the spoon into the sink and grabbing cling wrap, Serena was intent on covering the bowl and putting it in the fridge. She missed the expression on Tess's face.

Oh yeah, he had something else he wanted to control now.

"I'm glad you're staying for dinner. Except for Gabby and Rick, I think everyone's going to be here. Deke and Jake are even coming, and Dave and Steve. I did not, however, invite Chase." Suddenly looking unsure, Serena glanced at Tess to see how she was taking that news.

Waving away the comment, Tess responded without thinking. "That's fine, Serena. I have no interest in Chase other than as a fellow business owner and acquaintance."

Oops. How had that slipped out? Serena's look told Tess she was fairly pleased with this sentiment.

"And who is more your type, exactly? Rancher Deke? Deputy Jake? Or maybe Steve's lawyering turns you on. Or Dave keeping the roads in one piece for the community. Or maybe…," Serena drew out the provocative sentence, "you really do have a thing for Powers after all."

Flapping her hands as if she was trying to avoid an annoying insect, Tess gave a quick laugh. "No, not for any of the members of the wolf pack. And certainly not for Powers. Besides, it's not like he's hanging around here, other than for the project."

She should have known better once she saw Serena's big grin, because half a minute later, the front door opened and the men piled in. And Powers was the second one in the door.

Chapter 31

It looked like he and his brother were in the midst of an intense conversation, something that delighted Dane and pissed Powers off to no end. Tess was reminded of the explosive strength of the man, the flow of muscles under tanned skin and the glint of determination in his dusty brown eyes. His hands were held tightly at his sides and he looked like he was barely in command of himself.

When his eyes fell on her, sitting stock still on the stool and wishing she could lift wings and fly out of the room to escape, his gaze started to smolder. It wasn't rage she saw there, and that's what scared her.

It was desire, raw and powerful and unrestrained. He was so different from the Powers she'd grown used to seeing, a man intent on control, both of himself and of the situation.

Licking her lips to hide the panting need that burning look gave her, Tess spun around in time to see Dane sweep Serena into his arms and dip her for a giggling and fiery kiss. It didn't help. All she could think about now was Powers, wondering if his kisses would be as passionately playful when he wasn't continuously on guard around her in public.

"Welcome home, handsome." Serena straightened her clothes as Dane let her go.

"It's good to be home, despite the guy time. And look who I brought home for dinner and the night."

Powers was still scowling. Tess felt a shiver that made her wish for a blanket. Or maybe a parka. The heat in his eyes was having the opposite effect on her.

"Powers, I'm so glad you decided to join us. Everyone's going to be here. It's like the last big bash of the summer." And on Serena's final words, the front door opened again and Dave, Steve, Vince and DK, Deke, and Jake poured in.

Tess felt DK's hug but could barely respond. She stood pinned in Powers' sightline. When her friend frowned at her and followed her gaze to the man in question, she got a sudden smile and gave Tess a reassuring pat.

"Let's get this party started!" Vince slapped Powers on the back as he passed him by, then was caught in the same net of intensity that DK had stumbled into. When he glanced between the two, his smile got wide and crafty.

"Hey Powers, look who's here already. Tess." And he caught her up in a squeeze as he lowered his head to whisper in her ear.

"He won't bite, you know. Actually, I think he's nuts about you." With another squeeze, he headed for Serena and her hug.

She should move. She could just get up, say her god-byes, and drive herself back to town.

As if he knew what she was thinking, Powers shook his head slightly and held up a hand to dissuade her. She found herself mirroring the deep breath he pulled in, and as he let it out slowly, more distractions arrived.

Two bundles of energy disguised as boys ran into the room from the patio, dogs at their heels. The boys braked to a stop and started high-fiving the men as they walked down the line. The dogs rushed on, and the black Lab, DK and Vince's Fusion, bounded up to Tess and promptly put his paws on her lap for attention. Not to be outdone, Serena and Dane's golden puppy Trina tried to do the same.

Two dogs and a woman were more than the kitchen stool could handle. She felt it tipping over and made a grab for the counter, but her hands were full of enthusiastic slobbery greetings. Resigned to the insult of being tumbled to the floor, Tess braced herself for the impact.

Strong arms came around her as the stool slipped away, and she had the feeling again that she was flying, but for completely different reasons. Looking up, all she could focus on was Powers' face.

"It looks like I keep getting great excuses to save you, Tess." The hint of amusement in his tone was matched by the gentle expression in his eyes. Smoldering desire had been replaced by something that suddenly appeared much deeper.

She gulped, aware that all activity in the room had come to a complete halt to watch them.

"Ah, thank you. You always seem to be around during the very few times I need rescuing."

Knowing her annoyance was showing, Tess started to push away, giving him a clue that she could be set down on her feet again.

"Boys? How about putting the stool back in place for Tess?"

Powers' command was delivered without any intensity, but Jeremy and Will jumped to attention and set the stool on its legs.

"Sorry Tess. We were just playing with the dogs, and – "

Holding up her hand to stop them, she smiled at their explanation. "That's okay, I know how you two get when you're all fired up. Your parents are probably spending the first few days of their trip sleeping off the exhaustion."

The fact that Gabby and Rick wouldn't be leaving their bed for reasons other than escaping their active children was lost on the boys, but Powers got it right away. He grinned at her, and she shoved a little harder.

"Powers? I think you can put be down now."

A corner of his mouth quirked, like he was trying not to laugh.

She didn't want to admit that she liked being held in his strong arms, and she was amazed that he seemed to be doing it so effortlessly. However, it seemed to have restored his good humor. With a wink, he set her down gently on the stool.

"Ah, Mr. Ashland? We're sorry you had to catch Tess and everything."

Jeremy stood to one side, with Will shaking his head in agreement. They looked up at Powers with their heads back, as if they were trying to see the face of a giant.

Tess saw the smile on Powers' face transform into something whimsical and light. He crouched down so that he was eye-to-eye with the boys as he regarded them solemnly.

"That's okay, guys. I kind of like catching Tess. But you have to be careful when you run in with the dogs, okay? The dogs could get hurt too."

The kids nodded with rapt attention, not saying a word. Behind them, though, Tess heard a triumphant snort.

"See? What'd I tell ya. He's hooked."

Dane growled at Vince's remark.

Tess watched in growing fascination at this side of Powers she'd never seen, He kept his voice gentle with the boys even as he advised them. They were still watching him as if he was a strange new creature and they weren't sure what to make of him.

She wasn't either.

He stood up and patted them each on a shoulder, before adding, "And don't you think it's time you called me Powers?"

*****

Deke stood next to Powers and watched the heated game of softball taking place across the front yard. When the ball almost hit the back of his pick-up, Powers cringed as he fielded it and tossed it back to the pitcher.

"Sorry, I told you I'm not very good at sports." Mac waved in apology. Roxy took that opportunity to latch on to her boyfriend, kiss him, and tell him that he threw like a girl, right before she winged the ball with precise speed and direction at DK to tag Vince out as he tried to steal second.

The men on the sidelines chuckled. Since there were more men in attendance today than women, Mac was stuck on the women's team. And despite that, the women were winning.

"They work, you know? I had my doubts. A lot of the town did, but they've got a special something."

Powers turned to look at Deke in surprise.

"Roxy and Mac? They seem like they've been together forever. I didn't know differently until Dane filled me in a couple of weeks back."

Shaking his head in agreement, Deke took a pull on his beer. "Maybe it's a case of opposites attracting or something. They just didn't seem to be pulling in the same hitch, if you get my drift. But there's no question that they have that special something." He took another pull, turning to watch Powers carefully. "Kind of like you and Tess."

Powers snorted, even as his shoulders bunched defensively. He fought it at every turn. They were too different, as if they were natural enemies. But when he least excepted it, he felt compelled to rescue her, even when she probably didn't need his help.

"There's nothing going on between us, past the construction project, and the mutual friends we hold important. Nothing at all."

Who was he trying to kid? The bond between them seemed to be growing with each passing moment. Holding her in his arms felt right, like he was meant to protect and defend her. The eager thrum of blood picking up speed in his veins warned him that he would be an even bigger fool if he continued to deny it.

Shifting attention away from himself, he decided that turn about was fair, given the situation. "I thought I saw some sparks flying upon occasion between you and Marguerite. More opposites attracting?"

When the other man balanced on the balls of his feet as if he was ready to run, but said nothing, Powers became curious. "Deke? Is something going on with you and Marguerite?"

Deke was already shaking his head in denial. "No, no way. We have a fight on our hands, a big one. But that's not what we were discussing. We were talking about you and Tess."

Powers wanted to follow the other line of questioning.

"Hey Powers. Time to strike out so that we ladies can do our happy dance."

Roxy taunted him even as Mac gave her an indignant clap on the butt for the ladies remark. Handing his beer to Deke, Powers' eyes settled on Tess playing catcher.

Oh yeah, like he was going to strike out now.

Chapter 32

Snipping off spent rose heads was satisfying, doubly so when you could already see the promise of another round of buds shooting up. Tess leaned across the bed without thinking, lost in the Zen moment of tending to her garden, on a Sunday morning that stretched without commitment in front of her.

The gift of a day with nothing to do was rare. The gift of two days, counting Labor Day tomorrow, was even better. Not that she ever let the business range far from her thoughts, but at least she didn't have to open the shop and commit to the time. Her mind could wander wherever it pleased.

Unfortunately, it wandered back to last night too often for her liking. She felt vindicated when Roxy pitched her first ball to Powers as a strike, and Tess caught it with one hand. Tess fielded the next ball easily, and Jeremy, acting as umpire, had called it – 1 and 1. The swings Powers made were almost nonchalant.

He turned to grin at her then, crouched as she was behind their makeshift home plate. There was an implied challenge in his stance.

"Want to up the stakes?"

She barked out a laugh. She might look like a demure lady in her current life, but she'd played softball in high school and college, not to mention around the block growing up and at every family get-together years ago. And Roxy grew up a tomboy with one hell of a throwing arm. He didn't stand a chance.

Smiling smugly, she gave him a cocky smirk. "Sure. What did you have in mind?"

"What are you up for?" The challenge was obvious now. Honestly, she liked this playful and humorous side of him.

Still, it was better to be careful. "If – no, when you strike out, we drop the dinner."

The rapid change of his face from friendly to forced almost knocked her on her butt. As it was, she was sorry she'd said it. Part of her – a part she didn't want to give any credence to – wanted to get to know him better, despite the danger.

"And if – no, when I get on base, or better yet, score a run, we have dinner at the first opportunity. Like tomorrow night, and I get to pick the place."

His eyes had turned to dark flinty slits and the remainder of his face was so closed that it was almost a mask.

Still, Roxy knew how to pitch, and Tess already figured out his weak spots from his first swings. All she had to do was signal.

Tess set herself in her stance, confident that this would be quick. And painless for her, if not for him. She'd get her wish, getting out of the dinner she agreed to in a weak moment.

Roxy rocketed the ball towards Tess low and wide, and Powers swung hard at the speeding mass. And he missed. Jeremy called the strike without trying to hide the disappointment in his voice.

Smug once more, Tess signaled Roxy one last time. They disagreed, changed the pitch, and finally both shook their heads in agreement. Meanwhile, the men on the sidelines, led by Vince, began a ribald chant to pump up the batter.

She had to admire his focus. He ignored the men, seemed to be unaware of the jeers of the women who had now taken up a rival chant, and didn't even appear to notice Tess out of the corner of his eye. He toed the dirt, shifted into his stance and locked on to the pitcher.

When Roxy let fly, Tess knew it was a perfectly delivered ball. It was right in the sweet strike spot for a big guy like Powers, too close in and yet still legal. There was no way on earth he would hit it, and she'd be free.

The crack of the bat didn't make sense, and Tess checked the glove, expecting to see the dirty white ball waiting for her to toss in the air in celebration. But there was no ball, and she dimly realized that the chanting around the diamond had changed to yells of encouragement of different kinds, depending on your side.

And DK was heading for the woods, her eyes on the ball flying at a height and speed that rivaled anything Tess had seen outside a professional game.

"Go, you fucker, run! She's like a retriever – she'll catch it if she can get under it!" Vince was jumping up and down, waving Powers around the plates, while the love of his own life was swearing loudly and crashing through bushes at the edge of the field.

Roxy moved to third and yelled for DK to throw the damn thing. Tess covered home and prayed with all her might that DK would catch it, a clear if not easy out.

Powers rounded third, and as he barreled towards Tess, she noted the big smile on his face. She'd been snowed. And he was celebrating too early. She lowered her stance again and looked frantically for DK.

Her friend was nowhere in sight. In fact, Roxy wasn't looking for her anymore either. Everyone seemed to be watching home plate.

Noting that her heart rate had picked up fast, Tess made every effort to slow it down so she wouldn't boggle the eventual ball. Because DK was going to throw it in time, wasn't she?

"DK, damn it, throw the damn ball!"

All of the yelling stopped abruptly. Powers took the last few steps at an exaggerated slow pace, coming to home plate and making a point of jumping on it with two feet.

He stood there, breathing deeply, but not as hard as she was. Looking down at her with definite amusement, that odd quirk at the corner of his mouth, he put out a hand to pull her back upright.

"Why Tess, I've never heard you swear more than one word at a time. Looks like we're tied now."

Tied, like tied up in knots. She stared after him as he walked over to the group of men, low-handing them as he passed on the way to the cooler. At that moment, the ball came shooting by her, and hit her hybrid squarely on the trunk.

"Damn – sorry Tess. My pissiness at having to crash through the bushes and still miss the catch got the better of me. What was that, anyway? Is he a ringer?" DK bent over to catch her breath while the two of them eyed the men, now clustered around Powers, slapping him on the back and high-fiving him.

Roxy trotted up to them. "I would have sworn he'd miss that pitch, honest. Where'd he learn to swing like that?"

Powers turned around, obviously overhearing their conversation. He was grinning now, and it made him look a decade or more younger. And a thousand times sexier.

"Dane never mentioned how I could afford to go to college, did he? I got a scholarship – baseball." And he directed the epic force of his now-lazy grin on Tess.

This was the last thing she needed right now. She'd have to pay her debt, and it would come much sooner than she wanted. Too soon to get a shield in place to keep her safe from this more fun-loving side of him.

The sound of a hammer's crack against a nail brought her back to the present. She was standing in front of a bed of cosmos, one she'd deadheaded already. They didn't need her attention. In fact, she'd cleaned up everything she'd planned on in the backyard. That left the front of the house, and there lurked danger.

*****

Giving the nail a final whack to make sure it set deep, Powers stood back to admire his work. The steps were done, with a gentle widening from top to bottom like an old-fashioned hoop skirt, matching the elegance of the house. This house deserved character.

Just as flamboyant and artistic as its owner, and he grinned at the thought of the dinner to come.

"I didn't expect to see you working here on a Sunday."

He turned towards the side of the house as Tess came around the corner. She was dressed much like she'd been yesterday, denim shorts matched with a sleeveless tank top. Her hair was hidden under a large brimmed hat, and she had her gardening gloves dangling from one hand and a pair of pruners in the other.

No make-up, no artifice, and no smile either.

Drinking from the coffee cup near at hand gave him time to admire the view and think of an appropriate response.

"They're still working on the site today. Tomorrow everyone gets a holiday. The professor wanted to get as far as he can before the consultant arrives on Tuesday."

He wondered about her sudden nerves at his last sentence. She pulled the gloves through her fingers, getting dirt on otherwise pristine skin. It had faded from the Hawaiian brilliance it held at the beginning of summer, but tanned and tempting nonetheless.

He knew how it would smell, a subtle earthiness and florals that would remind him of the beauty of flowers grown in her garden. He wondered how it would taste.

Then he shook his head. He had no right. He didn't have time to explore a relationship, particularly with a woman who prickled every layer in him like Tess did.

"Oh, look at them. You changed them. They fit now. I didn't know why before but the old ones were never right." When she clapped her hands in happiness, his heart flipped.

Standing next to her, he took a subtle sniff. Yup, smelled like the flowers and plants in her garden on a warm summer day.

He took another longer slug of his coffee to keep his hands busy.

"I guess I need to see about getting some new railings made." She was frowning at the stairs, pacing to the side and back. "Can we reuse the old ones?"

Choking on a mouthful of coffee, the artist in him disapproved strongly.

"Not the old ones, no. They were about as exciting as the steps, Tess. What are you thinking?"

She stared at him, and he realized that he must have been looking at her like she suggested flowers should be planted blossom end down with the roots sticking up in the air. It was a good analogy.

When a sheepish smile started to spread across her face, he found himself grinning too. He couldn't help it. She was damned adorable in her gardening clothes.

"I wasn't thinking about design, you're right. I was thinking about the guy who likes to come around to the merchants and sue them for whatever he thinks he finds wrong – access issues for the disabled, steps that are too tall or too narrow, loose or missing railings. You don't want to know what I went through to build the ramp on the other side of the house, trying to put in what was needed while respecting the lines of the building. I don't need another problem once the retail week begins."

Placing his coffee out of harm's way, he walked up the steps and pulled out a measuring tape and notepad. "I'm going to make new railings today to match the old ones up here on the porch. The handrail will curve to match the steps, and the balusters will match what you have up here." He watched her out of the corner of his eye as he measured and made notes.

She looked completely befuddled.

"Why would you go through all that work?"

He smiled at her confusion. "Because when I do something, I do it right." Standing and descending the stairs, he stopped in front of her. "Don't worry, you'll be put back together completely by this afternoon. And we'll have plenty of time for our date tonight."

Her confusion cleared instantly, and he felt the atmosphere between them heat and chill in the course of a few seconds.

"About that, I don't think it's a good idea, Powers, and – "

He raised a hand to stop her. "You're not reneging on our deal – or rather deals – are you?" He waved a casual hand at the steps, confident that he didn't need to say anything more.

She sighed deeply and frowned at the stairs, her eyes following the flowing lines up to the porch.

"No, I'm not reneging. It's just that I don't date."

"Never? Not at all? Interesting." He hid his speculation as he turned away to fuss cleaning up scraps of wood.

"It's just that I don't have time for it. I have a full life, a business to run, and things I don't even have time to do now. Important things."

He let her run out of steam before turning. "Just for the record, I don't date either. I have a business to run, a foundation I'm still trying to understand, a brother I'm just starting to get to know again, and other things, important things, that I don't even have time to do now."

She had the grace to flush before she opened her mouth to argue. When he raised a hand to stop her, she snapped her lips shut and thinned them to a fine line.

Moving to stand within an arm's length forced her to tilt her head back to look up at him. He focused in on her golden eyes, suspicious now with more than a hint of heated anger.

"Tess, it sounds like we have a lot in common. Dinner should be – interesting."

He took advantage of her continuing silence to lean down and place a soft kiss on her tight lips. The bolt of energy that stabbed through him when their lips met nearly knocked him off his feet. He wanted to prolong the agony, but he had doubts that he could stop if he let it go on much longer.

Backing away slowly, he dropped his eyes to the ground littered with sawdust. He pulled his keys out and turned for his truck, unwilling to look back to see how she was feeling now. If she had the same stunned expression on her face that he bet was on his, dinner was going to be very interesting indeed.

Chapter 33

"Dane highly recommended this place. Have you been here before?"

Tess glanced around the ornate lobby, barely taking in the tall ceilings and intimate banquettes. She was distracted, and the reason for her mania stood by her side, giving his name to the young hostess. Even the girl seemed awe-struck.

After he'd fried her brain that afternoon with only a soft kiss, she'd stood frozen in front of her house, unable to so much as twitch. He hadn't looked back at her as he started his truck and backed out of the driveway, turning away from the downtown area for the local lumberyard. She was pretty sure she stayed in the same spot for a few minutes before someone tooted a happy horn and waved at her as they drove down Main. Moving only slightly faster than a jog, she took cover in the backyard and fanned herself.

She heard him return less than an hour later as she puttered in back, and the building noise continued in front, a whine that she took to be something related to a saw and the occasional drill biting into wood. Unwilling to heat her blood even more by sneaking a peek at Powers in work mode, she dug deep into her backyard projects. By the time she was done, her backyard was spotless of weeds and spent flowers and she was well on her way to exhaustion.

The midday quiet from the front steps pulled her unfailingly, but she resisted. Her shower felt good, her freshly picked salad for lunch tasted even better, and a book or a nap on the back porch seemed like the Sunday afternoon she deserved.

The problem was, she couldn't doze off, and after searching through her e-reader for words that would hold her attention, she gave up. She regarded her backyard thoughtfully. At least she'd gotten a lot of work done after her contact high from Powers.

Dinner was going to be a torture. She was already too attracted to him for her own survival. He was hard and unyielding and demanding, and she hated that in a man. She would be better off with someone like Chase, easy-going, slightly lost, and more than a little OCD. Powers seemed to know what he wanted, and as evidenced by all of his prior manipulations in Dane's life, he went after it.

On the other hand, he had proven himself to be charming and even funny upon occasion, much as she didn't want to give him credit for it. It was easier to resist the obstinate man than the one who made her laugh with contented exasperation. And they were linked.

When her cell phone chirped with an incoming text message, she raised it eagerly, hoping for a diversion from one of the girl tribe. But it was Powers.

'We're dressing up tonight. Hope you don't mind. Pick you up at 5:30.'

Debating whether to respond back saying she had a sudden migraine and couldn't make it, she started typing. And just as fast, the hint of a pain stabbed at her head. Okay, so the universe wanted her to go to dinner with the man or it was going to get even. Erasing and starting over, she confirmed the time and hit the send button.

Nothing more from him.

She replayed every moment she'd had with Powers since she met him at the engagement party. That night he'd been aloof and forbidding. The sight of him bare-chested on the beach before the wedding kept returning no matter how hard she tried to fight it off. The predatory look in his eyes upon occasion was a close recurring second. And the mysterious pull of his force last Christmas still had her puzzled. The stab of pain behind her eyes faded, and they drifted closed.

In the dream, she was flying, and Powers was running beside her. The rocky ground beneath them was strewn with recently upended trees and ragged plants, broken and battered as if they'd endured a torture. She could hear the keening of voices, men and women, and the cries of frightened children. Starting awake, she confused those sounds in her head with the chants she heard from the bones up the street. The sun was already beginning to sink, its angle lowering and telling her more than her watch could that she'd run out of time to beg off dinner.

She settled on a loose flowing pair of pants and fancy tank top, paired with an equally flowing scarf that could serve as a shawl or jacket. Debating heels or flats, she thought again about how much Powers towered over her. Heels it was. A woman had to use whatever advantages she could in situations like this.

Taking too much time over make-up and hair was out of the question since she'd squandered her primping time with her nap. The dream stuck with her until the sound of her doorbell roused her out of a staring contest with her own golden eyes in the mirror.

What was she doing with him, and why on earth was she doing it? It was like she couldn't help herself.

"Hello Tess." His eyes traveled the length of her body slowly – too slowly for her comfort – as she stood in the open door. When his eyes settled on her face, he quirked a corner of his mouth into a half-smile and added, "You look as exotic as your ancestors tonight."

The word caught her attention, but it wasn't enough of a distraction to miss her own eyeful. She'd seen him in slacks and a logoed button down shirt for work, and in jeans and another Ashland polo for his site activities. She'd nearly drowned herself in her drink when he walked out of the ocean in jams, and when he stood beside Dane in the traditional all-white wedding garb of Hawaii, she had a hard time avoiding being caught in a stare.

But what Powers did for dress-up was borderline illegal.

His hand on the small of her back gave a light push, and she realized she'd been daydreaming too long. The hostess was leading them to a table. Glancing up at him as he held the tablecloth so she could slide into the banquette, she gulped discreetly at the way his shoulders fit his suit jacket. The open collar of his shirt only made the formal attire that much sexier. He had danger written all over him.

Sliding in next to her, he raised his head just in time to catch her staring, and he smiled.

"You don't seem the any worse off for being windblown. I didn't think about warning you that I'd have the top down on the convertible."

She stuttered and hated herself for it. "It was fine. It felt wonderful, and I always carry a hair band with me, just in case." Now why had she shared something as inane as that?

He shook his head again. "You have all that hair, and I didn't think. Forgive me?"

The two final words were almost whispered as he watched her. When she nodded, his smile returned, satisfied and at ease.

Searching for her own ease was a lot harder.

*****

Powers sipped his Hangar One and watched Tess stir her martini with its stick of olives. The waiter, an earnest young man who seemed to spend most of his time tableside staring at Tess, assured her he stuffed the olives with blue cheese himself. The way he gawked, Powers was sure he would have said he'd raise the cows, milk them, and make the cheese if he had to.

But then, he could understand the boy's predicament. He was struggling to keep his cool around Tess too.

Her golden eyes captured him the moment she opened her front door. When she stared at him, Powers wondered if he'd forgotten something, like maybe something was growing out of the top of his cropped hair. But then she shook her head and turned to picked up a purse on the table inside the door, and he had a chance to catch his breath. He needed to get himself under control.

"Look at the steps. You did finish them today. Do you always do what you say you're going to do?" She'd stood at the caution tape he left up at the top of the flight, waiting for the second coat of paint and sealer to dry.

He felt himself puff up at her rare praise.

"I try to. If I don't, it's not because I didn't make every effort." Why did he feel like it was imperative that he impress her?

As he walked her down the ramp towards the driveway, he kept his hand in the small of her back, just because he wanted to touch her. He didn't think she'd accept him taking her hand. Besides, he wasn't a hand-holding kind of guy.

Conversation was sparse on the drive down the hill, primarily because a convertible on the freeway forced yelling as the only alternative. Once they'd exited and turned into the light shopping district where the restaurant sat, he'd been content to listen to the jazz station and glance over at her from time to time.

Her face in profile was even more regal. It should be immortalized on something. Changing expressions chased across her chiseled features, the one he noticed most often being a confused but determined frown.

The enthusiastic waiter paused at their table, inquiring about how they enjoyed the appetizer before whisking the empty plate away. Tess returned to her casual stirring of her drink, taking an occasion sip. Powers felt like she was actively avoiding looking in his direction.

Taking another sip of his drink, he sat forward and put a light hand over one of hers as it rested on the table. Surprise registered on her face as she looked up at him. But she didn't remove her hand.

"What did you do before the flower shop?"

His question seemed to divert her, and her eyes stopped darting to their joined hands on the white tablecloth.

Sighing, she picked up her drink with her free hand and took a larger than normal sip before turning back to regard him with neutral casualness.

"I went to college and got a degree in landscape architecture. That was what I originally thought I'd do. Along the way, though, I fell in love with plants of all kinds. It was inevitable, I guess, given than my grandmothers on both sides were huge gardeners."

It was the first time he'd ever heard her mention anything about family, even in those larger gatherings of all of her friends. Curious now, he leaned further forward.

"Where did you grow up? Were you around them a lot?"

She shrugged and gently released her hand from his, leaving him to run a reluctant thumb over a crease in the tablecloth before looking back up at her and waiting.

She gazed into the middle distance of the dining room, watching nothing in particular. Maybe she was looking at memories instead. They seemed to sadden her.

"I knew them both well, though I saw much less of them once I was in high school. I moved away from my family when I was sixteen." And she stopped.

Again, flashes of remembrances danced across her face. Their waiter picked that moment to return with their entrees and the wine Powers had ordered to accompany their dinners. As the young man reminded them of the multitude of ingredients and preparations on their plates, Tess brightened. Whatever distressed her about the past, Powers wasn't willing to quiz her about it. There would be other times for that.

The idea surprised him. He hadn't been considering anything past this night. Now he suddenly couldn't get his mind off it.

Beside him, Tess made a small moan of pleasure as she bit into her salmon. The sound speared through him and settled in his lap, stirring him as nothing else had in a long time. Well, nothing, that is, except Tess.

"Do you like salmon? You do? You have to try some of this. Here." And she put a bite on her fork and held it out to him.

She could have been feeding him cardboard and he wouldn't have been able to tell the difference. He was captivated by the raw pleasure in her big eyes, almost glowing with excitement over something as basic as a well-prepared meal. When he nodded his agreement with her opinion, he found he couldn't break their locked gaze.

Her hand was still in the air, the now-empty fork extended. And her lips were open on a small gasp.

"And how is everything? Are you enjoying that salmon? Isn't it amazing?" The smiling waiter popped back again and stared openly at Tess. Powers snapped out of his trance as Tess turned slowly to the man and blinked a few times before giving her approval.

Powers cut into his veal with a vengeance, aware that he was trying to avoid cutting into the waiter instead. He'd interrupted a perfectly amazing moment.

"Would you like to try some of this veal?" He held out a small portion of meat and sweet potatoes for her. When she hesitated, he coaxed, "Come on, turnabout's fair play."

She grinned at that, but when he tried to feed her like she'd done for him, she put her fingers on his fork and gave it a small tug. When he released it reluctantly, she brought the bite to her lips and closed around the food. Then her eyes closed as another little moan of appreciation escaped her.

God, that was sexy as all hell. He couldn't remember ever considering a shared dinner part of foreplay before, but Tess forced new ideas to grow inside him without an effort.

Looking at the sizes of the servings in front of them, he wondered how many more of those sexy bites they could work in. Taking a sip of wine, he watched her take another enthusiastic taste of salmon, and felt the primitive beat speed his blood.

Chapter 34

Tess was surprised – no, scratch that, amazed – at the wide range of topics they covered over the course of dinner. She'd been uneasy sitting beside him when the appetizer platter arrived, nervous that she was drinking her martini too fast but feeling like it wasn't fast enough. Careful with the wine, she found herself relaxing not because of the drink and food, but because Powers was turning out to be a disarmingly charming man.

They discussed their work, finding common ground in the feeling of passion they each carried about their professions. Musing on the bones in the ground brought her only a twinge of discomfort, and as soon as Powers placed a hand over hers when he signaled the waiter for dessert menus, it disappeared completely. By the time they finished their coffee, they'd been there for almost three hours.

The only topic that they each shied away from was any discussion about family. After Powers' questions, Tess made sure that anytime he wandered that way again, she diverted the conversation. And the one time she asked him about his upbringing, he gave her a noncommittal answer and said it was a topic better left for a less enjoyable evening.

It sounded like he was trying as hard as she was to avoid painful explanations.

As he turned smoothly off the freeway ramp to head the few blocks to Main Street, Tess watched his hands, assured and competent, on the steering wheel. He wasn't casual about his driving, and he didn't seem to have anything to prove in traffic. She would have expected him to have a short fuse when it came to slower vehicles and less respect for the speed limits. He left his suit jacket on for the trip back, and even the act of driving didn't ruin the fine cut of its lines. He could be taken for a banker or an attorney. Only the rough calluses on his hands gave away the fact that he worked alongside his crews whenever he had the opportunity.

Her heart rate picked up as they got closer to her house. The pounding in her head was back too, along with faint cries and complaining voices. The bones were sending their message, any time she grew close to their resting place.

Her fingers dug into her temples as Powers pulled into her driveway, putting the car in park right behind her hybrid. He shut off the engine and continued to stare forward, his hands again gripping the steering wheel but more tightly this time. What on earth was he waiting for?

The pounding in her head grew louder once again.

Abruptly, he turned to her, his face a tense mask. "Wait here."

He nearly slammed the door on the way out. As he disappeared around the bushes that marked the corner of the old Victorian, Tess used her time to smooth her ruffled hair and try to still the noise in her brain. The insistent chanting returned with force this time, and she closed her eyes in an attempt to find a calm place to hide.

She jumped when his breath tickled her ear.

"Want to be the first?"

Her eyes flew open on his words, nerves rubbing raw against the staccato pitch of the voices. She only wanted to go upstairs and lie down and pray that the ancestors would leave her alone tonight.

Turning brought her face to face with Powers and his quirky smile as he remained leaning over her. One hand was on the car's door handle, and the other was extended to take hers and help her out. His lips, full and sensuous since he wasn't currently grimacing, were only inches away from hers. She flashed back to those lips, wrapping around the spoon of *crème brûlée* they shared for dessert. Licking her own, she saw his expression change from playful to serious in a heartbeat.

The sharp yank to open the door only surprised her for a second. His hand was insistent, pulling her up and towards him as he retreated a pace. Once she was on her feet, he tucked her hand into the crook of his arm and followed the driveway to the street's main sidewalk.

"What are we doing?" He was walking her away from her entrance.

"Don't you want the full effect?" His voice was gruff with an edge of humor.

Strolling along the street and coming to the walkway leading to the front door, Tess felt peace descend. Her steps became lighter as the voices receded. When Powers spun her to face the house, she all but forgot that only moments before she'd been feeling like the top of her head would explode.

"The old lady looks pretty grand now, don't you think?"

Powers turned her towards the house, his tone light but his body tense. She had the fleeting thought that he was hoping for her approval.

When she looked at her house, she gasped in surprise. The old Victorian always looked elegant, but now that missing something, the one thing it needed to be over the top, was there.

"Oh, they're amazing! Powers, how did you do all of that today?"

She heard him exhale too fast, like he'd been holding his breath. Keeping her eyes on the steps, she began to walk towards them slowly.

"It's like she was all dressed up for a party but wearing old sneakers on her feet."

Behind her, Powers chuckled. "Good analogy. I always thought Painted Ladies should have all of their dignity restored. Otherwise, what's the point?"

Now she turned to him, only realizing then that he was standing close to her side with his hand resting on her elbow. She was forced to tilt her head back to see his face, and she felt at a distinct disadvantage.

"Are you referring to the building's less refined early inhabitants?"

He laughed at that, a deep belly laugh that had her insides curling up with pleasure.

"You mean when it was a brothel? No. I was referring to the nickname for these old Vics, that's all. But if the sneaker fits…"

His voice trailed off as he stared at her. The playful expression faded from his face, eclipsed by that serious tension again. His head dipped closer to hers once more.

"I don't want you to feel like you were cheated here, Tess. I told you I'd make good on the repairs to the steps in return for dinner. I enjoyed making them something special for you."

He hesitated and continued to stare at her. She felt like he was the predator and she was the prey, and there was little she felt she could do to change their positions.

When his eyes dropped to her mouth, her own lips opened without any prompting into a small sigh. At any second, she thought he would pounce, and she didn't care if she was the target.

Leaning closer, he continued, "I liked dinner with you even more."

*****

What was it about this woman that had him under a spell? He intended to replace the stairs to her front porch with the same style and footprint they'd had before she fell through the rotted boards. Somewhere along the way, his subconscious decided that they needed to be better than before, matching the lines of the old building and emphasizing the grace of its original design.

And the beauty and grace of its current owner.

The antique-styled street lights reflected in her golden eyes as she continued to watch him, carefully sizing him up. If he stood here much longer, he'd forget that they were on a public street in front of her place of business, and despite the late hour on Main Street, anyone could come by.

Tucking her in more tightly against him, he led the way to the steps, making a big flourishing bow at the base.

"Madam – and I use that term with the greatest respect – would you like to be the first to glide up your new stairs?"

Tess grinned at him, and it was all worth it. The hard work to finish the railings today and the delays on the site that allowed him to do it and the dinner he'd found himself enjoying more than he had any meal in a long time.

She stifled her grin and tilted up her chin, sticking her nose in the air. Putting a gentle hand on the railing, she took the steps one by one to the top. On the porch, she turned to Powers and gave a regal nod before her grin peaked out again.

He smiled back, relieved that she liked them and content for a moment that he brought her a gift she enjoyed.

She took two steps towards the front door, key already in hand, before he saw her steps falter. The hand she put out to steady herself was waving in empty air, and Powers only had a second to react before she started to tumble to her knees.

"Tess, god, what's wrong?" He wasn't even sure how he got to her side so quickly. Dropping down beside her, he wrapped an arm around her shoulders to steady her. Her face was etched with grief and her vibrant olive skin paled.

"Why didn't you tell me you weren't feeling well?"

She attempted to wave a hand in his face like she was shooing him off. "It just started."

"Just started? When did it just start?"

She kept her eyes closed but looked annoyed with him. At least it was putting some color back in her cheeks.

Slowly she opened her eyes, and he recognized the crinkles and strain on her face. She must have a migraine.

"It started when we pulled off the freeway, and it got worse the closer we got to…"

She broke off, worrying her lower lip with her teeth and glancing past him down the street. When he eyes swung back to him, she looked resolved.

"It got worse as we got closer to the ancestors."

That stopped him.

She shoved his arm away and stood up, still shaky but clearly putting steel in her spine. He had to admire her pride. She wasn't going to give in, just because he was a handy place to lean. Her display didn't last long, because before he could think of what to say, he saw the flash of pain across her face. She put out a hand to grip his arm, and he covered it with his own, fighting the urge to carry her inside.

Her expression stopped him. The pain was gone, but she was still frowning, looking down at their joined hands. Pulling hers away, she stepped back and paced the length of the porch. In the overhead light, he could see the crease of pain return. He was already walking towards her to grab her when she covered the distance back to him and slipped her arm around his waist under his jacket.

"That's what I was afraid of." Her voice was so low, he had to bend down to catch her murmur.

"What are you talking about, Tess? None of what you're saying is making any sense. Maybe we need to get you inside where you can – "

She waved off his words. Her eyes were fiery again, her head tilted back to stare into his face.

"Kiss me, Powers."

He started, not because of what she'd asked but the way she'd said it. It was a command, not a request.

His eyes dropped to her lips, full and lush like her gardens. He wasn't sure what was blossoming between them. He'd planned to take things slow and let whatever it would be between them grow naturally.

"I said, kiss me."

The ferocity of her words forced him to act without thinking. He bent his head further, and she grabbed his cheeks and lined up her lips with his before he had time to pull in air. When their lips connected, his body lit on fire.

Tess had her eyes open, the golden gleam watching him even as she began to ravage his mouth. Her lips were open and she forced his to part as well. When their tongues met, the electric charge volted up even higher, and he was only dimly aware that he'd wrapped her in his arms and lifted her off her feet, pressing her against him.

The current running between them charged to his lungs and made it hard for him to breathe. Blood rushed to his head before cascading down his spine and settling below his belt. In any moment, Tess was going to realize he was aroused and hard and pressing against her belly. And she'd probably be pissed.

Her bones were delicate under his hands, and he made a conscious effort not to crush her in his arms. When did he get so strong? Right now, he felt like he could lift the whole house and hold it high above his head.

She broke the kiss long before he was ready to let her go. Staring at him, she didn't struggle, and he was conscious that she felt as light as a feather in his arms. When the passion in her face faded back to a frown, he slid her down his body until she stood on her own. Her brief flicker of surprise at the thick bulge in his slacks was followed by yet another frown.

"Come inside. We have to talk."

Chapter 35

She bet that the last thing he wanted to do right now was have a conversation. It was the last thing she wanted to do too. What she really wanted was to take a fast climb up the stairs to drop him on her bed, followed by long hours discovering if either one of them would beg.

When she locked the front door behind him and turned off the porch light, his eyebrows rose before that quirky grin crossed his face.

"Why Tess, are you planning to keep me here?"

She didn't even bother to respond to the rumble of challenge in his voice. Climbing the stairs slowly, she unlocked the door to her private quarters. His steady tread was right behind her, and when she flicked on a light to illuminate the hall, his hand covered hers.

Whipping her around to face him, he kicked at the main door to shut it as he pulled her against him. His back slammed into the door, sending it crashing closed with a whole lot of force. Then he picked her up off her feet and he kissed her.

It was fast and unavoidable, like an autumn wind that tore leaves from the trees and sent them soaring. She felt the power bunched in his muscles and the significant hard ridge behind the zipper of his slacks. Heat pooled in her as well, and she felt the melting sensation of pleasure begin to pound in areas that hadn't seen any betraying action in a long time.

Only when Powers held her in his arms did she feel like this.

Wrapping her tongue around his in a sensuous dance, she felt him shift, walking away from the door and heading unerringly to her bedroom. That snagged her libido back from a soaring cliff and had her pushing him away gently. When he only tightened his arms, she shoved with more insistence as she turned her head away from those too-tempting lips.

His frustrated sigh was a gale in her ear as he slowly lowered her until her feet touched the floor. His quiet groan as she scraped over his heavy arousal made her shiver. Riding that would be the pinnacle of pleasure. She knew it, even though she'd only imagined what he would be like as a lover.

Demanding. Commanding. Strong.

But she would be protected and safe. She wasn't sure how she could be so sure, but she knew.

He didn't let her go, opting instead to tuck her under his chin and hold her there. She couldn't help but compare the strong beat of his heart was under her ear with the angry pounding of the voices earlier.

"I should be going." The rumble of his voice sounded through his chest, and she heard the regret in his tone.

If he left, the voices would return. More importantly, if he left, she doubted that he'd let her this close again. He had as much pride as she did. At some point, she'd push him away once too often.

"You should stay."

His stillness communicated his surprise more than any words would have. Tension flooded into him and reached out to her. Her blood crashed through her veins in response.

He let her step away this time, his arms falling to his sides. His face was a mask of control, the neutrality of his gaze in contrast to the burning light in his eyes. She thought she could see him bristling.

"It would be better if I left now. I can't give you what you need."

His words shocked her into stillness. How could he say that, when she didn't even know what she needed?

Taking matters into her own hands, she stepped back until her legs touched the edge of her bed, and dropped the gauzy fabric that had served as her jacket for the evening. She didn't even blink before her hands reached for button and zipper at the hip of her skirt.

Powers' hands were clenching and unclenching at his sides now, and a tic started to jump at the corner of his mouth, the same corner that he'd been quirking at her in amusement all evening. When the rasp of the zipper's teeth filled the room, he raised a hand. On another man, it would look like a plea. Coming from Powers, it was a command.

"Wait."

Tess took another deep breath and stopped to see what he was going to do. If she stood like this too long, the drumbeat of desire would be replaced by the chanting of the bones once more. She could already hear them at the edge of her thoughts.

With movements that mirrored the pace of hers, he stripped off his suit jacket and threw it without looking over the back of a chair. He unbuttoned his cuffs, staring into her eyes. Then he walked forward until he loomed above her and put gentle fingers in her hair, tracing the silver streak as if it fascinated him.

"I'm not good relationship material, Tess. You need to know that going in."

As he waited, she noticed his gentle pulsing energy. It seeped from him and surrounded her, and with it, any echo of the ancestors disappeared completely.

"I may not be good relationship material either. I'm not asking for that, Powers. I want tonight. We'll figure out what comes after when we need to."

She shivered as his hand continued to stroke down her hair, the other coming up to trace her cheekbone and the line of her jaw. The more gentle he became, the more she wanted him to hurry. The ache he built inside her was more than painful. It was volatile.

Chapter 36

Somewhere along the line, he'd lost control. The soothing softness of cotton as he rolled to watch Tess sleep was more than he deserved. He'd vowed to be gentle and in his soul, he knew he'd protect her, no matter what.

It had started so benignly, him tracing the streak of light she carried in her hair like a badge of dignity. His eyes wandered to her lips, and when her tongue wet them, he was lost.

He remembered her hands traveling up his arms and pulling him forward as he gripped her hips. Her arms wrapped around his neck, and he lifted her once more. Her delicate bones hid strength and power and resolve. When her mouth latched on to his, he could only lose himself in the burning sensations and barely keep from growling. His next clear thought was how soft her skin felt under his eager fingers, and how he could spend hours exploring her mouth alone.

He meant to be gentle, but her fingers clawing into his buttocks urged him faster than he thought was possible. Then her hands were soothing his back and cupping his neck. The contrast between fierce and gentle was addictive as sin. His hands traced her body and cupped her mound, feeling the searing heat. When her fingers wrapped around his erection, he matched her move for move, watching passion chase across her face in brilliant waves.

"Come for me, Tess."

She fixed him with an unblinking stare, her golden eyes glowing in the dusky light. When her mouth opened and she cried out his name, he thought he'd lose it right then like a high school boy.

Curling her body into his as she quieted, she hid her face from view. He wrapped her up in his arms and rocked her, knowing that each sway let her feel how hard and hot he was. But he didn't want to rush her.

Finally, she peeked up at him, and he expected shyness or embarrassment. Instead, she looked triumphant. Damn, she was singularly glorious, all mussed hair and rosy skin and a small smile playing at the edges of her lips.

Despite an almost painful erection, he had to smile back. He couldn't remember feeling this fulfilled, or this happy. Not in a very long time.

"I got carried away."

His smile grew larger. He was pleased he could satisfy her to the point of screaming. He had a feeling few men were every allowed close enough to break through her air of regal calm.

Reaching across him, she opened a drawer in the bedside table and pulled out a condom. His smile broke a little. She was prepared. He hadn't been.

Watching her tear the corner of the package in her teeth, he growled. There was something so damned sexy about her mouth, something about that blossoming smile that got to him every time. He was as hard as a diamond, and when she started to roll the condom down his length, he stopped her with an unsteady hand.

"Let me." If he felt her fingers flex around him one more time, he'd explode. His heart was beating like a riot out of control and he didn't feel responsible for his actions.

Instead of waiting for him to finish the process, Tess leaned up and grabbed his face, running her lips along the seam of his before penetrating and easing her tongue into his mouth. He got lost in the feeling of her tracing his teeth before she withdrew and took his tongue with her, allowing him to return the favor. He rolled with her until he was pressing her into the blanket, her heat cupping him like her body was made for him alone.

She felt so fragile underneath him, and he was aware that he had to be crushing her with his weight. He rolled them both again and she pushed rougher hands against his chest to raise herself and look down at him.

"What's wrong?" Concern mixed with hyped up desire ranged across her features, and he couldn't resist taming that streak of silver again.

"Nothing. I just don't want to hurt you."

She shifted, letting the tip of his arousal rest at her hot entrance.

"Does this feel like I'm in pain?" And she took him deep in one sharp stab.

He couldn't move, wouldn't have been able to if the house was on fire. The shock of her tight grip on him was unlike anything he felt before. She rocked slowly and took him in deeper, her breath coming in short gasps when she reached the hilt, and he fell into her rhythm without being able to think.

Her face became otherworldly, the depth of her eyes claiming him even as she reached down to kiss him. They were soaring, and she clutched him close to her as her keening met his moans. When she let go and tightened even more, he called out her name hoarsely and grabbed her in a death grip.

Watching her sleep now, he knew he shouldn't wake her. In fact, he should get up, dress, and leave her a note before driving back to his condo and arranging to have his head examined. But he was already without an conscience when it came to her. She'd grown under his skin and the roots she set were deep and unyielding.

She stirred and ran a hand down his body to his ever-hardening erection. Her eyes were slits as she looked at him in the thin light, and before she could move, he reached across her for a condom, rolled it on, and was inside her before his next breath.

*****

"You could stay for breakfast."

Powers zipped up his slacks and looked around for more clothing. One sock was inside out, gripping his shoe. The other was missing, and she suspected one of the cats – probably Tigger – had taken it for a new toy.

He avoided looking at her, and that cut her. With each piece of clothing he added, she felt the distance between them grow.

Exactly what had they done last night, other than heat up the sheets in ways that she'd never experienced before? Their lives were now complicated by intimacy, and they still had to work together. And they were part of an extended family with expectations about holidays and life events and daily interactions.

If this had been a mistake, she was stuck seeing him again, whether she wanted to or not.

Deciding that his silence was something she had to break, if only to establish some ground rules between them, Tess stood up and let the sheet fall behind her on the bed. It would be too weird putting on last night's dressy clothes again, and she wasn't even sure she would find her underwear without a search. But moving to her closet across the hall meant walking by Powers, almost completely dressed and looking as handsomely formidable as ever.

Screw him.

Oh yeah, she'd done that already.

Willing herself not to blush as the memory of how she'd taken that first initiative last night, she straightened her spine and lifted her chin, determined not to give him the satisfaction of seeing how much it hurt to have him ignore her now. She swept past him and out the bedroom door as he slid into his loafers barefoot, having given up the hunt for his second sock.

"What's that?"

His shocked words stuttered her feet for a second and her heart for longer. He followed her across the hall into her walk-in closet as she yanked open a drawer to find a t-shirt. When he laid a too-warm hand on the curve of her hip, she stopped midway with the shirt ready to pull over her head.

"It's an eagle."

"I haven't seen it before."

And when would he have? She didn't have it in an obvious place, and it wasn't something she showed off with the clothes she wore on a daily basis.

"Why did you get a tattoo?"

"It was a spur of the moment thing." It hadn't been, but she wasn't going to begin a discussion about the real reason and its symbolism, because that would lead them back via yet another circuitous route to her involvement with the bones.

"Coffee, at least, if not breakfast?" She pulled on panties and shorts before turning to him.

"It's not like you to do anything on the spur of the moment. At least not something that – permanent." He filled up the doorway and sucked the air out of the room. He frowned at her as if unsatisfied with her brief explanation. Already he could read her too well. If he was able to find the chinks in her shields after only one night together, arm's length should be the closest distance she would allow him in the future.

Aiming for humor, she tried out a smile, and was happy when he no longer compressed his lips, even if the serious light was still in his eyes.

"I don't consider coffee, or breakfast for that matter, something – permanent." She hesitated on the word to make light of his concern.

Eying her for another moment, Powers shook his head, and she relaxed a little more. He was going to drop it.

"I don't have time for breakfast, though coffee would be good if I can get it to go. I have to pick up my truck and finish the rest of the repairs on the porch. Next week, I can start the shingles that need to be replaced."

It was her turn to frown.

"Powers, you don't have to fix anything more. I can hire someone around here to take care of it. I'm sure you have better – "

He raised his hand to stop her with such a ferocious expression on his face that she broke off in surprise. Drawing in a breath to steady herself, his scent enveloped her. The subtle fragrance of his soap, missed with sweat and sex and her. It turned her bones liquid and heat traveled south to wet her.

"At least tell me what I owe you for the work before you start it, okay?"

The feeling of being prey again washed over her as his eyes sharpened. Not that she was necessarily complaining. Then he blinked, and the neutral distant air rode his face again.

"You want a contract?"

She nodded her head to agree, brushing past him to get out of the confining space and down the stairs, where the expanse of the shop could steady her. When she moved through past the employees-only sign on the back door and entered her modern kitchen, he trailed along like he was on a hunt.

Grinding coffee beans and filing the reservoir of her espresso machine, she turned to find him prowling the room, examining the workmanship on the cabinets and staring at the view out her back window.

"When was it built?"

Finally, a safe topic. "The previous owners added it on when they first bought the house. It was in a sorry state when I bought it and the location's not the best, since I live upstairs, but I've made it work. At least I don't have to carry groceries up a couple of flights."

"What do you do with the third floor?" He rummaged through her cabinets and came up with two mugs while she loaded coffee grounds into the machine.

It was too damned domestic.

"I have a sitting area up there, but mostly I haven't done anything with it. There are four rooms on the second floor, two on each side of the stairs. They might have been subdivided before, but the previous owners renovated that too. They used this as a house, not a place of business."

Handing him a mug, she watched him sip the brew, trying not to focus on the way his throat worked as he drank it down. He watched her over the steam from the mug, his face again his usual neutral mask.

"Do you have that to-go mug I can borrow? I'll bring it back to you when I return later."

Opening another cabinet, she pulled one out, and deftly brewed another serving of coffee to add to that larger mug. When she put her hand out for the cup he clutched, he took another quick sip before handing it over, his eyes on her face as she moved over the sink to add it to the plastic.

"I don't want to go yet, Tess, but I think it's better if I did."

She should have expected the stab of pain his words caused her, should have braced herself for it. After all, it was one night and it was probably the biggest mistake she'd ever made in her life.

"It would probably be better if the town didn't see me leaving in the middle of the day, don't you think?"

She hadn't thought about that, the fact that his convertible was sitting in her driveway in the wee hours of the morning.

"At least no one knows my car. My truck would be a different story."

Completely confused now, she turned to look him full in the face, trying to figure out where he was going with this.

There was that small quirk pulling the corner of his lips, the same expression that had her heart flipping over every time it grew into a full smile.

Flustered, she picked up her mug and drank too quickly, scalding the roof of her mouth and causing her to cough. When he was immediately by her side, slapping her back to help ease the choking sounds, she tried to wave him off.

"Give me three hours. I have to drive home, shower and change, and pick up the truck from the office lot. Then I'll come back and put a second coat of sealer on the steps, and we'll discuss the porch repairs."

At least she stopped choking. Wiping the tears from her eyes, she moved to the opposite side of the room to get away from his heat. It surrounded her and cut off any clear thoughts in her brain.

"Today isn't a good day. The streets will be closed off for the parade."

"There's a parade today? No one told me. I need to tell security so that they're watching the worksite more carefully. We can't have anyone…"

She'd crossed out of the room and through her shop, unlocking the front door and opening it to stand on the front stoop. His words drifted away until he realized she'd left him alone, and when he came to join her in the sunrise light, he was frowning again.

"I'm going. The sooner I go, the faster I can be back. We'll figure this out then."

Her noncommittal hum evidently didn't please him, because he made a sound of disgust next to her. Watching the quiet street and checking out who might be observing their little interchange meant she missed the signs.

When he put a possessive hand on her waist to turn her to face him, she was going to protest. When that same hand rested for a moment on the tattoo under her clothes, her heart set up a primal beat. Then he swept it up her back to rest under her hair on her neck, closed tightly, and pulled her in for a searing kiss.

If she poured her coffee on him right now, it would be his own damn fault. He sucked all the oxygen out of her brain, even as his lips were gentle and persuasive. When he let her go, tapping her cheek with fingers that were too casual, she was sure she blinked up at him like an owl.

"Two hours."

He stepped backwards away from her and started down the ramp, seemed to have second thoughts, and turned to stroll down the new steps. When he got to the bottom, he turned again and gave her a penetrating stare, one that left her with no ability whatsoever to read his thoughts.

Chapter 37

He made it in under two, and he didn't even get a ticket doing it. Jake warned him that the highway patrol would be on maximum enforcement today, so he kept his speed just above the limit, despite the fact that he wanted to mash his foot to the floor and make the old engine roar.

He almost convinced himself that what happened last night – and this morning and multiple times at that – was a mistake, as he'd searched for his clothes in the predawn light. If he didn't look at her, he could pretend that it didn't matter. It was just mutual satisfaction between casual friends.

Except it wasn't. One night of sexual intimacy, and he was already feeling the few protective instincts that hadn't been engaged before on full alert. In fact, he felt that way for months, even before he kissed her. Before he touched her. From the first moment he saw her, curled up in that big bed and suffering in the darkness on that winter afternoon months ago.

He pulled into town, happy to see that he beat the time when the street would be closed off to traffic to prepare for the parade. Cruising past the front of the Victorian, he admired his own handiwork. The curve of the steps added another layer of refurbished beauty to the old girl.

Her car was still in the driveway, and he wondered if she, like him, had spent the past couple of hours examining every nuance of conversation last night, appreciating every glance and laugh, and savoring every sensation of the night. He got hard more than once thinking about it. It was more than the spectacular sex. They had a connection unlike anything he experienced before.

Tess was fussing in the front yard when he pulled in, his work truck dwarfing her little hybrid. She looked up in surprise, then pulled her phone from her pocket to check the time, ricocheting her gaze back up at him rapidly. When he walked towards her, she made a point of putting the phone away and returned to the bundle of flags in her hands.

When he stopped next to her, she kept ignoring him. When he took the bundle of flags out of her hands and replaced them with a piece of paper, she opened her mouth. But he put a finger across it before she could say anything.

"I brought you a contract."

She blinked at him, then looked down at the paper in her hand. When she read it, she frowned.

"This is ridiculous."

"No, I assure you, it's a contract. It's between you and me. You wanted to know what I expected as payment for the work to be done on this place, and there you have it. Let me know if you have any questions. I signed it already. You just need to add your signature."

When she eyed him like he was crazy, he shrugged. "What can I say? I'm not cheap."

And he turned back to his truck, a confident smile on his face. He knew she would be staring at him, and he added more swagger than usual to his gait as he crossed the front yard.

*****

"He wants to be paid in what?"

Roxy leaned forward in her chair on the front porch as Marguerite cackled in laughter. Tess knew she turned a particularly unflattering shade of magenta, as bright as one of her prize roses.

The piercing whine of a drill rang out in back, louder than the midday bustle from the approaching parade. When the noise stopped, the women shot more questions at her.

"That's reasonable, don't you think? I mean, come on. How much would it cost you to hire someone around here? And you can't fault his workmanship. The steps are gorgeous." DK nodded towards the new work, a few feet from where they sat.

"And it's not like it's expensive in the least. In fact, I think it's a great deal – for both of you." Serena capped off her statement with a broad grin.

Tess shook her head, wondering where things had gone so terribly awry. She expected Powers to fight the idea of a contract, so when he passed her that piece of paper, she almost dropped it in surprise. When she saw his price, she knew she was dug in too deep.

Roxy tapped her sandaled foot on a new unpainted board running across the porch, and let her face settle into a smug smile. "Maybe I'll ask him if he'd like to do some work on my place. After all, I can make it very – affordable – based on his rates."

When her friends exploded in hyena-type laughter again, Tess threw her hands up in the air.

"Don't you all have men who are missing you?"

DK leaned back, wiping tears from her eyes. "Oh man, this is just too great. Wait until I tell Vince about this."

"Don't you dare! That's the last thing I need, not to mention the grilling he'll probably give Powers." Trying to think up a diversion and failing, Tess turned to Serena. "You know how these Ashland men are. He's not serious, right?"

When Serena shook her head, Tess bit her lip to keep from screaming.

"I know how Dane is, but I don't know Powers well at all. Dane would be teasing you. Powers might be, but then again, maybe he means it."

"Means what?"

All five women swiveled to look down at Powers standing in the yard at the corner of the house.

Please, on the bones of the ancestors, let him not have been standing there for too long.

When four of the five women kept glancing between Powers and Tess, she tried to ignore them. She needed to put an end to this now, before things got completely out of hand.

"Powers, I didn't realize you were still working. Really, you don't have to do anymore." She fluttered a hand at the board in front of her. "I can take care of this myself."

He slipped his sunglasses on and made a production out of wiping the perspiration off his neck. It made her toes curl, thinking about how it would feel to let her tongue follow that bead of sweat as it crawled down the front of his torso. She knew how he tasted, and Roxy had nothing on her menu as addictive as the taste of Powers.

Scanning the closed-off street and his truck parked in her driveway, he seemed to be considering his options. His measured gait brought him around to the front and up the steps. He stretched his shoulders, and Tess felt nerve endings spark throughout her body.

"No, can't do that, I'm afraid. I ran into an unseen problem on the back, so I taped off the area so you won't fall into the hole. And since I can't get out now, I guess that work will wait for tomorrow or later." He ran his gaze across the women seated around Tess. "Where did you all park?"

Serena jumped up and grabbed a plastic tumbler from a side table, pouring a tall glass of iced tea and handing it down to Powers. When he thanked her and took it, drinking steadily until half was gone, Tess stared at his throat working above the collar of his logo t-shirt. She heard a small hiccup of a giggle, and turned to give Marguerite her best bored stare.

Her friend wasn't buying it in the least. Marguerite nudged her with her elbow. "Go ahead, you can discuss – what is it – the terms and conditions while the rest of us sit here and enjoy the show – I mean the parade, of course."

When everyone laughed, Tess spun in horror to Powers. His face told her nothing, but there was that little quirk at the corner of his lips. Those lips themselves weren't tugged tight in a grimace, so he must be enjoying the joke too.

"Oh, the hell with it. Powers, I can't have dinner – no, multiple dinners – with you as payment for the work you're doing. It's just not right." She drew out the last words for emphasis.

Powers shrugged and drained the rest of his glass, thanking Serena as he handed it back to her. His eyes remained hidden as he turned towards Tess. "The first two items on the contract will be completed by tomorrow – Wednesday at the latest. So I guess you'll still owe me for the first two payments." He smiled at her like he'd just won the prize in a very big contest before slapping gloves on his dusty knees.

"Where are the guys?" He tucked the gloves into his back pocket, which pulled his jeans way too tight in front, in Tess's opinion.

Serena had been staring at Tess in amusement during the interchange before she turned back to respond. "Dane is taking pictures somewhere. I'd guess along the parade route itself."

Roxy wiped the smirk off her face to add, "And Mac is hanging out with Vince someplace, probably with Steve and Deke and more of their wolf pack. I thought I saw them two blocks up on the right, at the corner." She let her eyes slip over to Tess before she finished. "And they're all coming back here afterwards, so if you want to stay around with us and wait..."

Tess jumped up before Roxy had a chance to finish, grabbed Powers by the elbow, and all but pushed him down the steps. "I'm sure Dane would love to spend time with you, being you brothers are so close and all. Here, I'll phone him and find out exactly where he is for you." She pulled the cell from her shorts pocket as she followed him down the steps, shooing him away with her hands.

There wasn't a sound from the women behind her. She was sure they were all watching with rapt attention. The parade might include elephants and they could be dancing at this very minute in front of her shop, and no one would notice. The little drama with Powers was more than enough to keep them occupied.

He stopped and turned, and when he did, she ran into him with no hint of grace, waving her arms to keep from upending. A protective brace came around her, and Powers pulled her into him. She felt the immediate intense heat that licked every place they touched, and places that they didn't.

"I always seem to have to catch you for one reason or another. Why do you think that is?" The deep growl of his voice did nothing to calm her. In fact, it brought out every hungry instinct. She wanted to tear into those muscles and hang on for one hell of a ride.

When he took off his sunglasses, she read the extreme pleasure in his eyes. He was enjoying himself too much, damn it. When his gaze dropped to her lips, the look became predatory once more. His tongue slipped out to lick his own, and all she could do is watch.

"Why don't you like our contract, Tess?" He voice was low, so low that she had to reach up on tip toe to hear him over the approaching bands.

"I can't – I mean – it's too expensive."

When he tipped his head back and let out a long rumbling laugh, she wanted to hit him. Damn, he flustered her like no one else could. She completely lost any sense.

Then still chuckling, he took her chin in his big hand. He tipped her head back and dipped down to her level. The whisper of his lips against hers was gentle and all too brief. Then he chucked her under the chin and took three steps back, not smiling at her but not looking away. When he reached the sidewalk and its crowd of onlookers, he was quickly lost in the madness.

Chapter 38

"Here to carry my camera bag for me?"

Powers glowered at his brother, but he was grateful for the distraction. If he thought any longer about Tess and that last kiss, he wouldn't be able to waddle in public without giving himself away.

She wasn't happy with his payment conditions. He thought they were fair. He laid it out in simple terms. For each major task he completed, she'd go to dinner with him. That could add up to a lot of dates, considering the shape her house was in.

"A big strong guy like you can carry your own bag. I'm just here to appreciate the ambiance." He gave his brother an extra squeeze during their man hug to let him know he was teasing.

"So, how are you doing with the work on Tess's place?" Dane delivered his question with vague curiosity, but Powers knew better. His brother was feeling smug. When he lifted the camera to focus on a shot of kids who had decorated their wagons and bikes, he was grinning.

Pretty soon, everyone in their extended group would know what was going on. Hell, he wouldn't be surprised to find out that Vince knew already, and along with him, the rest of the wolf pack.

He should probably step back and get away from this town and the people who were all too willing to pull him into their circle. Dane had said it before – Powers was isolated. He thought he liked it that way.

Without warning, a picture of Tess naked in the predawn light rose in his mind. Her skin glowed like dusky fine china and the long curtain of hair with its silvery streak swayed with every delicate move of her body. Except she wasn't all that delicate. In fact, she was made of steel.

Except for her claim about the voices. An icy finger of uncertainty traced through his bones.

Dane stood and changed lenses on the camera body, glancing over at Powers as he did so.

"You haven't answered me. Does that mean it's going well, or it's going badly?"

Powers shrugged, unwilling to respond. He didn't know how it was going, unless you counted the fact that he was turning into a panting idiot every time the woman was closer to him than a football field. Or closer than his thoughts.

"Hey, Powers, long time no see, man." Vince clapped him on the back and Mac stuck out his hand, saving him from carrying the conversational football for the moment. Both were talking – fast and at the same time – about their idea for a documentary about Flynn's Crossing. They were arguing about the right approach and trying to pull Dane into the middle.

It would be a fortuitous time for him to escape. While he couldn't get his truck out, he could easily slip into the crowd and find a place to watch the proceedings. He'd drive out of town as soon as the street re-opened. He wanted to put some distance between himself and Tess.

"You're staying for the block party, right? I hear it's a great time. The street stays closed and everyone sets up a barbeque and there's live music." Mac had dropped out of the discussion, coming to stand next to Powers and watch a fire truck roll by with delighted children hanging from the windows. This was followed by their friend Deke and a group riding horses dressed in Western garb, a gang of people with decorated lawn mowers, and another high school band.

It took him a minute to process it. "How long does the street stay closed?"

Mac shrugged. "Don't know – I didn't ask. Roxy's is closed tomorrow, so we're in no rush. Not that I don't want to spirit her away someplace more private, after missing her for so long. But I'm content to be anywhere she is."

He looked like a man who was content, his face serene with a trace of a racy smile as he contemplated his time with Roxy.

"Hey Mac, you tell him. Won't it be easier if we re-enact the street scenes, like parades? If we have to wait until a full year passes and film things as they happen, we won't get this out right away." Vince was gesturing wildly with his arms, oblivious to the activities behind him. If he wanted to get the feel for a parade, it would be better if he turned around and watched it.

The chill came as he was having those unkind thoughts. It started as a prickle at his neck, then the hairs on his arms stood up as well. Someone was watching him.

Powers started scanning the crowd, though what he thought he would find he wasn't sure. The chilly feeling continued unabated, and as he ran his eyes over the people, his gaze collided with Dane's. His brother shot him a questioning look.

"What is it?"

Powers didn't want to answer, but Dane locked a tight grip on his arm.

"Someone's watching me." Powers felt stupid admitting it, but the sensation was too strong to ignore.

Dane's expression changed to confusion, but he gave the briefest of nods. Together, they turned so that they were facing in opposite directions to scrutinize the people around them. There might be people – a lot of people – looking their way. Or those people might be watching the parade and just happen to be facing in their direction.

"Guys, what's going on? Powers, man, you look like you've seen a ghost." Vince's voice was hale but uncertain. Soon, he too was examining faces, though his gaze kept returning to Dane and Powers as if he needed a clue about what he was looking for.

"Powers, what's wrong?"

Mac's question was more direct. That didn't distract Powers enough to stop his inspection. Gradually, the prickly feeling dissipated, and as it did, he found himself shaking.

Chapter 39

"You have to remind Ashland that he doesn't have a change order clause in this contract. We negotiated that because the project is so small. Or at least we thought it was going to be small." The man standing in her display room chuckled, and it didn't sound exactly humorous.

Tess felt a growing annoyance with Chase. He'd shown up bright and early on Tuesday morning, wanting her assurance that she would accompany him to the construction site when the Native American cultural consultant was scheduled to arrive and review the status of the bones.

The good news was that she'd avoided thinking about them for over a full day. In fact, she'd realized with considerable joy that as long as Powers was nearby, or she was thinking about their odd connection, the otherworldly chants were negligible or non-existent.

In this morning's light, her ability to ignore the situation any longer was gone. Today all sorts of shit would hit the proverbial fan, and it was going to splatter far and wide before the damn thing got turned off. This morning the voices were angry, and no amount of thinking about Powers drove them off.

"Chase, I'll be at the site. I'm sure Powers realizes that he can't ask for additional money just because the work is delayed. I doubt he's even thinking about it. He's got other much bigger projects to think about."

She doubted he was thinking about anything else today, though. His actions told her as much yesterday, when he was corralled into joining the street party. The party was in full swing by the time Deke joined them.

Everyone made appropriately amazed and complimentary noises over the new front steps. Vince went so far as to ask if Rick and Gabby had discussed their planned house remodeling with Powers yet, and Mac asked if he did new house construction too. When Dane broke in to point out that Ashland Construction usually did much larger projects, both men shut up, but Powers had been gracious enough to say that his company would be happy to look at any viable projects for his brother's friends.

"What, we're not good enough to be your friends too? Wolf pack, man, and you're part of it." Vince punched him on the shoulder, then threw a companionable arm around the other man's shoulders. Tess appreciated the momentary look of panic on Powers' face because she recognized it. He was being dragged into their fold, and he wasn't sure it was the right place for him to be.

Powers looked almost grateful when Deke put a beer in his hand and changed the subject. His eyes raised to hers, and the sudden jolt of intensity had her shifting uncomfortably. The thought of his hard body pressing hers into the depths of the bed came up unbidden and she was sure she blushed as her whole body heated and liquid pooled between her thighs.

"I do not like him either."

Marguerite put a glass of wine in Tess's hand, gesturing to the two men with her own.

"Wait, what? You don't like Powers? I thought you were one of the multitude pushing me his way." Tess was happy to be distracted, even if the subject was still the man reducing her to ashes.

Marguerite made a vulgar noise and shook her head. "No, that other one, that Deke person. I have decided that I do not like him." Her French accent became more pronounced with her disapproval.

"His family has been on that land for generations, he works hard, and he's easy on the eyes. What's not to like about Deke?" Moving closer in curiosity and dipping her head so that they looked like they were cooking up something, Tess waited for her friend's contribution.

"He rubs me the wrong way. In fact, I think you could say that he and I are at *une impasse*, a deadlock. We do not agree, and it is war." She took a sip of her wine and glowered at the men.

Intrigued at what could be causing this much drama in her already over-dramatized friend, Tess opened her mouth to ask but was beaten to the punch.

"Powers, on the other hand, is everything you could hope for, *ma cherie*. You should go after him. It already looks like he could eat you up for lunch and still want more for a late night snack." The undercurrent of teasing laughter in Marguerite's voice made Tess look towards Powers sharply. She sincerely hoped that he couldn't hear them. After last night, it would be nothing but embarrassing.

"Tess? Did you hear what I said? Ashland needs to be made aware that we aren't paying him a penny more, not even if that site sits as it is until next spring."

Tess popped back to the present with Chase's vehement words.

"By the way, I noticed a strange car sitting in your driveway yesterday morning, early. Did you have company?"

Chase's innocent expression didn't fool her. He was being nosey. Tess thought about giving him a piece of her mind, fuming more than a little that he was presuming to question her activities. The fact that he'd probably accuse her of sleeping with the enemy – which she was after all – provided a good reason for her to keep her mouth shut. But inside, she allowed her anger to put a tick mark against any future with Chase in her mental tote book.

He was still watching her, curiosity evident on his face, when his cell phone rang. Squinting at the display, he put the phone to his ear and with only a brief hello for the other party.

"Okay. We'll be there." Hanging up, he gestured with the phone to the front door. "That was Kevin. The cultural consultant is due at ten o'clock. We'll walk over there now, and get a coffee at Brew Bank on the way. Come on." And he headed for the door.

Tess stayed where she was. She knew who was coming, when, and what would happen. He didn't have to tell her, and he certainly couldn't expect her to follow and do his bidding.

"I'll walk over there later. You don't need me there as soon as he arrives. He'll be busy for a while anyway. First he has to do a purification ceremony, and then he'll examine the bones. He has to talk to the professor, and he'll discuss the site with Powers too I expect." She stopped when Chase turned at her front door, frowning.

"And how do you know all this? Have you been at one of these visits before?"

She didn't want to explain the ins and outs of her understanding. Instead, she waved him away. "I know what's expected, that's all. I'll see you there later, and if he's ready to render an opinion about what happens next before I appear, feel free to text me and I'll hurry over."

Her dismissal didn't seem to sit well, as Chase opened his mouth to argue. She pointed, for once not bothering to soft-coat her annoyance. Domineering men with expectations that women would follow their commands, whatever nonsense they said, were getting on her last nerves.

*****

When the state said they were sending a cultural consultant, Powers hadn't expected a local Native

American tribal leader to be that person. The Chief, and Powers couldn't help but think about the man as anything but, was majestic, even in regular street clothes. There was something about his bearing and the respect his companions showed him spoke of his leadership. He also looked vaguely familiar.

When the chanting over the bones began, the Chief's voice raised to a keening pitch, with the others surrounding him matching notes until it sounded symphonic. It was mesmerizing watching their deliberate movements, some appearing more ancient than the bones themselves. In his mind, Powers could imagine them in feathered robes made of the finest animal hides, dancing around a blazing fire while ancient spirits whirled through the air.

As the sounds began to fade, he felt a spirit near him too. It wasn't the malevolent watcher from yesterday during the parade. This spirit felt gentle and warm and tugged at his heart.

Turning, he found Tess standing at the back of the crowd out of sight of the chanters. Her eyes were closed, and she was mouthing the words along with the men as they danced around the construction site. She didn't seem to be aware that she was following, though her eyes opened slowly as Powers continued to stare at her as if she could feel his gaze.

At this distance, he couldn't read what was in her eyes, but the soulfulness he felt emanating from her unsettled him in ways he didn't like. She was part of this world. He was not. But she was convinced that these bones were a connection between them.

"Mr. Ashland? Can we have a word with you, please?"

The Chief stood a few feet away with the architect and the archeology professor. The county coroner joined the group, and Wolford inserted himself circle. The feeling of excitement was palpable in everyone but the Chief.

Approaching the small group, Powers noticed that the consultant looked serene, an expression similar to the one Tess usually wore. Of course, he hadn't let her wear it much recently. The thought almost made him grin among the agitation.

The professor looked beside himself with excitement, and the coroner wore a look of excited curiosity. The architect looked distinctly uncomfortable. Whatever the verdict was, Powers had a premonition that he wasn't going to like it either.

Taking the lead, Dr. Shakiff said, "Mr. Ashland, Chief Ross has examined the site. I have shared with him our findings estimating the age of the bones and their distribution across this soil level. Kevin has been kind enough to share the soil geology and other pertinent facts as well. The Chief has some questions first, and then he will be ready to render an opinion about what needs to happen next."

Bowing almost ceremoniously, the professor took a step back, leaving the Chief and Powers in the center of the small circle. The fleeting sense that they were about to negotiate a treaty passed through Powers before he had time to examine the idea.

"Mr. Ashland, my people appreciate all that you have done to offer security and protection to the site during this process of examination." Chief Ross gave a stately nod, and Powers wondered if he'd stepped back into a different time.

"The bones are definitely Native American, based on the tests already performed by Dr. Petry." This time the regal nod was sent in the coroner's direction. "And their age has been confirmed as predating the founding of the town of Flynn's Crossing."

That was new, at least in confirmation. And he had a feeling that it didn't bode well for being allowed to continue on the project any time soon.

"Thank you for the information, sir." Powers couldn't help himself. The man glowed with authority. His eyes, a deep brown with large flecks of gold and red, seemed to blaze in his face.

Shuffling to make his stance wider and pull up to his full height, Powers copied the man's nonchalance and crossed his arms over this chest. This was dragging on too long.

"You said you had some questions, Chief. We want to cooperate in any way possible. What information can I provide for you?"

When the man's face began to split into a knowing smile, Powers blinked. He felt like he was the butt of a rude joke, and he didn't appreciate the sensation. Still, there was nothing overt or obvious about what the Chief was doing. It was a sensation, and it crawled across his skin like an insect, something he couldn't see and couldn't shake off.

Chase took that opportunity to move forward. "Yes, Ross, let us know what we can do to help fill in any blanks. The sooner we can move this along, the better."

While Powers agreed, he didn't like the guy's tone. It sounded disrespectful and bordered on rude.

The chief seemed unconcerned, however. His face remained serene as he ignored Chase and the others and examined Powers more closely. It was like he was taking inventory of the man in front of him. Powers fought the urge to stand even taller. In all of his days having to face up to his own father, he'd never felt an inspection this acutely. When the slight smile became more knowing, Powers had the sense he'd been tested and passed.

While Chase was still almost bouncing on his toes next to them, both Powers and the chief ignored him. It was the two of them, eyeball to eyeball. Without knowing why, Powers felt every protective instinct rise up once more. This was about so much more than the bones on the site.

"You said you had some questions. I'm ready to answer them." Forcing himself to return the chief's benevolent gaze, Powers waited.

With an only slightly more pronounced knowing smile, the chief gave a small nod. Around them, the professor and Chase were shooting questions of their own. He waited until the noise died down of its own volition.

"Oh, it's not you I need to ask the questions of, Mr. Ashland. There is someone more powerful who has the answers I seek."

Frowning, Powers was uncertain where this was supposed to head next. Kevin moved forward, already offering to respond, but the chief waved him off with a little gesture. He stood waiting, as if he had all the time in the world.

They didn't have all the time in the world, and he was getting a little tired of these games. Powers was ready to express the anger that was rising fast inside him. He could only be polite for so long.

Opening his mouth to demand what the hell this was supposed to mean, Powers stopped when a hand caressed the middle of his shoulder blades. Without turning, he knew who that hand belonged to. He'd felt her presence behind him during the whole exchange.

With a quick pat that could only serve as a warning, Tess appeared at his right and stopped, inclining her head in a slow nod until her eyes were on the ground. Then she lifted her face up, and her noble bearing had him staring, forgetting their surroundings.

"I believe that I am the one who has the answers you seek."

Regarding the chief without saying a word, his warrior goddess waited. They all waited. Finally, the chief nodded in turn and gave a full-faced smile.

"Hello Daughter."

Chapter 40

She felt vaguely ill but refused to show it. It was inevitable that it would come to this. The only Native American cultural consultant in their region was her father. Only a profound fluke would have sent anyone else to review these bones.

"Why didn't you tell me?"

Powers bent his head next to hers when the exclamations of everyone around them gave him cover. His words were angry, but he didn't appear to be mad at her. Instead, the harsh tone was directed towards their situation.

Turning slightly so that her lips were hidden from view, she answered in the only way she knew how. "You wouldn't have understood."

"Try me."

Okay, maybe he was mad at her too.

Shaking her head, she focused on the man who had raised her, trying to convince herself that she was strong enough to stand up to him now. For years, he had demanded that she follow the old ways. When she decided at it wasn't for her, he disowned her. In fact, her siblings had as well.

"Daughter, it is good to see you. You look well." He put out a wrinkled hand to touch the streak of silver hair running down her hair. "You have kept your mark."

Backing up a step ran her straight into Powers, hard and unyielding behind her. His arm came around her, and since she was in no danger of falling, she could only assume he was being protective – again.

Shrugging with a nonchalance she didn't feel, Tess put a restraining hand on Powers' forearm in warning. He was watching the Chief with suspicion, the anger teaming right below the surface. When she squeezed it again, she felt him take in a long breath and relax with effort.

Her father looked between the two of them with interest.

"Ah, so that is how it is? How long have you known?"

Tess frowned at the old man. Clearly he was losing some of his edge, because he wasn't making any sense. But instead of calling him on it, she chose to push slightly against Powers' arm until he let her go. Flashing him a warning glance, she moved past the Chief towards the bones.

As soon as she was no longer in contact with Powers, the chanting that had plagued her all morning grew loud again. The ancestors were, if anything, even more angered by the ritual of the blessing and the activity surrounding them. She could even hear the laments of the children, noisy and fretful and unfocused.

She felt like she was leading a parade. Her father followed in her footsteps with Powers right on his heels. The coroner, professor, architect and Chase brought up the rear. All around them, people pressed against the protective fencing to watch.

This would now never go away. Her background would be exposed, and with it, any hope of a simple normal life would go with it.

"What do the ancestors say?" Curiosity brewed in her father's voice.

Instead of responding, she focused on the blaring cacophony in her head and tried to make sense of it.

Maybe if she found a way to bring them to whatever resting place they deserved, they would leave her alone. But there was an element of malevolence in them that she felt creeping into her living bones while they shrieked and cried.

She didn't realize that she was swaying until she felt Powers beside her. He eased her back against him, and she took strength from his warm body and sure hold.

"I think that this conversation would be best held someplace where we can all be a little more comfortable."

The voice booming at her back was controlled. She supposed she could be grateful to Powers for trying to make things easier on her. Even if he didn't understand what was happening, he could feel her distress. His head dipped towards hers and his eyes bored into her, telling her without any doubt that he didn't want her to cross him on this.

Her father eyed them both again with greater speculation. "As you wish. Perhaps we can find a room where we can meet?"

Chase came bustling forward, tossing a strange look at her as he passed and offered Brew Bank Bakery as an option. When Chief Ross inclined his head in acceptance, Chase started leading him down the street and away from the site.

"What is going on, Tess?"

She could feel Powers bristling with the words.

"It's a long story, Powers. And it's not all that interesting. Trust me when I say that my father is not in the least bit happy about my involvement in this. But I was chosen."

"Chosen? Chosen for what?" His frustration grew by the minute, shown in the dark swirling questions in his eyes and the tight hand he clenched around her upper arm. There was no fear, which surprised her. Most men would be afraid of what she was, even if she fought it every day of her life.

*****

Talks had been completely unproductive in his opinion. Rather than talk about the removal of the bones, the chief kept probing about their source, asking Tess repeatedly who they belonged to and what she knew.

He could see the stress building on Tess's face. She hid it well, but the more the chief queried her, the greater the tension grew in the room.

"I don't mean any disrespect, sir, but I don't see how this is accomplishing anything. The bones have to be moved to allow for the construction to take place. Shouldn't we be discussing this instead of trying to figure out who the people were?"

When the chief swung his head at Powers' question, he could swear the old man had a hint of a smile on his lips. Then he returned to that hard stare between Powers and Tess, finally shaking his head in obvious satisfaction.

"You are the one, then."

Tess roused at this. "Father, stop speaking in riddles. Powers asked you a valid question. Why aren't we talking about moving the bones and then figuring out who they belonged to when we have the luxury of time?"

When the old man just smiled more broadly at her, tsk-tsking as he did so, the flash of true anger on her face surprised Powers. This was pissing her off, maybe even more than it was him.

"I will do some research of my own. You tell me that they are not our ancestors, or the ancestors of our brothers. This will take more consideration. We will meet again – next Monday."

Chapter 41

"I don't get it. It was your father? You never talk about your family, other than to say that you're estranged from them. Why did he come here now?"

Tess closed her eyes, even though her back was to Serena and her friend wouldn't see her expression. It was almost impossible to explain this without sounding like a modern day lunatic.

Opening them again, she aimed for calm. She'd been doing a lot of that this week, while trying to preserve her sanity.

"He's a cultural consultant, so it's no surprise that he was called for this project. In fact, he is an expert historian on the tribes that once inhabited this region. He swore that he had no knowledge of a burying ground, but it's unusual to have so many bodies discovered together like this."

Circling around the island in Serena's kitchen, Tess grabbed an apple and made a production out of biting into the red surface. She'd been thinking a lot about the bodies, finding that their cries had become more plaintive over the last few days. At least they were silent at night.

Because at night, she was thinking about Powers.

He'd been just shy of furious by the time everyone dispersed. While his precious control was well in place, she could sense the waves of emotion coming off him. Chase and Powers both wanted to speak to her after the meeting, and when she'd announced that she was returning to work, they both trailed after her, Powers on her right and Chase on her left, all the way up Main.

"Tess, we have to get this project moving. We can't have the street blocked over the holiday season." Chase seemed to think that she had some control over this.

Powers, on the other hand, wanted to know why her father kept insisting she knew something more about the bones.

Closing the front door of the shop and locking it in their faces, she was rewarded by seeing them both look dumbfounded before throwing snarling glances at each other. Let them fight it out. She had bigger things on her mind.

While Chase left only one message about the project on her phone later in the day, Powers was unrelenting. He finally gave up on Tuesday after leaving six messages on her personal and business voicemails. On Wednesday, his first call came at 7 am, and when he texted her at 6 pm and wanted to know why she hadn't responded to his seven other messages that day, she gave up and told him to call her again.

"Powers, I'm sorry, but there isn't anything to discuss. I can't control what my father does, even though he makes it sound like I can."

"That isn't why I called, Tess. I want to make sure you're okay. You looked everything from shell-shocked to pissed off yesterday, with a lot of misery in between. Is there anything I can do?" Genuine concern coated his tone.

Momentarily speechless, she moved the cell phone away from her ear to stare at it before bringing it back up to listen.

"Tess? Are you still there? Did you hear me?" Now Powers sounded pissed.

"Yes, I heard you. I'm sorry, it's been a confusing couple of days." Not to mention the fact that she'd had little sleep in that same period, replaying in her mind the night they'd spent together instead.

It had been the most stirring night of her life.

His new tone soothed her, even as his words did not. "You still owe me a dinner date – two in fact. And I'll be working on the shingles this weekend, so…"

Her confusion vanished in an instant. "Powers, it isn't a binding contract. After all, who gets paid for labor and materials by taking their client to dinner? I don't expect anything from you." And the sooner she pushed him away, the easier it would be to deal with her own attraction. Once he had the full story, he'd be revving his engine to get out of town.

"Are you planning to eat the core too?"

Tess focused on the apple in her hand, now chewed to the seeds. Serena stood on the other side of the island, watching with an amused expression on her face.

"I was thinking about the construction project." She threw the core in the compost jar.

"Yeah, I'm sure you were. I'm sure that it makes you look flushed and dreamy and a little bit adrift." Serena's gentle teasing was overtaken by her growing smile.

Tess eyed her sharply, knowing what was coming next but without any way to dissuade her friend.

"Only Powers makes you look like that. And he has for months."

Waving a hand to ward off the discussion, Tess toyed with the other fruit in the bowl without looking up at Serena. "It doesn't mean anything. He doesn't make me look any particular way."

Shaking her head, Serena turned away. "Face it, he's under your skin. Or should I say, in your bones? He's worried about you, Tess." Serena's voice was muted, gentled, no doubt, so that she wouldn't scare Tess out the door.

Sighing, Tess brought her gaze up fully. "I don't think that's possible. He regards me as a curiosity, nothing more."

Serena shook her head in disagreement. "No, he's worried – enough to call Dane last night while he was driving to ask if we'd heard from you."

Feeling slightly ruffled that now the man was calling her friends directly, Tess was about to ask for more information when Dane himself walked into the kitchen.

"There she is. Powers was looking for you yesterday." He gave her a welcoming kiss on the cheek before pulling Serena into a fuller embrace.

Glowering at her best friend's husband seemed to do no good. He just broke into a big smile, one that made you forget the scary scar on his face and his watchful eyes.

"He's worried about you, Tess."

She swatted at the comment like it was a buzzing gnat.

"I told him not to worry last night."

"Oh? You talked to him last night? That must be why he hasn't called and asked me to drive to your shop today and camp on your doorstep until you appear."

She wasn't sure what caught her attention in Dane's teasing expression. Perhaps he had a little of that same endearing quirk at the corner of his mouth that Powers carried. She'd never noticed it before. On Dane, it was goofy.

On Powers, it was irresistible.

The hot ache of need unleashed itself. Wanting him was different from needing him. And she could fight want on its own terms.

She hadn't noticed Dane's face grow sober as he watched her. When he continue to stare, she shifted uncomfortably, sure she'd let something of her rampaging thoughts cross her face.

"You two need each other, you know." His voice was quiet but firm.

Flapping her hands again seemed like the wisest thing to do. If she opened her mouth, she'd say something stupid about mutual needs and where they led.

Like straight to her bedroom.

"Look Tess, Powers has lived a pretty isolated life. I know, it doesn't seem that way. He didn't move to a cliff and live like a hermit, like I did. He isolates himself with work, with lots of business enterprises and the drive to succeed at everything he does. Our father did that to him, the bastard."

It was Tess's turn to stare, and her surprise was underscored by Serena's small gasp. This was the most Dane had ever said about their father, and evidently the vehemence in his voice was new to Serena too.

"Ask him about our parents some time. I know that's why he stays alone now. Sure, he has women chasing him, but they never stay around long. He finds ways to push them away." Dane hesitated, as if weighing if he was revealing too much. Then he leaned closer.

"This is the first time that I've seen him doing the chasing. You push his buttons, and it's been fun to see him with all the questions and none of the answers this time around." Then Dane smiled and looked only slightly sorry. "Hey, so forgive me, but I am the younger brother, and it's nice to see that for once, I can rub his nose in it."

*****

She ended up spilling the rest of the beans to Serena and Dane, about the current state of affairs with her family, her reasons for splitting from them, and her strange connection to the bones.

She left out the part about her equally strange but strong connection to Powers.

But they convinced her that she needed to discuss this with Powers. Frankly, she had little choice. He kept calling, and since they spent hours on the phone, she couldn't deny that they anything to talk about.

Which is why, as Friday's business hours were drawing to a close, she was debating what she would wear tonight on her next pay-back dinner date.

The flute music played as the front door opened, and she glanced at the clock to see that she'd missed the top of the hour. When she turned, she was surprised to see Chase standing in the doorway, wringing his hands in anticipation.

"Hey, Tess. How are you? We haven't had a chance to talk all week."

True, she'd been letting his calls go to voicemail.

"Listen, the girls are with their grandmother tonight, so I'm free. We can go get some dinner, have a chance to catch up, maybe get a nightcap here or at my place. Let's go." And he turned to head for the door.

Really? Did he really think she would drop everything because he was suddenly free for an evening and wanted her attention?

"Chase, I have plans for tonight."

He spun around again, his face crestfallen. "Oh, I didn't think…" He started over. "I mean, I didn't hear from anyone that you had plans, so I just figured…"

He trailed off again. Her frustration was growing faster than the weeds in her yard, and she allowed it to play across her face.

"Chase, you can't make assumptions. And you have to stop assuming we're going to go out. This isn't right.

There is nothing between us, nothing but friendship and business."

True, at one time she'd thought differently, but it had only taken one long and lovely night in Powers' arms to convince her otherwise. Even if Powers didn't last, she wasn't going to settle for Chase.

Chapter 42

He paced the entry foyer, checking once more that the intercom appeared to be working. Tess was supposed to be here twenty minutes ago. There wasn't any traffic that would hold her up. He knew. He checked that three times already.

Powers didn't think she'd stand him up. When he insisted that they have dinner in Sacramento, she'd been just as insistent that she would drive herself down the hill. All of his work to convince her that he was happy to pick her up did nothing to dissuade her.

The least he could do is provide her with a parking space. His penthouse came with two. Since his work truck stayed at the yard with the others, he only needed to park his convertible in the private garage. Tonight, Tess's hybrid would be sitting next to his Mercedes.

Just as he hoped Tess would be sitting close by his side. Very close.

He'd selected and discarded a number of restaurants for tonight. Then he thought about having something sent in. But in the end, he decided that it would be more personal – and more impressive – if he cooked. He spent as much time at Whole Foods puzzling over the menu as he had on the original possibilities for restaurants.

He glanced at his watch again. Twenty-three minutes late now. He thought about calling her, but he didn't want to distract her when she was driving. Besides, he knew she wouldn't stand him up. She had too much class for that.

The intercom gave its discreet buzz when he had marched himself across the dining room and almost all the way to the kitchen. He raced across the condo, coming to a sliding stop in front of it.

Pushing the button, he was gratified to see Tess's face fill the screen.

"Hello? Powers?"

He pressed the button, trying to keep the relief out of his voice. "Tess, you're here. I'll buzz you up. Top floor."

That sounded pompous. She could do that to him. Around her, he wanted to be as important as possible, even while he kept her safe from harm.

Throwing open the front door to the elevator lobby, he took a moment to run a hand over his hair, bristling as usual, and smooth his buttoned shirt. He'd opted for casual in an effort to set Tess at ease. Somehow, it wasn't making him feel any easier though.

When the elevator door opened, she stepped out and glanced in the opposite direction up the hallway. After scanning the other penthouse door, she finally flashed back to him. He wanted to think that the first expression on her face was one of pleasure to see him. But she covered it up so fast, he could have been wrong.

Damn.

She was heart-stopping gorgeous to look at. A few days without setting his eyes on her and she seemed to have become even more stunning. Tonight she wore dressy jeans that hugged her curves and made her legs seem longer. The sleeveless top was some kind of shiny material, and she had a light jacket thrown over her arm. The big purse over her shoulder was woven, hinting at her Native American heritage. And her long hair was pulled pack in a clip set below her neck, creating a loose ponytail that made her facial features stand out in stark contrast.

Remembering his manners, he stepped forward and took her hand, not in a handshake but to hold in his, pulling her towards him. When she looked up into his eyes, he forgot that he was going to greet her and welcome her into his home. All he could think about was pulling her close, inhaling her unique floral scent, and kissing her full lips.

*****

It was there again, that hungry predatory demeanor. It was as if he could eat her in a few fast bites. Eagerness was in the hands pulling her forward and lifting her up on her toes, even as his head came down.

The touch of his mouth jolted her, even as it was chivalrous. He ran his tongue across the seam of her lips, a whisper of a touch, allowing her to make the decision. Let him in or turn him away?

It wasn't even conscious thought that led Tess to open her lips and let her tongue sway with his. He pulled her in tighter against him, and she relaxed into the embrace, reveling for once that while he was big and strong, he could temper it, respecting her own strength and power. She felt the burgeoning length of him rising as he pressed closer.

The ding of the elevator door closing brought her back. They were in a public place, on display at any moment. While it added spice to the kiss, she didn't want to put on a show.

Pulling back reluctantly, she gave him a cautious push. He lifted his head and regarded her thoughtfully, running his tongue across his lips as if he was savoring her taste. His eyes were pools of darkness, deep enough to drown in if she so much as dipped her toes.

"Hello." She gave him an apologetic smile, sorry to break up their clench.

He loosened his grip, running a hand down the length of her hair once before wrapping it loosely around his hand. Letting it free, he ran fingers along the lustrous stripe beginning at her temple.

"Hello." Somehow, he added depths of meaning to the simple word.

Taking her hand, he walked backwards through the open door and pulled her with him. He lifted the purse off her shoulder and took her jacket, placing both with care on a chair in the entry hall. Then he took both her hands, drawing her into the open room behind him.

Her eyes were locked on his and would have stayed that way, except for the glare of sunlight hitting her. It drew her gaze to the windows behind him. As if he knew what to expect, he stopped in his tracks, grinning when she gasped in astonishment.

"Yeah, that's what got me the first time too." Turning to stand beside her, he followed her eyes to the view.

It stunned her senses. From the sweep of the Sierras to the east, bare of the snow that would soon cloak the mountains, to the lazy bends of the Sacramento and American rivers and the sun falling lower over the intercoastal range to the west, the vantage stole her breath.

"This is amazing. I'm surprised you get anything done when you're here. I'd be distracted by everything I can watch."

She felt his eyes on her even as she took steps towards the beckoning windows. When he didn't respond, she turned to find him staring at her with undisguised lust.

It might have been safer to have him pick her up at home.

"I am – distracted, that is. But it isn't by that view right now."

The low rumble of his words caused an answering echo of need to reverberate through her. That wasn't why she was here. Or was it? She'd taken very little time to examine her rationale for agreeing to meet him at his penthouse.

Watching him shake his head as if to clear it, she turned back to the windows, no longer conscious of the dramatic perspectives. She couldn't see his reflection in the glass, though she heard him moving around behind her.

"Drink?" He held a glass of bubbles to her right, the heat of his arm below his short sleeve reaching her bare skin. There was no reason for the raised goose bumps it generated.

"Thanks." Her husky tone betrayed her, and she cleared her throat to put things back on even ground. "So, have you lived here for a while?"

When silence met her question, she turned to him. He was staring at her again, this time with a gaze that held both desire and regret. Damn the man, his moods shifted in every light breeze, bobbing around as much as an unstaked flower.

Exhaling a deep breath, he took two steps back before breaking her gaze, stopping once he reached the leather couch and its glass coffee table. She missed his intensity instantly.

"When I realized that I would be staying in Sacramento for an undetermined amount of time, I decided that hotel living was getting old. This place was on the market for a steal, given the economy. I walked in with the realtor, had the same reaction you did to the view, and made an offer on the spot."

Waving a hand in silent invitation, he waited for her to sit before he sat as well. The distance between them on the couch could have spanned half the world. Tess ached to move closer.

Why did she react to him so strongly? Ever since her father's comment about Powers, that he was 'the one', her unease had grown beyond reasonable proportions.

She didn't need 'the one'. She needed a return to quiet, her garden, and her simple life.

"It's been quite a week, hasn't it?" The grumble behind his question made her smile.

"Yes, and next Monday is even going to be more interesting. I wonder what the decision will be." The smile hid her worry that the bones would need to remain in place until conclusions could be drawn about who they belonged to.

She felt him shift next to her, and his hand covered her fists, clenched tight in her lap. Pressing her knees more tightly together did nothing to make the sudden bolt of desire from making itself known.

"So, you have a father."

She almost giggled at the statement.

"Yes, I do. So do you, I understand."

He was turning her smaller hands in his much larger ones, feather touches and traces of scars and lines. His fingers tightened slightly with her words, but for once, she didn't feel him retreat when he sighed again.

"Yes, I do." He paused long enough for her to bring her eyes to his face, but he was still watching their linked hands. Sighing again, he continued.

"He's actually a big part of the reason I'm here, in California, I mean. Him, and Dane, and my son."

He dropped a hand to pick up his wine glass, releasing one of hers when she tugged mildly so that she could do the same. She leaned back to watch his face. She was curious. He had never discussed his reasons for moving out of Oregon.

Dropping her other hand, he snaked his arm across the back of the couch, letting it rest on her shoulders and tucking her into his side.

It felt so right – perfect, in fact. The sun lit up the city below them, and the condo was quiet except for the sounds of their breathing. It felt peaceful.

"Dad and I don't get along. That's understating the situation. He wants to continue to hold the reins of the family construction business, and he only grudgingly allowed me to carry the name down here when I made a point of saying that my reasons for moving were because Dane needed our support." He sipped the wine again, though she doubted he tasted it.

"Dad doesn't approve of Dane's profession, and he considered it Dane's own fault when he was injured. I was furious with Dane too, but for completely different reasons." She felt him shake his head. "When he was hurt, he wouldn't let me help."

Tess absorbed his words. She couldn't see his face, since he'd tucked her head under his chin, but she could feel the rumble of emotion under the words.

"It's important for you to fix things, isn't it?"

His chuckle reverberated under her cheek.

"I'm in renovation and construction, so yes, that's what I do."

She poked a finger into his ribs and was rewarded by a hiss that could have been the edge of a laugh.

"I mean, you like to fix people. Like you tried with Dane." She waited a beat. "And like you're trying to do with me."

She held her breath, waiting to see how he'd respond. His temper could flare up, or his control could kick in and he'd push her away.

Or he could grab her in his arms and kiss her nearly senseless, like he had at his front door. That had her vote.

The blare of a kitchen timer broke the moment. His arm tensed around her before he let her move back a few inches. She made an effort to straighten but he held on, tilting her chin up and placing a light kiss to her lips. It was quick but tender.

Tess blinked back the sudden wetness in her eyes.

When he leaned back, Powers had a wry grin in his face. "Saved by the bell."

Chapter 43

"I'm stuffed. Those potatoes were amazing. What do you call them?"

Powers leaned back in his chair, watching Tess over the rim of his wine glass. Her eyes were half-closed and she had a hand on her flat stomach, high enough to allow the top she was wearing to ride up and give him a tantalizing view of an inch of her olive skin.

It would be warm and smooth, like heated silk, like her back had been under that Hawaiian sky, like all of her had been that night in her bedroom.

He was hard thinking about it. He'd been hard, in fact, since they sat down at angles to each other at the corner of his dining room table. Grateful that he'd put all of the serving dishes in its center, he didn't need to stand up and give himself away.

Until now.

"It's my mom's recipe. She had a fancy name for it. I just call it scalloped potatoes. The secret is the sauce, I will tell you that though. But you have to earn the recipe."

He liked to tease her, he found. She never took offense and only got riled up in the best possible ways.

Her eyes opened wider when he issued his challenge. "Earn it? How? Do I get to wash up, is that it?" She made a big show of pushing back her chair and huffing in mock disgust. "I guess I can do that. You cooked, after all, and the steak was perfectly prepared."

He pushed back his chair to match hers, but when she reached for his plate, he wrapped a hand around her wrist and gave her a little yank. The fact that she landed squarely in his lap made him suck air before she settled.

There was no way she could miss his need for her now.

Her golden eyes flashed with mischief as she watched him. Throwing an arm around his neck, she shifted again, and the agony of having her bottom pressing closer made him grin at her. Her laughter trilled, and he knew that he was in deeper trouble than he thought.

He wanted to freeze the moment, Tess with her sparkling eyes as her arms tightened around him, her lithe body making him feel big and strong and undeniable turned on. It wasn't just her body, though. It was her spirit, proud and courageous and seemingly invincible.

She needed his protection. He wasn't sure how he knew it, but Powers was convinced that her survival depended on him.

The idea made his grin fade away. He examined each line and valley of her face, tracing her cheekbone with a finger and coming to rest at her earlobe, playing with the dangly hanging there. There was no way he would ever push her away. The act, even its very idea, was impossible to contemplate.

Tess's smile faded along with his until she was watching him solemnly. Her hands stayed linked at the nape of his neck and she toyed with his hair. Shifting again, she brought her face closer to his.

He could spend the next hundred happy years staring into those eyes, watching her lick her lips as the tip of her tongue darted out, feeling her press against him until he was ready to explode from that alone. It would take him years to get answers to all of the questions her had about her, and he wasn't even done figuring them out yet.

God, he'd fallen in love with her.

The concept, so quickly presenting itself on the heels of his desire for her, stunned him.

She seemed to notice the change in him, because she frowned. He shook his head wordlessly, and he lowered his lips.

Hers parted on a gasp when he touched her. He planned to kiss her, but the beat of her pulse below her ear was too tempting. He wanted to absorb it, take that spark of energy into himself until his heart was set at exactly the same pace.

Her skin was tender, and he swore every nerve ending jumped under his lips. When she gave a vague moan, it made him feel stronger than he ever had before. The atmosphere in the dining area, charged by an hour of sexual tension masquerading as dinner, suddenly heated to a new level.

Her head fell back against his arm, laying her neck bare. His lips traveled there, tasting her, feeling her pulse pick up another tempo, a wilder one this time. His own heart noticed, and when he finally moved from neck to lips, there wasn't a cell in his body that wasn't completely aware.

He loved her.

*****

From the moment he strode into her life, Tess knew she was in trouble. Even when she told herself she hated him, she knew. When he made her furious, she sensed that part of it was because he was the one.

He was the other half of her legend, and she didn't want to depend on him.

When she'd dripped some of that excellent sauce from a forkful of potatoes to land at the corner of her lips, the feel of his thumb as he'd laughingly wiped it away made her long to pull it into her mouth and suck. As he'd told her about his father, his strict ways and how he feared becoming more and more like him the longer he stayed under his control, she ached for the boy she saw beneath the honesty. His dedication to finding a sister long lost said volumes about his loyalty.

When he held her like this, like she was a precious treasure that he couldn't wait to claim, her body surged and she almost stripped naked and took him, right there at his finely made dining room table with the remains of dinner all over it.

Her heart got it, though. As much as she tried to push him away, first with anger and hatred and then with sheer force of will, he was already embedded deeper than any arrow her ancestors sent flying.

She loved him. Of course, she wouldn't be able to hold on to him, not when she revealed the strange voodoo world she came from. He'd run back to his native Oregon – or at least assign the construction in Flynn's Crossing to someone else to oversee.

His lips were sinfully rich, spiced with the steak and blue cheese butter, the luscious potatoes, and their wine. Those flavors were just undertones, though, to the taste of the man himself.

Monday it would all be over, because she knew what her father would ask of her. There was no way to know who those bones belonged to unless she could reveal their souls. And to do so, she'd need to reveal herself.

When he broke the kiss, she was shaking. She felt him throbbing through his jeans and hers. She wanted it, all of it and all of him, for the next few hours.

Looping her arms tighter around his neck, she stared hard into the blazing dark eyes that missed nothing. The desire she saw echoed her own. There wasn't any question where this was heading.

"Take me to bed."

She felt him shake when she said it, saw the flash of relief followed by burning heat that made his face look predatory. She shivered in response. This was exactly what she wanted.

When she shifted to get to her feet, his arms only tightened around her. She knew he was strong, but he got to his feet with her in his arms and strode down a hallway.

Powers shouldered through an open door and laid her down on the king bed, following her quickly to cover her with his body, linking their lips again even as he linked his hands with hers. His arousal pressed into her as he stretched out, rolling to her side.

"You are the most beautiful thing I've ever seen." His words whispered into her ear as he nuzzled her neck. "You are the most amazing woman I have ever known."

With a full body shiver, she wiggled her fingers to encourage his reluctant release. He growled his pleasure, though, when she pushed them under his shirt to run over his ribs, his lower back, and finally up his chest. Undoing the top couple of buttons opened up flesh for her to explore, and when her lips met his skin, he swore.

She intended to be tender, to take it slow and easy, but things were spinning too fast. When he reached for the hem of her tank and pulled it up, she could only raise her arms and help him, pushing her hair out of the way when it tangled in a shoulder strap. He stared at her, but not are her lacy bra, which she expected. He was looking into her eyes.

"You take my breath away." The murmur of his voice washed over her, and she felt her skin prickle as if he was caressing it.

He shifted again, running an unsteady hand down her front, a finger dipping between her breasts and the back of his hand running down her belly until he came to the button on her jeans. When he paused there, he looked up at her, questioning.

She covered his hand with hers and released the fastener, pulling the zipper down and laying back so that he could tug the jeans off. When he murmured this time, she felt powerful and invincible. He prowled across the bed towards her on all fours, his expression greedy and menacing in its tension.

She felt exactly the same way.

"My turn – or should I say, yours." She tried to hide the shriek of need in her voice, but it was there for him to hear. His voracious smile only pushed her further up in the stratosphere until she was panting. He brushed aside her bra and panties so fast that she barely noticed, and she rose to her knees to run her lips down his neck to the collar of his shirt as he sat in the middle of the bed.

The hand he put on her hip was unsteady, and she reveled in that. She crawled around his body, kissing and sucking on any bare skin she could find until she was pressed against his back. Bringing her arms around him, she took her time releasing each button on his shirt, caressing the skin and hairs underneath until she could hear him gasping as hard as she was.

When she had the shirt open, she began pulling it off his shoulders in a slow shimmy. She didn't want to give in to her frantic pulse and rush things. When she was alone again, after he left her, she wanted to have deep memories of every second they were together for the lonely years ahead.

Running her lips along his shoulders, she saw him grip his hands tightly at his sides. His chest fell in rapid movements, and she closed her eyes to enjoy the feel of his skin under her lips. His muscles were hard and his skin so soft, and the contrast was killing her. When she pulled the shirt sleeves over his fists and threw it to the side, she finally opened her eyes to take in the contoured expanse of his back.

It drew her gaze in a second. It was potent and vigorous and forceful. Its fangs were barely concealed in an expression that could only be called menacing.

The dark eyes of a wolf stared at her from the tattoo on Powers' shoulder.

Chapter 44

The moon had long since moved out of sight in the sky, but he was unwilling to close the blinds. Soon, too soon, the predawn light would begin over the mountains. But even that wasn't enough to drive him away from her side. She slept restlessly next to him, and he tightened his arms as reality flowed through him.

He thought she'd seen the tattoo already. He made no effort to hide it in Hawaii or when they'd been together before. But when she uncovered it last night, her cry of distress forced him to swivel on the bed to see what was wrong.

She had one hand over her heart, the other clapped over her mouth, and her eyes were wide with shock. Her reaction frightened him.

"Tess, tell me what's wrong and I'll fix it, I promise."

Shaking her head at his words, her hand finally dropped from her mouth, but her eyes were no less startled.

"Why do you have that?"

The question puzzled him. She had ink too. He wasn't sure why his tattoo caused such a big reaction.

"It spoke to me." It was the truth. He'd taken one look at it and knew that it was something he wanted with him always, even if he never had any interest in marking his body before.

She shook her head, seeming to agree with him, which was even more confusing. Coming to some sort of decision, she pushed him back on the bed and reached for the zipper on his jeans. The rasp of its descent sent him spiraling, and her eager hands pulled away denim and briefs in one quick movement before she straddled him.

"Wait." He clamped damp hands on her thighs, holding her still. "Tess, tell me what's wrong."

Because something was wrong. Tears were streaking down her cheeks, and he could tell she was upset. The near violence of how she quickly disrobed him panicked him.

"Nothing. It's nothing. Please, Powers." She flexed her strong legs in an attempt to complete their union.

Now it was his turn to feel violent, because he wanted more than anything to drive himself into her and let her blazing heat wrap around him. Her hands tightened on his legs, her short nails biting into his skin as she tried to free herself enough to move.

Hoping that one hand would be enough to delay her, he reached across the bed to a nightstand and yanked open the drawer, relieved to find protection close at hand. When she grabbed it from him and rolled it on with eager fingers, his eyes crossed. And when she dropped over him in one movement, a higher shriek and lower rumble filled the room.

Powers tightened his arms around her now, trying to make sense of it. It was the best sex of his life. He never felt this in sync with any other woman. It was like their spirits were joined in some mysterious way. When Tess came on another small scream, he couldn't help but roar his own approval as he followed. She collapsed on top of his heaving chest and he held her so close that he thought he might crush her bones. That's when he realized she was crying softly.

"What's the matter, sweetheart? Tell me what's wrong." Even if he felt damn close to tears himself, the connection between them so powerful that it vibrated in every corner of his soul, he had to understand why she was distressed.

She never told him. When he shifted to curl her into his shoulder, her hand crept around to cover the tattoo on his shoulder. He rested an equally protective hand on the eagle at her hip. And somehow, that was enough to quiet them both and they slept.

Her restless mumblings woke him. The words were unintelligible, but the level of misery was clear. Hoping to calm her, he ran his hands lightly down her back and pulled her closer, tugging the blanket around them in a warm cocoon.

"Tess, it's all right. You're safe. I'm right here."

She became more agitated at his words. There was no way to get around it – he needed to wake her out of her nightmare. He just wasn't sure he wanted to know if he was the cause of it.

"Tess, wake up. You're having a bad dream. You're okay, sweetheart. It's all okay."

Her eyes popped open with an expression of horror, dashing a frantic gaze around his bedroom before coming to rest on him. When they did, she frowned before squirming in his arms.

"I should go." She pushed away from him.

"No, you should stay. What were you dreaming about?"

Pain, horror, embarrassment and finally resignation flitted across her features as she tried to put more distance between them. He tightened his arms in response.

"Tess, I have something to say, something you may not be ready to hear. But I have to say it."

"No, Powers, there's nothing to say. Let me go. I shouldn't be here."

It sliced his heart to shreds to hear that. He wanted to keep her safe by his side, and she wanted nothing to do with him. But he had to convince her.

Tipping her chin back so that she was forced to look at him, he realized that he had never been surer about anything. "Tess, I love you."

She stopped moving immediately, watching him with unblinking eyes that looked dangerously close to tears again.

"You don't, you know."

The words surprised him.

"I do love you. I think I did from the second I stumbled upstairs at Christmas last year. Ashland men don't fall in love easily and we don't fall out of it either. So get used to it." He added a teasing quality to his voice in the hope that she would lighten up.

But she was shaking her head. "It won't last."

When it seemed she would try again to get out of his bed, he rolled them over, letting his weight rest on his elbows as he traced her face and played with her hair spread across his pillows. The streak of silver in her otherwise black mane fascinated him, and he couldn't help but run his fingers through it.

"What about your son's mother? Didn't you love her?"

This was a hell of a conversation for the rising dawn – and that wasn't the only thing rising – when the beautiful woman he loved was hot and soft underneath him.

"No, I never loved her. We conceived Chris, and I needed to make sure he was cared for, so we married. I tried to make it work, and I think she did too. But we were grateful only for our son. And in the end, I was too much like my father to be the kind of husband she wanted." He hesitated, knowing that this didn't sound like a ringing endorsement to take a chance on a relationship.

"I'm not that man any more, Tess. That's why I had to leave Portland, why I had to escape that environment. Dane's been telling me that I isolate myself in my work, and I thought he was ridiculous. But I've come to see that he's been exactly right about it. I don't want to be isolated anymore."

He couldn't help himself, he had to kiss her. The touch of her lips alone was enough to keep him occupied for hours on end. When she put her arms around him and pulled him closer, he felt a small tug of victory. Tess finally broke their hold.

"I have – feelings – I guess that would be safe to say – for you."

He tried not to grin, and he flexed his hips to let her know how he was feeling at the moment.

One corner of her lips rose in a half-smile. "And I can tell what you're feeling."

He let his grin show now, and her own peeked out as well.

"This doesn't solve anything, you know." Her smile slipped and he kissed her, hard and fast. Trouble was back in her eyes, along with that painful resignation he didn't understand.

"Tess, I love you, believe that. I understand if you don't feel you can explain how you feel about me, yet. But I can be patient."

Okay, he could try to be patient.

She dropped her eyes, tracing lazing circles in his chest hairs and teasing his nipples until he was sure his body would explode.

"You can't change my mind."

He opened his mouth to argue, determined to have her believe him. His heart ached with the thought that perhaps she had feelings for someone else. That Wolford character? The jealous surge in his chest made it difficult to breathe. But he could change her mind. He could –

Her fingers came to rest on his open lips as she gave him a knowing smile.

"You can't change my mind, Powers, because I already know that I love you too."

Chapter 45

The coffee in her mug had grown tepid, ignored as she examined the metal in her hand. The condo key Powers insisted she take yesterday morning burned her fingers as she stroked it. Everything it symbolized meant the world to her, and soon that world would be destroyed.

"How about if I trim back this tree on the north side – like way back?"

She turned from contemplating the key and her coffee grounds to watch Powers round the side of the Victorian, his t-shirt sweaty and stuck to his body in a way that had her wishing she could drag him back inside to lick him from head to toe – again.

He took the mug from her hand, swigged the contents, and made a face.

"Your coffee got cold." Then he dropped a quick kiss on her mouth before moving to her small tool shed and disappearing inside.

It had been like this since yesterday morning, when she woke up from a satiated sleep that lasted long past her usual sunrise to find him watching her, a tender and delighted smile on his face. What he did with that smiling face after he kissed her had her heating up even hotter with the memory.

She didn't know what to make of it. He'd told her countless times now that he loved her. Her heart breached each time he said it, even though she knew that everything would change tomorrow. Once he knew her history, he'd be history.

There was no helping it, it hurt. She found the only man who made her feel like nothing was missing, and soon he would be gone. Of course, not gone completely, because she was sure that their shared extended family would require them to be together at points in the future. But by then he'd have moved on.

She never would.

Powers reappeared with a handsaw and heavy-duty loppers, and he cocked a questioning eyebrow at her. "So, is it okay with you if I prune the tree?"

She came back to reality with a start.

"I love that mimosa tree. The flower puffballs in the summer bring the hummingbirds, and in the winter, the seed pods sound like a babbling brook when the breeze hits them. Not to mention the shade – "

She stopped when he changed his stance to one of relaxed cockiness, one hip checked and a gloved hand on the other, the tools resting under his elbow. "I take it that's a no."

Smiling in return seemed like the only answer. She loved to see him like this, at ease and playful. He rarely seemed this carefree. This was a gift she could give him to remember their time together.

In fact, she loved everything about him. The way his thick hair with its brushy undercoat was currently standing on end was endearing. His insistence that she take the first of everything – coffee, bite of a meal, sip of wine – made her feel treasured. And when he pushed into her shower to share that with her, it turned into a contortionist adventure in the confined space.

"Seriously, much as I'd like to say it's not a problem, it is." His current shift to earnestness was yet another attractive quality. Damn the man.

"What's wrong with the tree?" She dropped her gardening gloves on the table when he wrapped an arm around her and starting walking her around the corner of the house.

"It's rubbing against the shingles. See the marks, there and there?" He pointed and frowned. "It's damaging the siding, and that means a risk of – "

"I know, you've already given me the lecture. Rot and insects and eventual water leaks. I get it. But I love this tree."

Actually, the tree was one of the reasons she'd fallen in love with the property in the first place. When she viewed the house for the first time, it had been in full bloom, an umbrella of yellow and pink flowers with bees and hummingbirds buzzing everywhere. It hadn't been as large then, and it was only in the past couple of years that she noticed it's natural shape was now reaching out to stroke the house.

He kissed her forehead, then returned to an examination of the tree. "How about this. How about if we compromise? I'll climb up into the tree and point to branches that I think need to be taken out, and you can stand down here and either agree or disagree. How does that sound?"

If he could compromise over the pruning of a tree, maybe there was hope for more understanding about the rest of it. She sure as hell didn't want to give him up. But it wasn't about her. Ultimately, he'd decide for himself. Unfortunately, she had first-hand experience with how that turned out.

The thought had her gripping his chin and bringing his face down to hers. When he laughed in surprise, she kissed him, hard. He dropped the tools and grabbed for her, pulling her close. They were both panting when he finally lifted his head.

"Deal", she whispered, and he chuckled. Her heart flipped again before settling in her throat. Pushing him towards the ladder, she turned and stepped away as if positioning herself to supervise. It gave her time to swipe at the tears falling from the corners of her eyes.

*****

"Nice to see you come up for air." DK's teasing tone made Tess wish she was the kind of woman to give a friend the finger. Wait, she was that kind of woman, and she lifted the appropriate digit in her friend's direction.

DK's belly laugh made Vince turn around out in the guys' makeshift ball field and miss the throw Deke arrowed at him.

"Safe!" Jake's bellow had Vince swearing, even as he smiled over at his woman, the undoubted glint in his eyes hidden by his shades.

"And now you're getting some of what you so rightly deserve. Oh Tess, I'm really happy for you." Serena looked so pleased, Tess didn't have the courage to deflate her happiness.

"We're just enjoying each other. There's no future in it, I'm certain."

In fact, Tess was trying to enjoy as much of today as she could. She wanted to tell her girlfriends that tomorrow, everything would change. They might not even recognize her based on the stories they'd undoubtedly hear. She hoped that the love they all had for each other was going to be enough so that she wouldn't lose them too.

"I for one am delighted that you have found someone to share your time with, my dear. You deserve it. Look, everyone has now found a partner, *non*?" Marguerite gestured to the women gathered around the pool as the men continued their noisy game out in the field.

"That just leaves you, Marguerite. Hhmmm, who should we bet on for you?" Gabby eyed the field speculatively, but since only three of the men out there weren't taken, there wasn't a lot to choose from.

"How about Deke? I think he's perfect for you." Tess sat up, then ducked back down into the relative safety of the chaise as she remembered how she was dressed. The bikini Powers convinced her was perfect for a day with their friends did little to hide her skin, and the cover-up felt shear on top of it.

"*Non, non, non!* I will never go out with that man. If you knew what he is saying I am guilty of – " Marguerite bit off the sentence as that man, along with all of the others, headed their direction.

Interesting. Tess enjoyed the momentary distraction from her own troubles to think about the implications. After all, she and Powers hadn't gotten along at the very beginning either. Nor had any of the other girl tribe members and their respective loves.

"I absolutely cannot frigging believe you cannot throw a damn baseball any better than you can throw darts. I mean, really Mac, who doesn't know how to play ball?" Vince grabbed a beer from the iced metal washtub, popped the top, and handed it to the offending player.

"I warned you, man. I always warn you. Why doesn't anyone ever believe me? I am not the physical type."

"That's because I say differently, honey, that's why." Roxy came out the French doors in time to grab Mac for a lusty kiss as everyone laughed. When she let him go, the world-famous movie star was blushing.

He wasn't the only good-looking man in the bunch. In fact, there wasn't a bad looking guy on the patio. Half of them had their shirts off already, and it appeared that almost everyone was ready for a dip in the pool.

Standing next to the table, Powers stared at her. Giving her a funny little smile, he reached for the edge of his t-shirt. When he lifted it over his head and tossed it at her, she caught it in surprise. When he stalked towards her with a huge smile on his face, she knew she was in trouble.

"If you'd like to keep that bit of nothing you call a shirt dry, you'd better lose it quick, sweetheart." Even as he whispered the words faintly, she was so focused on him that she caught every one. She pulled off the cover-up just in time for him to scoop her up off the lounger and stalk back towards the steps leading into the pool.

The catcalls and shrieks behind them were all good-natured and the ribbing they would undoubtedly get was going to be even more of the same. Tess didn't care. The feel of Powers against her, skin to skin in the cooler water, did nothing to chill her own heat. She was surprised the pool didn't sizzle and steam when they walked into it. And when his mouth locked on hers as he pulled her under, she worked hard not to laugh at the plunge of sensations.

"Wow, that was hot. Like a movie, eh?"

Tess heard agreement among their friends at Mac's statement, even as she kept her lips locked on Powers. When he finally let her go, his grin made her heart melt a little more.

"Yeah, pretty hot stuff, bro. I mean, who expected that you two would actually work out your differences enough to – "

Dane's words cut off when silence dropped over every member of the group. Tess thought maybe she'd let a little too much skin show, courtesy of the pool plunge, and grabbed for the bottom of her suit, then the top. But both were in place.

"Ah, wow. I didn't know you had ink." Dane picked up the thread of conversation, though the direction it headed in now was so different that it took Tess a moment to realize what everyone was staring at.

"It's nothing," she and Powers responded in unison, before giving each other an embarrassed look.

"Ah, Tess? It's not nothing. How long have you had that?" Serena moved forward on slow steps, as if creeping up on the eagle would keep her from scaring it off.

Tess felt herself color, realizing that Powers was watching her with exactly the same intense interest.

"I've had it for a while, since long before I met any of you, actually. Think of it as a rite of passage from long ago." And she hoped that would dismiss their scrutiny.

"Powers, I don't recall you ever saying anything about getting a tat. In fact, I'm not sure why I never noticed it before. Is this recent?" Dane crept forward almost as stealthily as his wife, only stopping when he reached the edge of the pool and crouched down for a better look at the wolf draping his brother's shoulder.

"No, it's not recent. It was something I felt I had to do at the time. What, do you have a problem with it?"

Tess detected the note of challenge in Powers' voice. The shift from hot lover to cold customer was so abrupt, the water should have frozen around them.

Pushing at the arms that still bound her, Tess felt Powers give way at the same time that a deep sigh escaped him.

The others were now gathering around the edge of the water, and rather than invite everyone in, Tess pulled Powers to the steps and out behind her. When they reached the top, they were passed from person to person to admire the artwork.

"You got the first wolf." Dane was smiling now, a full-on grin that minimized the brutal scar and made him look years younger.

She turned to catch Powers chuckling and wearing a sheepish grin.

"Yeah, I liked it so much that I wanted it with me always."

"What do you mean?" Roxy's question was accompanied by an almost reverent finger tracing the intricate pattern. Tess felt like she needed to slap the finger away – only a little.

Powers shuffled his bare feet and finally stood to his full height. When he did, the wolf rippled on his skin, and its intense eyes seemed to stare at each human surrounding it in turn.

"It was the first wolf photo that Dane sold for major bucks years ago. Dad didn't appreciate the work that went into that art. But I did. It called to me. I was so proud of it and of my brother that I decided I wanted it in ink." Powers grimaced in embarrassment at the silent attention surrounding him. When Dane suddenly grabbed him by the shoulders for a hard hug, everyone clapped.

"You don't know what that means to me, Powers. I knew you supported my work, but I never realized how much."

Tess felt tears welling up in her eyes as she noticed the moved expression Powers was trying so hard to hide.

"Ahem. And you, missy. When and where and why on that beautiful eagle?" Serena dragged a small patch of fabric on the bikini bottom down enough to see the rest of the eagle on Tess's hip.

She didn't want to talk about it. But she also knew that if she didn't say anything at all, it would be a continuing topic brought up in every possible discussion until her friends were satisfied with her answer.

"It's a Native American symbol, a remnant of my time in my tribe." That part was true.

"I never knew you did anything with the tribe or your family. You've been holding out on us." Roxy gave a mock stern look even as she smiled.

Tess shrugged, hoping to minimize the explanations as easily. "It was a long time ago, and it doesn't mean anything anymore."

Chapter 46

They pulled up to the Victorian, and Powers thought he could count on his fingers the number of words Tess uttered on the way back. She had been silent during dinner too, only responding when asked a direct question, and then answering quickly, as if eager to turn the attention away. A few times, he caught wistful misery on her features. When she noticed him watching her, she quickly shuttered the look and gave a smile that didn't reach her eyes.

As if they were silent by agreement, they each reached for bags and dishes and assorted odds and ends as they unloaded the car. It only took one trip between them, and soon, too soon in Powers' opinion, they were setting things down in the kitchen and on the hallway floor. Unspoken emotions rippled around them in air that felt increasingly thick, too dense to breathe normally.

Damn it, what was bothering her? The afternoon and evening had been relaxing, even with the abrupt shock of the group over their ink. It wasn't like they had covered their bodies with tribal art overnight. It was just – well, just two animal drawings. What was the big deal?

But he thought he understood, at least part of it. He never told his brother that he respected his work so much, he had it permanently etched into his skin. And she had never shared hers – either in the flesh or the thoughts behind it – with her best girlfriends. Clearly, they both had issues.

At least between the two of them, the secrecy needed to end – tonight. There were stories on both sides, things that needed to be shared. He didn't want another day to go by with something as monumental as this standing between them.

Once Powers made up his mind, he wanted to act on it immediately. He turned to reach for Tess, to pull her up the stairs to the intimacy of her bedroom, and explain all. And he wanted her to feel at ease enough to tell him whatever it was she hadn't been willing to say to her friends.

"Powers, no." She didn't struggle against his hand, but her feet were planted firmly even as she gazed at him imploringly. Her heavy breathing left him confused and agitated. He wanted to know why she didn't want to share the details, even with him.

Even though she loved him.

When she didn't move and didn't say anymore, he dropped the hand that had been clutching her upper arm. She took one slow step back, then another, putting up her hands as if to push him even further away. Then she turned and unlocked the back door, stepping out of sight on to the dark back porch.

No – to what? No to tonight? Or no to talking? Or no to them.

Anger spurted through him, chiding him for his sudden feeling of empty confusion. He thought he'd found the one woman who made his life complete. Instead, it seemed like all he had was more questions, and more uncertainty, and more distance.

Dropping the last bag to the kitchen tile made the unexpected clatter of metal and ceramic sound otherworldly loud in the confined space. She wasn't going to exit this easily, not the discussion, and not his life. His long legs ate up the short distance to the door and the width of the porch. He was going to make her talk, and they were going to have this out, once and for all.

But she wasn't on the porch. In fact, he couldn't see her at all in the dim glow of night. Flipping on the porch light did nothing to help, instead bathing the backyard in complete darkness outside the bulb's circle.

She'd disappeared, and he didn't know what the hell he was going to do about it.

*****

The espaliered apples provided a wall to hide behind, not that it was impenetrable. At least it would be difficult for Powers to see her out here. He sounded frustrated enough as he called her name, first softly, and then with more force.

Tess didn't want to end it. He was the one man who had come close to her heart. Of course, she thought she could trust before, but her destiny had frightened almost everyone off. Her family, rather than standing by her, had demanded that she embrace the hideous talent she was born with.

Even if it was painful and humiliating.

Tomorrow, it would all happen again. Short of running away from Flynn's Crossing, she didn't see a way out of it. If she was lucky, the worst that would happen would be name-calling. For others like her, there had been much worse.

"Tess, where the hell are you? Come back to the house. We need to talk."

The flare of a flashlight hit the other side of the apple trees and Tess resisted the urge to dart into the darkness as fast as her legs could carry her. There wasn't anywhere to hide. It was only running away.

"God, there you are. What's the matter? Come back inside. I promise I'll leave if that's what you want." Powers shifted the beam of light away from her face, half shaded by the tree limbs and verdant leaves. "Tess, please."

She longed to give in to the begging tone in his voice. She couldn't see his face, but she thought she could picture it. His confusion, his doubts, his desire. If she held on to one more night with him, it would help her hold her head up when he looked at her, aghast and disgusted, tomorrow.

Stepping out of the shadows took all her courage. Rather than pin her in the light, Powers shown it on his own face. Lit from below, it was primitive and savage and more than a little scary.

"I promise, Tess, that I won't do anything you don't want. We can just sit and talk." He hesitated, and confusion and sadness danced across his features to a rapid beat. "I want to understand what's wrong. I can help."

Dear man, trying to fix things even now. But there were some things that couldn't be fixed, no matter how hard anyone wanted to try.

Chapter 47

His hand fit over the eagle on her hip, covering it almost completely from wing tip to talon. He swore he could feel it beat at a tempo different from her heart. And there was a heat from it, a burning that scalded his skin even as he couldn't bring himself to move away.

Confused once more, Powers was at a loss about what he was supposed to do. Once he found her in the garden, he thought Tess would want to come inside, brew some of that herbal tea she was so fond of, and clear the air.

Instead, she'd wrapped her arms around his neck, knocking the flashlight to the garden's path, and kissed him like she never had before. Her taste was desperate, and inhaling the floral fragrance he'd come to think of as hers alone, he was assaulted by the myriad other smells of the night. She became one with the flowers of her garden, the damp earth beneath their feet, and the rich heaviness of the night air.

When she broke the kiss, her eyes hidden in the darkness, he wanted to ask her again what was wrong. But instead, she walked backwards for the house, pulling him along with her, only giving him a moment to capture the flashlight off the ground and shine it on the path to guide them. But she ignored it, sensing her way even in the pitch blackness.

Still silent, she led the way up the stairs and locked the private door behind them, pausing a moment to lean back against it and search his face. Whatever she was looking for, she seemed satisfied that she'd found it, because she pulled him into her bedroom and turned, beginning the slow process of stripping off her cover-up and her shorts.

He swallowed his tongue. She was always the most beautiful woman he'd ever seen, and when she uncovered herself for him like this, it was all he could do to keep from shedding his own layers in a rush and grabbing her to him. Instead, he matched her pace.

The seriousness never left her face. She didn't even smile when he tossed his shorts over his shoulder and they hooked on the ceiling fan. He swore she never even blinked those big golden eyes.

The heat of the eagle flared under his hand once more. Or maybe it was his overactive imagination, thinking about every position they'd taken each other in the past hours. Forcing him back against the wall, she all but climbed up his body, arms and legs like vices around him, as she rocked over him. He thought that the bed would collapse in their almost savage coupling after that. And then the peaceful and poignant last time, when her tears fell and he almost cried with her.

What was wrong with them? Hell, what was wrong with him?

Tess shifted her back against him. She didn't want to face him, but she wouldn't let his body stray across the big bed. Her breathing and the small twitches of muscle let him know she was still awake.

Sleep didn't seem to be a friend to either one of them tonight.

Smoothing the skin on her hip one last time, Powers lowered himself to the bed and tightened his arms around her. When she snuggled in and didn't fight him, he kissed her cheek and settled his lips near her ear.

"I want to tell you the real story behind my tattoo."

He felt her start at his intense whisper. Then she turned on her back and watched him warily. He couldn't shake the feeling that something was very wrong.

Sighing deeply, he moved so that he could hold on to her, cradling her body in his arms and throwing a leg over hers for good measure.

"Our mother died too young. She was the light of all of our lives. Sometimes I was jealous of Dane, because as the youngest, he seemed to get the bulk of her attention. Or Mandy, being a girl, got to do all of the girly things with Mom." He huffed out a snort of self-disgust. It was still hard not to be jealous.

"I spent most of my time with Dad. I'd go to the sites with him during vacations from school. Once I got older, I worked as a laborer, learning the business from the ground up. When I got even older, Dad would take me to the construction sites on the weekends and expect me to analyze what was going right, and what was going wrong. If I could guess how to fix a problem, he gave me some grudging praise."

"He doesn't sound like an easy man to live with." Tess stroked the hand that held tightly to her shoulder.

Powers laughed, thought there wasn't any real humor in it. "No, the only person who could get him to lighten up was Mom. She had a special way about her. We'd have these family grill fests on the weekends. Attendance was mandatory, unless you had a very good excuse. But Mom made them fun, and even Dad resembled a human being once she got him to relax. Those were perfect times."

He fought back the cloud of pain that still rose each time he thought about those times fading away, just as their mother's light had faded with the destruction of disease eating through her. But those damn barbeques continued, right up until the end.

"I wanted to please my father. I wanted him to tell me that he was proud of me and mean it." He fell silent, and Tess pushed off the bed to place her lips on his in a chaste kiss that held so much understanding, he felt the prick of tears again.

Settling back and curling closer into his arms, she asked, "What about your sister, Mandy? Serena says that Dane never talks about her."

He snorted, then stepped back to examine the memory. Maybe she was the sanest one of the family. "Mom died when I was eighteen. I'd finished high school and had worked hard enough to earn my partial scholarship for college. Rather than earning praise, Dad berated me for not making it a full ride, and just to prove his point, he made sure I would be paying the difference."

It hurt to peel away the layers of memories like this. He'd never told anyone the full story. Even others he had been close to from time to time only knew bits and pieces of it. In fact, he never discussed it completely with Dane.

There was something about this magic woman in his arms that helped him feel like he could become whole.

"After Mom died, Dad distanced himself emotionally from all of us. I never saw him cry for Mom, not once, not when we buried her or at the first Christmas or even on her birthday or their anniversary. He was always – stoic."

"So that's where you get it."

Startled, he pulled away from her, but her arms were now woven through his and she wouldn't allow him to move far.

He hated to think that he was still like his father by any stretch of the imagination. But Dane had called him on it more than once, and years ago, so had Mandy.

"You asked what happened to Mandy. The years between Mom's death and her graduation from high school were hell for her. Even I knew that, and I wasn't around that much. College and working to earn my way took all my time. I didn't stay in close contact with Dane either. Basically, I abandoned them and was grateful, I'm sorry to say, that I didn't have to live in that depressing and painful excuse of a home any longer."

"Of course you were grateful to escape. I don't think Dane blames you for that. The only complaint I've ever heard from him about his big brother is that you can't seem to stay out of his business." Her teasing tone took any sting out of her words.

Powers smiled ruefully. "Yeah, there's that. But you see, I wasn't there when they needed me. I was sorry about that, once I got older and could understand it. And once Dane was injured, all I wanted was for him to be able to be happy again."

Rubbing a hand over his heart, he thought about the abject fear of that phone call, the one from the Army chaplain telling him that as next of kin, he needed to know that Dane was in a military hospital in Germany, where initial surgeries were taking place. Once he was stable, they would transport him to Bethesda. He was entitled to every reasonable level of assistance, the disembodied voice had said. When the voice asked if Powers wanted someone to visit him for comfort, he'd almost laughed.

There hadn't been any comfort anyone could offer. He and his brother had drifted apart over the years, and he doubted this would suddenly bring them closer.

"Anyway, you know the rest, I suppose. I was only trying to help Dane when I meddled into his life here." Seeing Tess's teary smile, he kissed her once, hard, before adding, "And I like to think it had something to do with moving things along between him and Serena."

Tess chuckled too. "I believe it did, though Serena was pretty determined from the get-go." She grew serious again. "What about Mandy?"

He sighed again, cataloging that new source of friction with Dane.

"After Dane and Serena got together, and it looked like I was here in California for a while, I told Dane I wanted to find her. Mandy bore the brunt of it once I left for college. Dad was constantly angry. Dane knew how to crawl inside himself, but Mandy lashed out, blaming Dad for not getting Mom to a doctor earlier, testing his limits every day and turning into a wild child. If someone said it was bad for her or told her not to do it, it made her doubly determined to try whatever it was."

"Does she look like your mother?"

The question surprised him. He never thought about it, but now that he did, Amanda had been a young carbon copy of their mother. In fact, they used to tease her about it, and Mom had said it just showed what a beauty she would turn into one day.

When he told Tess this, she tsk-tsked him. "That makes perfect sense. She was a reminder to your father about what he lost."

Now why hadn't he ever figured this out?

"So Mandy left, I'm guessing?"

"Right out of high school. Graduated one day and gone the next. Dane and I hoped that she would come to her senses and return home. Or at least she would contact us and let us know she was all right. But in all these years, we haven't heard from her." He hesitated, before adding, "It's caused a rift between Dane and me. In fact, on some days, it's a chasm."

She stared at him, waiting for him to go on. When he didn't explain further, she turned her head and stared at the tattoo peeking over his shoulder. The ears of the wolf, it's intense gaze, and the drip of its fangs hung just in her view.

"And the tattoo?"

Shifting so that he could see it in the mirror over her bureau, he examined the lines and form closely. He hadn't looked at it, really looked at it, in some time.

"It was about the time Dane started to make a name for himself. Our father never approved of his profession. He didn't believe that it was a real job, and he certainly didn't believe it was something appropriate for one of his sons. In Dad's mind, the only thing that we are supposed to be doing is working in the family business, and helping him grow it larger. Of course, we don't have any freedom in how we wanted to do that. It's Dad's way or nothing."

Tess reached a finger up and smoothed his eyebrows. He didn't know why that felt so comforting, but it did.

"Dane worked in the construction business part time. Dad insisted he do it, so that he could learn what the old man described as a real trade. But Dane was always taking pictures. He went on this wilderness hike up in the Cascades, driving Dad crazy for the three weeks he was gone. When he came back, he was different. More centered, more intense, more driven. He quit the company. I guess he'd been saving his money, because when Dad asked what he would live on, he just laughed."

Lying down beside her, he pulled her closer. He couldn't see her face in this position, but he could feel her emotions.

"A few months later, Dane's picture of a wolf was featured in a travel journal, along with a story about his hike and other nature shots. The photos were so incredible, so lifelike and moving, that you swore you were there too. Dane made a name for himself in that first article. And I fell in love with the wolf." He paused, before adding sheepishly, "I enlarged the magazine print and framed it. It's in storage in Portland. I had it hanging in my living room there, and I got the tattoo as a tribute because it speaks to me."

He felt himself drift. Tess didn't ask anything of him, and for that, he was grateful.

"Dad never got my little brother, you know? He's got all of this creative energy and a huge heart. He's so unlike Dad. Mandy is too." He felt the tightness close his throat. "But me? I seem to be the most like him. And that scares the hell out of me."

Chapter 48

The heat of his body flared like the sun at her back. A heavy arm linked around her waist, and a large hand encircled her breast in casual possession. One leg was thrown across hers, as if even in sleep, he was afraid she would bolt.

She could wake up this way each morning, happy and grateful. But Tess knew that this too would soon be torn away from her.

He started to doze on his last admission in the wee hours of the morning. Powers' fear that he was too like his father to be of much use to anyone was palpable. And it explained so much. Like why he brushed off her comments about how natural he looked playing with Jeremy and Will. Or how he tried to keep his son Chris close.

For a man with a big heart, he gave very little care to himself. Luckily, he'd had no energy left to pursue his other line of questioning last night – the reason for her silence yesterday, the reason she ran from him when they came home, and the symbolism she read into their tattoos.

Her hair was trapped beneath his head, like she was the pillow he needed to rest. She smiled at the thought. Her body in tune to the rotation of the earth, she woke with the beginnings of daylight on the eastern horizon. It was time to get up, dress, and face the reality of the construction site.

She wanted him one more greedy time. Last night had been too perfect for words, and the memories would fill her heart until the day she died. She was hopelessly linked to Powers in every way imaginable, and there wouldn't be anyone else for her.

Pulling at her hair as she worked her legs free, Powers stirred and shifted to his back, keeping a hand on her belly as he did so. He protected her, even in sleep. Taking a moment to set this image of him in her mind, unhurried and relaxed, wouldn't hurt anyone, would it? She traced his features in repose with her eyes, following the curled hairs on his chest down to where they arrowed below the sheet to the wonder that he was below it. When she couldn't stand it any longer, she pressed a kiss above his heart, beating strong and true under her lips.

In her heart, she gave him the words one last time – I love you, Powers – and hoped that someday, he would look back on what would happen today and think of her kindly.

*****

He was racing fast through tall timber, seeking something in the sky, something that evaded his sharp eyes. The sun was bright, and it hid whatever he sought from his view. With a growl of frustration, he entered a meadow by a large river and stopped, scanning the blue expanse again.

The screech tore through him. It was troubled, in pain, and only he knew how to ease it. He didn't know why he knew this, but he did. He raced to the center of the clearing in time to see the bullet of a body diving towards the river. It would never survive the rushing torrents of water, even if it could withstand the crash.

At the last moment, it pulled up with a keen of pain. But it was too late. While it didn't crash, it was caught in the heavy curls of spring run-off toppling over boulders. The creature was pulled under, its cry of fright terrifying him into action.

He raced to the water's edge. It was stunning, cold and noisy and without rhyme as it tumbled and shattered in waves larger than him. But he needed to reach the injured one. It was his destiny.

Shuddering with the cold, he put a tentative foot in the water. Another cry, a scream this time, made him surge forward, even as his heart beat in his throat.

"Powers? Powers, you're having a dream."

A hand shook his shoulder. He wanted to stay in the dream, paralyzing as it was. He needed to save the creature. It was his purpose.

"Powers, you need to wake up now."

He shook himself clear of the weight of the dream, disappointed in some way. He thought it held something – important. There was a message, and he needed to understand it. But just as he wanted to hear it, he realized that it would change him forever.

Blinking rapidly to focus on something other than the metallic taste of fear in his mouth, Powers centered on Tess, standing in front of him completely dressed, make-up in perfect order and hair in a gentle curtain hanging along one side of her face. It was a face he could wake up to every morning for the rest of his life and never tire of it.

"Sorry. I'll get it together in a minute." He closed his eyes, which was a big mistake. The creature thrashed in the river's ferocity, its cries devastating to hear. He popped them open again, staring at Tess. It made him feel better, but like a failure at the same time.

Blinking harder this time, he zeroed in on her outfit. It was a dress, flowing down her body like a second skin to end at mid-calf. Intricate stitches rimmed the edges, and a pattern not unlike the sun covered the upper body. Her arms were bare, and she was holding out a mug of coffee to him as if in prayer.

She smiled at him, but it was a smile tinged with sadness. He wasn't sure what she was telling him.

"It's time to get up. We meet with the elders in less than an hour. And we don't want to keep them waiting."

She closed his unsteady fingers around the handle of the mug and leaned forward. The curtain of her hair brushed his cheek as she kissed him. Her lips were a sweet torment, and what he wanted – no, needed – most of all was to pull her back into bed with him and sink into her warm body until it wasn't clear where one of them ended and the other began.

Tess stepped back, but not before the silver streak from her temple folded around his cheek. It burned like he'd been branded, a pain he welcomed.

"We have time, don't we? Come back to bed, Tess." It was suddenly urgently important that he hold her, that she hold him, and that somehow, this would banish the unfinished business of his dream to a place where it couldn't hurt them.

She smiled, a small sad Mona Lisa smile that said everything and explained nothing, before taking a step back and turning, her flame orange skirt swishing around her as she walked out the door.

Chapter 49

What he'd come to think of as the whole gang had assembled at the construction site. Wolford fussed around Tess like she was a rare and precious jewel. Powers understood the sentiment, even if the actions made him wish he could wrap her up in his arms and carry her away from this circus.

The Chief arrived with a retinue of elders. Among the group, two old women, wizen to the point of being caricatures, talked behind their hands and stared with ill-disguised hostility at Tess. After an initial glance of alarm, Tess ignored them. Despite the flurry of people and activity around her, she seemed like she was alone on an island.

"I asked, Mr. Ashland, how long you can keep this site available for us to work on, once the ritual is completed?"

He'd missed something important, he realized with a frantic flash. Just as that passed through his brain, Tess's eyes met his. They stabbed at him, leaving him without a single coherent thought, except one.

It's time.

Except it wasn't his thought. It was hers.

"I am sure that we can come to a mutually satisfactory conclusion on this matter in the course of the next day." The Chief stood to the left, surrounded by other minions. To a man or woman, they were all dressed in elaborate outfits, the likes of which Powers had never seen except in programs about Native American rites. Come to think of it, it wasn't that different from the dress Tess wore today.

"But what will be accomplished from this ritual?" The professor rung his hands as he looked between them for answers.

"The peoples of the bones will be revealed, and once they are, we will know what needs to be done with them."

The Chief's words drew a fine blade of concern down Powers' spine. He felt it on every vertebrae. As if Tess felt it too, she shivered in her spot on the other side of the fenced area.

The coroner frowned. "I thought you would know who they belong to."

With an enigmatic smile, the Chief reclined his head in agreement. "As did I. But you see, there is no history of The Others here."

Suddenly eager, the professor leaned forward. "The Others?"

Nodding again, the Chief looked into a distance. "Not one of the tribes from this area. What you were able to show us through your test was that these bones do not belong to a race from the tribes who were settled in this area."

Powers felt the urge to speak, even though he immediately dreaded the impulse. He had the sensation of falling and knew that landing would be excruciatingly painful.

"Why are they called The Others?" His voice boomed, even to his ears.

The Chief turned to regard him thoughtfully. Instead of answering, he turned again, this time to stare at Tess. When she lifted her chin and stared back at him, a shadow of a smile tipped up one corner of his lined mouth. When his old eyes rested on Powers again, the other corner tipped up as well.

"They are not of our world. They are descendants from a tribe that was outcast. Few can interpret what they have to say."

A flurry of whispers rose like the wind from the minions, and they talked between themselves in harsh tones, casting furtive glances at Tess.

What the hell? He took two steps towards her before he realized that she was shaking her head at him, trying to turn him back.

"What kind of ritual are we talking about?" The professor rubbed his hands in glee, and his students typed madly into their cell phones, no doubt sharing the news about the awesome experience they were about to have.

He couldn't take his eyes off Tess. She seemed to glow with sudden power.

The Chief smiled now, somewhat ruefully as if the joke was on him. "It is not I who will perform the ritual. I do not have that ability. But someone else does, if that person is willing to use it." He stared into the distant trees and fell silent.

No one talked then, not the elders, who were to a person staring at their feet, and not the students, poised with fingers ready over their phones. The professor was perplexed, the coroner frowning, and outside the security fence, the silent crowd milled impatiently.

The sudden heat in his tattoo was the warning. From the day it had been completed, he thought of it as a talisman. Up until now, it was a sign that he could be closer to his brother. But now, he wondered if it meant something else completed.

"It is I who will commune with The Others."

Her voice was clear and determined. Powers felt Tess tremble, even across the space. The shiver of intensity raced along his nerves and settled in the pit of his stomach, a heavy cold stone of despair.

"And I will speak for them."

*****

She willed her knees not to shake, just as she forced steel into her voice to strengthen it. Keeping her eyes on the back of her father's head, she waited. For once, she wished that he would turn and look at her with approval on his face, but she doubted that would ever happen.

Tess didn't dare look at Powers. She felt every emotion running through him, anger and confusion and raging fear. The last had her puzzled. He had no idea what this meant to her, or to them.

The elders burst into loud whispers now, openly staring at her. She stood taller under their scrutiny. Some nodded sagely. Others were almost indecent in their mockery. They expected her to fail.

The Chief did not turn, nor did he acknowledge her words other than with a small nod of his head.

"And he will be your guardian."

Tess started at her father's words. The guardian was a sacred role, one she anticipated he would fulfill himself. But he was nodding towards Powers, even as he still stared into the trees.

"What do you mean by that?" Powers bristled as the words left his tight lips, their grim line a message in itself. He didn't believe.

The Chief turned to regard him thoughtfully. Tess wanted to intervene. It was not what she expected, and certainly not something Powers would agree to.

"When Daughter speaks to The Others, it is your responsibility to bring her back."

Tess caught Powers' gaze and shook her head slightly. He didn't want to be part of this, and she didn't want him to be privy to the upcoming activity. But he moved forward until he stood in front of her. His body shook with rage, and disgust blanketed his features.

It was as she expected. She was already turning away from him when he asked in a harsh undertone, "What is it you have to do?"

Chapter 50

"As the legend has it, the eagle flies far and wide, gathering wisdom and knowledge, and brings back sources of enlightenment." The Chief's voice took on the singsong quality of a storyteller.

Powers had to force himself to stand still to listen. The disrespect the old man showed to his own daughter was completely unacceptable, but that didn't mean that he could let his rage storm out either. Even now, Tess stood apart from everyone else with her back turned.

"When the eagle seeks vision, it flies to the sun to gather light, to reinforce its powers and its magic." The Chief now stared at Powers frankly. "Its guardian, a wolf of great strength and cunning, follows it from the earth, and when the eagle falls from the sky, paralyzed by what it has seen, the wolf retrieves it and brings it back to the elders so that its message can be heard."

The symbolism was too real. Did the old man know about their markings, about the totems each of them had chosen?

"Leave him out of this." Tess's harsh voice pulled everyone's attention. Powers caught the vicious expression that accompanied her declaration.

The Chief inclined his head to indicate he'd heard her, but he didn't bother to turn. "Daughter, you have chosen, and he has chosen. It is destined to be."

Silence fell, and in it, Powers sensed her barely controlled fury. Her hands opened and closed at her sides, her unadorned nails digging into her palms. If her eyes had been lasers, the Chief would have disappeared in a cloud of ash and flames.

"Then tell him the rest of the fable, so that he can choose with full knowledge."

A chill of apprehension clutched him by the throat.

Inclining his head again, the Chief turned to pin Powers in his ancient gaze and continued. "The eagle and the wolf each mate for life. It is said that they are fated to be together, even at the price of turning their backs on their own species."

The old man stopped and everyone waited once more. When he folded his hands in front of him and bowed his head, Tess huffed out a screech of frustration.

"It is the wolf's job to protect the eagle on its vision quests. Once it soars and is filled with wisdom, the eagle cannot see, as its eyes have been burned of bad spirits by looking at the sun. If the wolf does not guide it home, it is fated to roam the skies for eternity, unseeing. And the wolf will return to its lonely journey across the planet, left without purpose."

Tess's voice fell to a whisper on her final sentence. When she met his eyes, Powers felt her icy desolation. She watched him carefully, and when he did not respond, she shook her head sadly.

"This has no meaning, Father. I will enter the underworld and talk to the bones of the ancestors. Once I learn why they are here and what they wish, I will return and tell you. But as to the rest, leave Powers out of this."

*****

"What do you mean she has to do some kind of voodoo?"

Dane's tight grip anchored Powers in place when he would have stomped off.

"I told you everything I know. Tess isn't discussing this with me. I'm glad that you brought Serena and the others. Maybe they can talk some sense into her."

They turned together to watch the tight clutch of women, Tess in its center. There was a lot of gesturing and an argument in process. Finally, Tess threw up her hands in dismissal and stormed away from the group in a sentiment foreign to her nature.

Shaking off his brother's restraining hand, Powers marched after her. Dane followed on his heels, still trying to calm him.

"Rituals and rites are important in many cultures. It sounds like that is what's happening here. There is a ceremony that needs to happen before the bones can be moved to an appropriate resting place."

Their longer legs ate up the distance to Tess as she all but ran down the street, the flame-colored dress fluttering around her. Serena and the other women trailed in their wake. Powers expected Tess to climb the steps to the Victorian's front door, but she turned instead and banged through the garden gate, disappearing around the back of the house.

"Tess, damn it, wait." Powers banged the gate open mere seconds behind her, leaving Dane to play the part of polite gentleman and hold it open for the women behind them.

Rounding the corner, he saw the flash of orange now making its way through the rows of flowers at a midpoint in the garden. It stopped suddenly, and Powers knew that at last, he was going to get a chance to be face to face with her.

"Don't, Powers."

She was turned away from him, but her voice carried on bleak notes as he approached.

He had to touch her. Even if he didn't believe in the power of legends or destiny, he had to hold her.

When he closed a hand on her bare skin, the heat scorched him. It flashed through him, nearly knocking him off his feet. Turning her towards him, her golden eyes were blazing when they locked on his.

"Don't what? Don't tell you that this is just a ploy, some kind of game to delay things longer? Or that the supernatural mumbo-jumbo is only that, nonsense? Or that I wish like hell that you'd thought to clue me in on your special talents before I found myself bound to you?"

She recoiled at his last words.

He watched the delicate workings of her throat as she swallowed before opening her mouth to reply. "You aren't bound to me. I release you, Powers, from whatever hold you believe I have over you."

Funny, but her words didn't make him feel any better. He dropped her arm, severing even that connection. The more intimate one, the one that let him share her feelings, still tied them.

"What kind of show, exactly, are you expected to perform?"

*****

He didn't believe in her, that part was obvious. Worse yet, he ridiculed her special gift, the one she swore she would never practice again. But if she did nothing, the voices would stay in her head and their urgency would only become more pronounced.

"It isn't a show. This is a Native American ritual of passage, talking to the spirits of the ancestors to determine what action needs to take place in the present. In this case, it means talking to the spirits that belong to the bones to ask what occurred and where their final resting place should be."

Powers snorted and shook his head in derision. "What are you, a witch doctor? Or just a witch?"

That hurt, with more pain than she believed she was capable of feeling. Pulling herself up to her full height, she stared back at him defiantly, unwilling to let him see how much his words destroyed her.

"I am a spiritual healer." She waited to see what he would torture her with next.

He shook his head, digging at the dirt with the toe of his work boot and examining the ground. "Have you done this kind of thing before?"

"Yes." Of course, he didn't need to know that it had been decades since the first time, in high school, when it turned her into the laughing stock of the school. Her father had taken this as a sign that she should return to the old tribal ways, when all she wanted to do was be normal. Years later, a decade ago, another ceremony that brought the ridicule of her peers cemented her resolve and turned her away from healing. And with that, her family shunned her.

"Damn it, Tess, I don't believe in this magic stuff."

Her gaze riveted on him as she felt him withdrawing. But he wasn't looking at her. He glanced up to the sky at a dense wave of clouds on the horizon. Dropping his eyes, he flicked his wrist to look at his watch. Finally, his eyes fell on her.

They pierced her heart, already bleeding from his disbelief. His face lacked expression when he asked, "When will you do your voodoo?"

Shrugging off his ridicule, she turned away so that he couldn't take any satisfaction in her pain.

"Tonight, at sunset."

Chapter 51

He couldn't bring himself to stay away. He wanted to, because of the knowing smile on the Chief's face. But in the end, she drew him with her like he was the root to her flower. Cutting that tie would mean that they would both die.

"This is some serous shit, man," Vince said, shaking his head in disbelief. "I've seen these kinds of rituals before. The person goes into a trance, and there's a lot of scary words and drumming, and they don't look like themselves. It's like they're possessed."

Dane nodded in agreement, settling the camera more comfortably in his hand. "I photographed one and it was a shock to see the change. The before shot of what they looked like, and the during. Even the after was different. That healer said that every trance changed him, and not always for the better."

No wonder Tess hadn't told him about this.

The sun was minutes from dropping below the horizon, and still he was frozen in place. Tess stood at the edge of the bones, dressed as she had been earlier in that flame-sun dress, holding a feather in one hand and clutching a large rattle in the other. Everyone maintained a distance around her, alone and silent with a forlorn stoop to her shoulders.

Frankly, he was terrified.

"I want to help you," he'd whispered urgently, as she walked through the security fence a short time ago. Despite his misgivings, he loved her. And the more he learned about what was about to happen, the more frightened he became for her.

"Please, no, Powers. This is going to be a spectacle, and you won't want to see it. Leave now, please." And she passed him by.

"It is time." The Chief nodded to a circle of drummers, and as Tess began to shake the rattle, they picked up a slow and steady rhythm. She turned in a small circle, finally coming to a stop when she faced him.

Her face was solemn and anything but serene. He could feel a range of emotions coursing through her, even at this distance. Her eyes rested on his for a moment, and he thought she mouthed the words 'I'm sorry' before she closed her eyes.

Dane and Vince maintained a running commentary in low voices, but he tuned them out. His whole being focused on the woman across the cleared space. She was chanting now, swaying slightly as she increased the pace of the rattle and the drummers matched it. They too were chanting, and the Chief stood with his eyes closed, mouthing the words.

Powers felt her inside his heart. She was soaring, unable to help herself, pulled towards bright light and kinetic heat. He found his eyes drifting shut, and he thought he could understand the words she was saying, even though he didn't speak the language.

He heard his friends suck air and fall silent behind him. Forcing his eyes open, he sought out Tess, and found that she'd knelt next to the bones, the rattle now silent and her graceful sway no longer in motion. But he realized what had stunned the others.

It was her expression. Her eyes were open, but she didn't appear to see what was in front of her. Their golden color glowed, intensity and predation in her gaze. Her hands extended in front of her and her fingers curled, like the talons of her totem. Even her voice changed, becoming a quiet screech as she held what appeared to be a one-sided conversation.

His shoulder burned, his tattoo feeling like fresh ink as the needle applied it. Dropping his eyes closed again, he felt her presence inside his head. And with it, he heard The Others.

*****

Tess knew what the trance would feel like and had prepared herself for that sensation of being in two worlds at once. She felt the press of the crowd outside the security fence, heard their shocked silence, and could even smell the dirt beneath her knees. But she wasn't present herself.

Instead, she was with The Others. And they were speaking to her.

"We were taken as spoils of war," said one ancestor. "We were taken from our home by the big water and brought here to serve the masters."

"Who took you?"

Another ancestor brushed Tess's question aside. "It matters to no one. We were taken, and when our work each day was done, we were forced here, to the edge of the river. They put us in cages and locked us in each evening, only releasing us at dawn to work once more."

"What is your tribe?" Dimly aware that the drumbeats were fading, Tess felt an urgency to get this over with.

"We are of the tribe of big water. Our name has no meaning to you."

It was like guessing what should come next in a string of riddles, and she was getting a little impatient.

On that wave of emotion, she felt him. Even standing a distance from her, his solid presence brought heat to the mark on her hip. With him there, she had the courage to begin the free fall.

"What is it you desire to be at peace?"

The ancestors were silent for a moment. Finally, a young soul spoke.

"We were made to die here. When the waters of the river rose in the great storm, the masters abandoned the village and left us in our cages to drown. Our bones lie where we fell. It is not our way."

Tess felt the pull of gravity speeding her to a nasty landing. Riddles, more riddles.

"What is your way?"

An old soul brushed across her psyche, his restless spirit blocking her path. "We are meant to transform into the fish of the seas, bountiful and abundant. Our bones must sail on the big water. That is the peace that we seek."

Tess felt the earth rushing up towards her, but she could no longer see it. Her perception reduced to a pinpoint of sensation and the air rushing by as she fell. Just at she thought she would hit and burst into a thousand pieces, she felt a bite close on her neck and pull her up.

Then everything went black.

*****

"They were slaves."

"Slaves? What are you talking about?"

Dane's voice was in his ear, and he opened his eyes to focus on Tess, swaying again in a more agitated fashion than before. Alarm was on her face, and even the Chief looked concerned. Resounding drums echoed off the surrounding buildings, matching the rapid beat of his pounding heart.

"Where did you get the idea about slaves?" Vince's question from behind him was perplexed.

Powers opened his mouth to explain, then realized that whatever he said was going to sound stupid. Tess was speaking in a language none of them could understand. But he heard each of her questions and the replies as clearly as if he stood in the middle of the discussion.

He couldn't take his eyes off Tess. Her alarm had changed to fear. Taking three strides forward, he almost reached her side when she gave a cry of horror and passed out.

He wasn't sure how he caught her before she fell into the bones. He cradled her, willing her eyes to open and her breathing to slow.

"Tess, honey, wake up. You're safe. It's Powers. You're safe."

He rocked her gently in his arms and felt some relief when the terror left her face, even as her pants of agitation continued. Her eyes remained closed as the drummers broke off.

The abrupt silence shocked him into action. Lofting her slight frame in his arms, he backed away from the bones before turning.

The Chief walked forward. "You may leave her here, with us. Once she wakes, we will discuss what she has learned."

He couldn't believe it. The man had no regard for his daughter. Wasn't he concerned that she fainted?

"I'm taking her home."

"We must learn what she knows. She does not need to be coddled."

Turning to face the old man, Powers felt his rage rise. Biting back words that would only make the situation worse, he shared instead what he had heard.

"They were slaves, kidnapped to work the land for their masters. They came from a tribe that lived on the coast, I'm assuming the Pacific. And they want to be buried at sea."

No one around them said a single word. The Chief looked shocked.

"You know this how?"

"I heard every word she said, and what they replied. So you have your answers."

"You understood their language?" This question hit his back as he strode to the gate in the fence.

Dane and Vince were already parting the crowd, Serena, DK and the other women pushing ahead of them. Everyone was silent, and Powers saw a couple of people cross themselves as if to ward off evil.

He cursed their narrow-mindedness silently before bringing his thoughts up short. He hadn't been any better than them, up until he'd followed the lilt of Tess's voice in his head and the shadowy replies of the ancestors. If he hadn't experienced it himself, he might not have believed it either.

Chapter 52

She felt like she was floating, the gentle rocking movement at odds with the rapid beat under her cheek. Voices murmured around her. Exhaustion made thinking impossible.

"She's waking up," a woman's voice said.

"Tess, honey, come back to me. Come on, open your eyes."

The rocking motion stopped. The urgency in the voice communicated itself to her. She knew the voice.

Powers.

Forcing her eyes open took an effort, but when she did, she was rewarded by his worried face only inches away. When he leaned down to kiss her, a shiver ran through her.

"Welcome back."

She blinked again, trying to focus. His mouth was tense, a slash across skin paled to gray.

He was carrying her down the street. Her friends were around them and they were heading some place with great purpose.

Home. That's right. Home.

"You can put me down, I can walk." She struggled, but his arms only tightened around her.

"You don't weigh anything. You've been through an ordeal. I'm carrying you, end of discussion." The declaration brought color back to his face.

He climbed the steps, the same ones he'd rebuilt for her, and she realized that the rest of the group hung back.

"Please, come in. That is, if you want to. I know that seeing something like this," she waved back in the direction they'd come from, "can be scary."

Serena surged forward, followed by DK and Gabby. Dane already had the front door open and was inside, turning on lights, while Vince held it for Powers and the rest.

"Forget scary. That was terrifying to see. How can you do that?" DK's short hair was standing on end, like she had the fright of her life.

"How are you feeling, sweetie? Can I make you some tea?" Serena bustled towards the kitchen.

"Forget tea. Do you have anything stronger in the house?" Vince disappeared down the hallway with Gabby and Dane in tow.

Tess shifted, waiting for the wariness to leave Powers' face.

"You can put me down now. I'm fine." Nerves jumped in every cell of her body. "Besides, I have to go back and tell them what I learned."

A peculiar expression crossed his face. "That can wait. You need to rest." And he started up the stairs, holding her as easily as carrying a child.

*****

"Not the bed. If you take me to the back porch, I agree to stay down for a little while."

Her request was delivered in a small voice, edged with exhaustion and loaded with sadness. The quiet 'please' she added as an afterthought made him pause and look down at her. But she was intent on the collar of his shirt, toying with the ends and unwilling to meet his gaze.

Relief that she opened her eyes and didn't look any worse for the experience warred with confusion about how he could link his mind with hers so easily. He only wanted her to feel safe and secure with friends fussing around her. Once she was settled, he could make his escape and find a quiet corner to contemplate what happened.

Heading through the hallway to the kitchen meant that they ran the gauntlet of their friends, clustered around the kitchen counter as they poured drinks of varying potency. Conversation stopped when they walked in. Even Dane stopped fiddling with his camera long enough to give them a curious look. When no one said anything, Powers felt Tess fidget, pushing against his arms. He got the message, letting her legs slide down his until her feet touched the floor.

"You have to see these pictures. They are frickin' amazing." Vince took a long draw from his glass of amber liquid.

"You took pictures?" Tess sounded decidedly put out as she leaned around Powers to glare at Dane. "That was a sacred ceremony."

Dane raised a hand to stop her. "I only took pictures of your face, not of anything else. I suspect you've never seen yourself when you're doing one of these. Oh, and I took pictures of Powers too."

That was more than he wanted to hear, and it halted his subtle retreat for the door. He hadn't figured out how he felt about things yet. If he didn't believe that Tess had special powers, how the hell could he understand the foreign words that were spoken? And how could he hear what was going on in her mind?

"Why did he take pictures of you?" Tess turned her glare on him now.

"I don't want to discuss it. I have to go."

Hitting the hallway fast, he took the coward's way out. He heard the exclamations behind him, and Tess called him back. But he needed to get out of there before his head exploded from the irrational thoughts flowing through it.

Chapter 53

Tess sat back on her work stool, admiring the combination of flowers that graced the ornate vase in front of her. Things were blessedly quiet. Even the voices of the ancestors no longer haunted her. But it brought her no peace.

One other voice that she would like to hear remained quiet as well. In the three days since Powers made his quick exit, he hadn't called, hadn't returned her messages, and hadn't visited the job site. In fact, he had one of his anonymous engineers there instead, providing support to the archeologist and his students as they removed the bones with painstaking attention to detail.

In the end, it was Dane who explained what happened, even as he showed her the pictures he'd taken. The metamorphosis of her face during the trance did look like a possession. She definitely didn't look like herself.

But it was Powers who staggered her. His face was eerie, with a barely contained savage scowl, his eyes closed and his lips moving. Dane told her that his brother chanted right along with her, though there was no way he would know the words. And then the big shocker.

"He understood what you were saying, what they were saying – the ancestors. He told the Chief and the others while you were still out cold."

"But how could he understand that? Even if he somehow figured out what I was saying, he couldn't hear their replies." She bit her lip, sudden realization coming to her.

Dane eyed her shrewdly. "He linked to you in some way."

Shaking her head, she thought back to their strange connection, reminded of the many times it seemed that he could read her mind, and she knew his.

Tracing the petals on a dahlia, she realized that this was why he no longer wanted anything to do with her. She was cursed, and being together would only remind him that he was doomed too.

The tinkle of the flute music signaled an arrival, and her heart leaped into a faster staccato in hope. But the man who entered was the last person she expected to see. Recovering her tongue and her manners took long moments, enough time for him to stare at her before nodding once and turning to examine the contents of the flower shop.

She stood, but was unable to move further. The fragrances of flowers that had been pleasant moments before were now stifling. Old sadness mixed with new disappointment moving through her.

"Father." She wasn't sure what she wanted to say next. Before this week, she hadn't seen him in over ten years. For him to appear here now was nothing short of an omen, and she wasn't sure she wanted to know what it portended.

He strolled the front area of the shop, stopping by pillars and pedestals, pausing to examine an old wood birdcage from different vantages, and sniffing a bouquet of roses in a wildly colored ceramic vase gracing a table. In everyday clothes, she could almost forget that he wielded such power over their tribe. He had served as its leader since she was a girl, and yet today, he seemed older, more fragile, and less sure of himself.

"You have done well, Daughter. I hear wonderful things about your business."

He stood on the opposite side of her worktable, eyes not on her but on the display she just finished creating. Nodding as if he approved, he finally looked into her face.

"And you have grown even more beautiful."

She didn't know how to respond to that.

"Thank you, Father. And you're well?"

He shrugged, indicating with the seesawing of his hand that things were so-so. When he cleared his throat, she braced herself.

"I've brought you something, a peace offering." The hand behind his back appeared, and in it, a Brew Bank Bakery bag hung, loaded to the top.

The Chief had the grace to look sheepish. "The men at the shop said these are your favorites."

*****

"So you see, there was always a risk that we would learn nothing from the bones, other than confirming through DNA that they were Native American in origin. What you did solved many problems. Now the ancestors can return to the final resting place they deserve."

They sat on her patio, the midday sun making her gardens seem over-bright when compared to the shade of the trellis and vines overhead. She had accepted his gift in the same spirit in which it was offered, a quest for peace. When she made them both tea and they settled into the padded wicker chairs, he explained the complexity of moving ancient burials when there was no information about their source.

"I am happy I could help, Father."

He watched her carefully, looking every single one of his seventy-odd years even if he still held his head proudly with a regal carriage that looked immortal.

"You have a wonderful gift, you know. I wish that you would use it more often."

This had always been the source of their friction. He wanted her to exercise her talent at every opportunity. She would only do so under duress.

Rather than answer him and ruin their fragile peace, she sipped from her mug, letting her eyes rove over the lush contours of her plants. In the quiet, she heard him sigh.

"At least embrace your destiny when it comes to your man."

Tess was shocked. The last thing she expected to hear from her old-ways father was advice on her love life.

"If you mean Powers, he's no longer in the picture." She licked her finger and gathered crumbs of her pastry on the tips, taking great care to get ever single tiny piece. When her father didn't respond, she glanced up to find him watching her gravely, even as a hint of mischief danced in his eyes.

"He is the one, you know. I can see it in the way he looks at you, in the way you look at him. More than this, however, he completes your gift. He is the one who guards you when you cannot guard yourself. He would not have been able to speak for you if that was not true."

She thought of the countless times in the past months when Powers was the only one who could banish the voices and bring her peace.

"He doesn't believe in our ways. He must make his own choices." Her throat tightened on the words and she blinked rapidly, hoping to stave off the tears that threatened.

Her father stood and crossed the patio, bending over to kiss her on the forehead, at the base of the silver streak that had marked her as gifted from her birth. "He will choose well and wisely, I have no doubt." He paused, his expression fond. "He will choose love."

She blinked in surprise.

Straightening again, he moved at a dignified shuffle to the edge of the sunshine. He stopped, surveying the gardens and again nodding his approval, a smile on his face as he turned to her.

"Your mother would like to see you. Your sister and your brothers as well, and all of their children, and your cousins and aunts and uncles. I would like to see you again in our family home. Think about it, if you would. We still have Sunday supper at midday each week. You are welcome, as is your young man."

The constriction in her throat became a vice grip of emotions. He gave her one last smile and walked away, his hands grasped behind his back as he raised his creased face to the sun.

Chapter 54

The setting sun shone on the rivers, reflecting their pristine beauty even as boats and jet skis cut across their surfaces. Birds flew, flocked and settled in the tall trees of the city. On the streets, the bustle of early evening dates, people linking arms and laughing as they made their way between the bars and restaurants and entertainment, began to pick up.

The vodka did nothing to warm him as he sipped it, watching the vignettes of activity on the streets below. Everyone seemed to have someplace to be, and someone to be with. Everyone fit in, except him.

Ever since the ceremony on Monday, since he could no longer deny the fact that his attachment to Tess was more than a simple love affair, he'd felt destroyed. What hurt worse was Tess's silence. Since he escaped from her home after ensuring she was safe, nothing.

She had given up on him, on them. And she was the better off for it, he knew. This way, she could heal and find someone who could give her the love and attention and belief she deserved.

He would only hurt her, losing himself in his work and isolating her like his father treated his mother. Even if she could tease a smile out of him, eventually she'd tire of working so hard to make him happy.

And there was the link, that otherworldly connection the two of them had. It couldn't be healthy to be that in tune with another person. What if something happened to him? How would she survive it if they were so close?

How would he survive it with the tables turned, knowing that only she breathed life into his dull and boring routine? He was a coward, too afraid to risk exposing himself to her rejection. Besides, he hadn't had faith in her when she needed him most.

The next sip of his drink emptied the glass. Powers studied the pile of paperwork covering the dining room table. He'd been ignoring things quite a bit lately, hypnotized by the spell that was Tess as he delegated major decisions to his managers. Not that they minded, and not that they had done anything wrong. But it was his company.

Pouring another shot was a fine idea, considering that he couldn't concentrate. What was she doing right now. Was she surrounded by her friends? Or maybe she was out on a date with that Wolford character. The idea brought a bitter taste to his tongue.

Lost in his musings, he jumped when the buzzer sounded on his door. Not the chime for the door in the lobby, but the one on his penthouse door. When a knock followed the buzzer, he frowned at it, tempted to yank the door open to see who was this persistent. But a key turned in the lock, and he went rigid.

He could catalog on one hand the people who had a key to his place. And he didn't want to see either one of them.

*****

His car was in its slot in the garage, so if he wasn't answering the door, he must have gone out for a walk or down to the gym. That was how she rationalized letting herself in. She would wait for him.

When the door swung open to reveal rooms bathed in lights, she froze. The door continued its inward swing, and she stood in the hallway, bent with her hand out after turning the key, her other arm loaded with take-out bags.

The snarl of frustration was familiar, even as her eyes landed on Powers standing across the living room. His puzzled grimace changed to a frown as his eyes narrowed.

"What are you doing here?"

His voice held that same growl, the deep timbre making her bones vibrate, though what she felt wasn't fear. The longing to walk into his arms and wrap herself around him was so strong, she puffed out a pant instead.

Putting steel in her spine, she straightened and gestured with the bags. "I brought us dinner." Pausing for a response that didn't come, she added, "I thought we could talk."

He slammed a glass on a side table hard enough to have the clear liquid splash on the polished surface. When he prowled towards her, she made herself stand still, even as her senses shrieked that she wanted to meet him halfway.

Grabbing her free hand, he yanked her inside the penthouse and slammed the door behind her. He extended his hand, palm up.

"The key, please."

Her heart cracked at that. The key was a symbol. She shouldn't be shocked that he no longer wanted her to have it.

Tossing her head to fling her loose hair over her shoulders, she dropped it into his waiting hand. "You'll probably want to change your garage code too, so that I can't stalk you there either."

She brushed past him, ignoring the beauty of dusk falling outside his windows, and headed for the dining room. There was no room for food, so she turned back to the living room's low glass table and dropped the containers there.

The room was quiet. The only sounds were her own hissing breath and his harsh pants of air behind her. His silent strides could bring him to her side without any hurry.

"I brought Thai. I can leave it if you prefer. I know you don't want to see me." She stared out at the spot on the distant horizon where the sun sunk behind the intercoastal mountains.

His sudden sigh conveyed a variety of emotions, confused frustration predominant in the mix. "It's not that."

The words halted her as she glided towards the door. She turned to look at him.

The pull of impossible attraction was there, as was the feeling that he was part of her destiny. Without him, she would survive, but it would be an incomplete and haunted life.

Running a hand through his already tousled hair, he huffed out another sigh and gestured to the bags on the coffee table.

"Would you please stay for dinner?"

*****

Her face haunted his dreams and every waking minute. Seeing her in the flesh only added to his misery. The agony of needing to touch her only added to his uncertainty.

He didn't deserve her. He loved her, but he hadn't believe in her magic. But then how could he explain understanding the ancestors' voices?

To give his hands something to do, something other than grabbing her and hauling her curves up against his body, he rustled through the kitchen, finding plates and silverware and napkins. When he turned back to the living room, she had returned to her contemplation of the horizon, turning east this time. Over her shoulder, he could see a rising moon, full to the point of bursting.

She turned as he clattered everything to the glass, and her face in profile was outlined by that moon. The primitive picture she painted burned into his mind in a second, and with it, he felt every last barrier drop.

Whatever she was selling, he'd buy it. If she really believed they were meant to be together, he'd agree. Anything to keep her in his life.

"I never thanked you." Her quiet words startled him out of his thoughts.

"For what?" Since she didn't seem inclined to move, he joined her at the window, staring down into her face as she examined the sky.

"For telling the elders what they needed to know when I couldn't. That was very – brave of you."

Her hesitation on the word surprised him even more.

"Brave?" He nearly choked on the word. "I couldn't seem to stop myself. It was only later that I realized how impossible it was."

Turning towards him at last, she spread her arms to encompass the room, the view, and it seemed, the universe. He was reminded of the spread wings of the eagle on her hip, the proud tilt of her chin a memory of its nature, and her knowing eyes holding so many promises.

She smiled, a small movement that tipped the corners of her lips up only a fraction. "You see? Brave." She put out a hand to him, her smile now full of love. "Fly with me, Powers."

His heart cracked open on her words. Slowly, he returned the smile, the first real joy he'd felt in days. If this was his destiny, he'd take it, and gladly. When she soared, he'd be ready to catch her.

Sliding unsteady fingers into hers, he pulled her closer. His hand broke free to trace the silver streak in her hair, finally cupping her cheek. When she lifted her face, he dropped his head and said against her lips, "My destiny."

Epilogue

"It's too bad you can't twitch your nose or something and get all of this dirty work out of the way." DK dropped a broken wooden shingle to the growing pile on the ground.

Tess sighed. Her friends had taken her admission of her spiritual healing powers remarkably well, all things considering. No one ran screaming and no one disowned her. It didn't seem to be doing her flower business any harm either.

"It doesn't work like that, I already told you." But she smiled to take any bite out of the words.

"But you have to admit, that would be cool. Hhmmm, maybe there's a character idea in this." Gabby nearly fell off her perch on the neighboring ladder as she concentrated on that thought.

Behind them, Tess heard the men laugh.

"Hey, I don't see any of you up here laboring away. What gives?" She focused on Powers, standing with an arm around his brother's shoulders. Dane was staring with fixed attention at his wife Serena's backside a few feet away.

"Careful, you get too much of an eyeful and those peepers might just pop out of your head." Serena laughed with the delivery, and winked at Tess.

So normal. Even Powers seemed to be taking everything in stride.

After the night she'd let herself into his condo, they'd talked for hours, made love for hours more, and spent all of Sunday and most of Monday curled up together.

He still didn't understand how their whole linking thing worked. Frankly, neither did she. But she'd been raised to believe in things that couldn't always be explained. Powers, being Powers, wanted to understand everything in detail.

She squeaked when strong arms wrapped around her from behind and lifted her off the ladder. Tucking her into his arms, he carried her a distance away from the crowd. When he turned back to the house, he kept her locked in his embrace.

"Put me down. People will see." Not that she really minded.

"Oh all right. But I want you to stand here and look at the house for a minute." He paused, as if suddenly unsure. "I have a proposition for you."

Nerves raced along her spine. "Powers, we talked about this. Now is not the time. We're too new to – "

He stopped her with a finger across her lips, smiling. "I agree. But I have a different idea, if you'd like to hear it."

She nodded, though his words did nothing to ease her concern.

Turning her towards the house, he pulled her back against him and wrapped his long arms around her, much as he had that night at the fireworks. She snuggled closer, calmed by his presence and knowing that whatever he had to tell her, it would be okay.

"What do you say to moving your shop to the new building?" When she gasped, he tightened his arms. "Hear me out. The first floor is perfect for it. It has lots of light, great display space, and terrific parking. And I would move my own office to one of the suites on the second floor, so we'd be close together at work."

She opened her mouth to protest, but suddenly she couldn't think of a single reason why this wasn't a good idea.

When he spun her around, he continued on in a rush as if he was certain she was going to protest. "And then I'd move in with you in the Victorian. We can turn her back into the stately residence she deserves to be." His face was tense as he waited for her to say anything.

"But what about your condo? And your business? Don't you need to stay in the valley?"

He shrugged, and some of the tension left his body. "I can commute. Most of the time, I'd be rotating between construction sites anyway. We can keep the condo if you like, since it's almost like a perch in an aerie. And I know how much you like the sky, even if you don't always want to soar."

Her heart flipped over at that. He could accept her for who and what she was. "And where will you be?"

"Right here on the ground, ready to catch you when you're ready to be earthbound again."

The grin on his face told her he knew he had her. Actually, the idea of him in her bed every morning, waking up to his rugged face, and sharing the simple pleasures of a life built together, was incredibly appealing.

"On one condition." She raised an eyebrow in challenge.

He responded in kind, the grin growing wider. "Name it."

"I'll tend the garden, and you can climb up the ladder and rebuild the house."

He laughed, loudly and with so much pleasure that all of their friends stopped what they were doing to turn and look at them. When he picked her up and twirled her in the air, her hoot of laughter joined his.

And beyond them, their family and friends clapped in approval.

THE END

Excerpt from WINE INTO WATER

If you enjoyed *Blooms on the Bones*, stay tuned for the next book in the Flynn's Crossing series, ***Wine Into Water.***

And here's a sip:

She peeked out from behind the stout trunk, its red bark smooth against her cheek. She liked this kind of tree. Rubbing against its sun-baked contours reminded her of comfort, something she hadn't felt in a long time. Even hiding in the brush, she remembered the clean smell of herbs and flowers from warm, delicate skin. An echo of laughter in her distant memory made her stomach jitter like it was full of ants and tears pricked so sharply that she closed her eyes.

The sudden sharp crack forced her to abandon the sensations and startled her eyes open. The tall man at the edge of the clearing brought the large thing in his hands down on the tree lying in front of him, hard enough to make little pieces of wood fly in every direction. One more resonating whack and the log on the ground severed into a length as tall as he was. He glanced over his shoulder in her direction, and she froze, the same stillness deer used to hide in plain sight. His lips pulled into a tight line as he shook his head and hefted the log on to his shoulder.

She followed him up the hillside. Though he carried a load and she only needed to creep along behind him, out of sight and stealthy, her breathing labored and her heart fluttered as hard as a rabbit's. Near the top of the mountain, the man stopped in a clearing and stacked the log on the rest. He was too near her water, the only place where she'd been able to settle. The day he'd examined her bed, nestled in the torn roots of a long-dead pine tree, she'd run so deep into the forest that it took her long hours to find her way out again. When she crept back to the cool spring, the man was gone.

Since then, he'd returned periodically and continued to stack logs. The shape was vaguely familiar to her. A house? But why would he build here, when he already had a house, a much bigger house, down at the bottom of the hill? This was her place. It was the only place she still felt safe.

The man had skin like hers, but that didn't make her trust him. The first ones had skin like hers too, but they talked funny. And her mama and papa were covered with blood and unmoving as the strangers dragged her sister and brother away. She hid in the woods for a long time after that, learning how the small animals escaped detection and surviving on forage. She made their habits her own until the voices of her family faded into a blurry memory.

"Où es-tu?"

The man's voice, coarse but gentle, perked her ears to attention. The words were familiar but lost to her. A musical quality in his tone soothed her. She raised her gaze to find him staring straight at her, as if he could see her hiding in the tall grasses. He moved slowly now, laying down the tool in his hand and staying in a low crouch as he approached.

"Où es-tu?" He called it again in a singsong tone. But he was looking right at her. He knew exactly where she was.

Her heart fluttered again, her body yearning to creep out of her hiding place and move towards that lovely sound. He was close enough now for her to see kindness in his gray-green eyes and sadness cut into the deep lines of his face even as he wore a small smile.

"Nous allons prendre soin de vous, ma petite fille."

Her mind struggled to understand his words. Little one. Care for her. But others had said something like this, and it made her anxious. She shrank further into the grasses but couldn't help the nervous twitches of her body.

"*Venir.* Come. Little girl – food."

She knew these words. The last brought a rumble to her belly and a longing to reach out a hand to him. She watched his face screw up in concentration as he continued to crawl towards her slowly.

"De famille."

Family.

She cried out, her vision blinded by memory of the red shooting from her father's neck, her ears filled with her mother's screams to run, run as fast and as hard as she could. The men laughed and grabbed *Maman*, throwing her to the ground as they pulled at her dress and apron. She kicked them, her pointy-toed boot crunching into bone and flesh, and soon the men were yelling in anger. Then they held her mother down and she covered the swell of her belly as they cursed and raised a knife in the air.

She screamed like the wild thing she had become and crashed backwards through the undergrowth, the tall man's curses ringing in her ears as she bounded into the forest. Running on instinct, she burrowed deeper into densest shrubs, tearing at her dress and scratching her arms so that she was bleeding too, just like her parents. She stopped only when she could no longer move, when her legs had no strength and scalding tears blinded her eyes. And there she lay, wishing that she too could die.

About the Author

I love to hear from readers, so feel free to contact me through my website, www.yvonnekohano.com, or directly on Facebook as Yvonne Kohano, on Twitter @yvonnekohano, and at yvonne@yvonnekohano.com. Please leave an honest review of this novel at Amazon, Goodreads, or your favorite book discovery site of choice.

Yvonne enjoys channeling her characters' voices and passions as they overcome real world problems and discover love. Her Flynn's Crossing contemporary romantic suspense series is set in a fictional northern California foothills town not unlike the one where she used to live. Of course, the beauty and wonders of the Sierra Nevada Mountains and the surrounding counties play costarring roles in her work.

The first six books in the Flynn's Crossing series follow the developing love interests of the girl tribe, a group of successful women who work through real world conflicts and challenges to find acceptance and love - with some suspenseful happenings thrown in! In the next six books, single guys in the wolf pack find their true loves, but not without their own issues to conquer. Periodically, Yvonne will be adding seasonal novellas to the series, featuring the first person voice of a character from one of her previous books experiencing an event that we can all relate to.

www.ingramcontent.com/pod-product-compliance
Lightning Source LLC
Chambersburg PA
CBHW051330250626
47155CB00007B/2539